TOR BOOKS BY ORSON SCOTT CARD

ORSON SCOTT CARD

SEVENTH SON

TOR®

A TOM DOHERTY ASSOCIATES BOOK
NEW YORK

SEVENTH SON

Copyright © 1987 by Orson Scott Card

Cover art by Dennis Nolan
Cover design by Carol Russo
Maps by Alan McKnight

A Tor Book
Published by Tom Doherty Associates, LLC
175 Fifth Avenue
New York, NY 10010

www.tor.com

Tor® is a registered trademark of Tom Doherty Associates, LLC.

ISBN: 0-812-53305-4
Library of Congress Catalog Card Number: 86-51490

First edition: July 1987
First mass market printing: April 1988

Printed in the United States of America

20   19   18   17   16   15   14   13   12

To Emily Jan,
who knows all the magic
that she'll ever need

Acknowledgments

I OWE THANKS to Carol Breakstone, for her help in researching folk magic of the American frontier. The material she found became a rich mine of story ideas and details of life in the frontier period of the Northwest Territories. I also made extensive use of information contained in Douglass L. Brownstone's *A Field Guide to America's History* (Facts on File, Inc.) and John Seymour's *The Forgotten Crafts* (Knopf).

Scott Russell Sanders contributed by putting in my hands a copy of his exquisite story cycle *Wilderness Plots: Tales About the Settlement of the American Land* (Quill). His work showed me what could be achieved through realistic handling of frontier life and helped keep me on the right track with my ongoing Alvin Maker project. And, though he is long dead, I owe a considerable debt to William Blake (1757–1827), for writing poems and proverbs that came so perfectly to Taleswapper's lips.

Above all, I am grateful to Kristine A. Card, for the incalculable value of her criticism, encouragement, editing, and proofreading, and for single-handedly turning our children into wise, kind, well-mannered human beings, who readily forgive their father when he is not a fit example of those virtues.

Contents

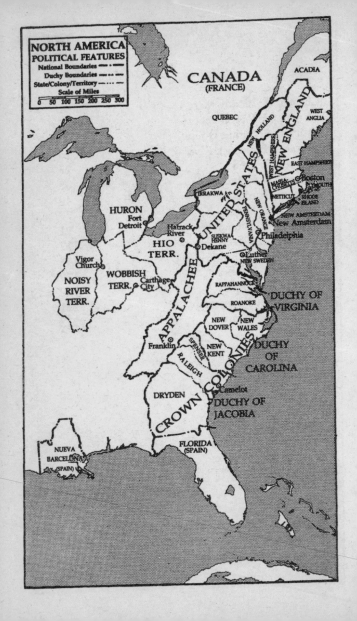

NORTH AMERICA
POLITICAL FEATURES
National Boundaries ▬ ▬ ▬
Duchy Boundaries ▬ ▬
State/Colony/Territory ▬ ▬ ▬
Scale of Miles
0 50 100 150 200 250 300

CANADA
(FRANCE)

ACADIA

QUEBEC

NEW HOLLAND

NEW ENGLAND

WEST ANGLIA

NEW HAMPSHIRE

EAST HAMPSHIRE

MASSA-CHUSETTS

Boston

PLYMOUTH

IRRAKWA

UNITED STATES

NETICUT

RHODE ISLAND

HURON

Fort Detroit

Hatrack River

HIO TERR.

NEW ORANGE

NEW AMSTERDAM

New Amsterdam

PENNSYLVANIA

SUSKWA-HENNY

Dekane

Philadelphia

Vigor Church

WOBBISH TERR.

Carthage City

Luther

NEW SWEDEN

NOISY RIVER TERR.

APPALACHEE

RAPPAHANNOCK

DUCHY OF VIRGINIA

ROANOKE

NEW DOVER

NEW WALES

Franklin

SPENSER

NEW KENT

DUCHY OF CAROLINA

RALEIGH

CROWN COLONIES

Camelot

DRYDEN

DUCHY OF JACOBIA

NUEVA BARCELONA
(SPAIN)

FLORIDA
(SPAIN)

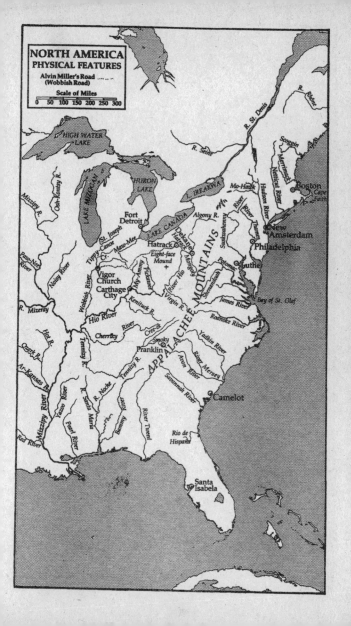

NORTH AMERICA
PHYSICAL FEATURES

Alvin Miller's Road ·· ··· ·· ··
(Wobbish Road)

Scale of Miles
0   50 100 150 200 250 300

HIGH WATER LAKE

R. Rhone

R. St. Denis

Scoggin

Merrimuc

Nettical R.

R. Seine

HURON LAKE

LAKE MICHIGAN

IREAKWA

Mo-Hawk

Hudson River

Boston

Cape Faith

Oeh-Kontoy R.

St. Joseph

Fort Detroit

LAKE CANADA

Algony R.

River Thames

New Amsterdam

Mizzipy R.

Tippy-Canoe

Mavo-Mee

Dekane

Philadelphia

Hatrack

Susquehanny

Paw-Nee River

Noisy River

Wobbish River

Eight-face Mound

Memony

Suther

Potomac

Shenenoah

Bay of St. Olef

Vigor Church

Mite Pikwanet

River Hio

Virgin R.

James River

Carthage City

Kentuck R.

Hio River

Roanoke River

R. Mizeray

Cherriky

River

Creeck

Yaddin River

Hot R.

Ozark R.

Tennizy R.

Smoky

Franklin

Avon River

River Mersey

Ar-Kansas R.

R. Noche

R. Santa Maria

Tennizy R.

River Tweed

Camelot

Mizzipy River

Yazoo River

Pearl River

Bonny

Savannah River

Red River

Rio de Hispana

Santa Isabela

1

Bloody Mary

LITTLE PEGGY WAS VERY CAREFUL with the eggs. She rooted
her hand through the straw till her fingers bumped something hard and heavy. She gave no never mind to the
chicken drips. After all, when folk with babies stayed at the
roadhouse, Mama never even crinkled her face at their
most spetackler diapers. Even when the chicken drips were
wet and stringy and made her fingers stick together, little
Peggy gave no never mind. She just pushed the straw apart,
wrapped her hand around the egg, and lifted it out of the
brood box. All this while standing tiptoe on a wobbly stool,
reaching high above her head. Mama said she was too
young for egging, but little Peggy showed her. Every day she
felt in every brood box and brought in every egg, every
single one, that's what she did.

Every one, she said in her mind, over and over. I got to
reach into every one.

Then little Peggy looked back into the northeast corner, the darkest place in the whole coop, and there sat
Bloody Mary in her brood box, looking like the devil's own
bad dream, hatefulness shining out of her nasty eyes, saying
Come here little girl and give me nips. I want nips of finger
and nips of thumb and if you come real close and try to take
my egg I'll get a nip of eye from you.

Most animals didn't have much heartfire, but Bloody
Mary's was strong and made a poison smoke. Nobody else

1

could see it, but little Peggy could. Bloody Mary dreamed of death for all folks, but most specially for a certain little girl five years old, and little Peggy had the marks on her fingers to prove it. At least one mark, anyway, and even if Papa said he couldn't see it, little Peggy remembered how she got it and nobody could blame her none if she sometimes forgot to reach under Bloody Mary who sat there like a bushwhacker waiting to kill the first folks that just *tried* to come by. Nobody'd get mad if she just sometimes forgot to look there.

I forgot. I looked in every brood box, every one, and if one got missed then I forgot forgot forgot.

Everybody knew Bloody Mary was a lowdown chicken and too mean to give any eggs that wasn't rotten anyway.

I forgot.

She got the egg basket inside before Mama even had the fire het, and Mama was so pleased she let little Peggy put the eggs one by one into the cold water. Then Mama put the pot on the hook and swung it right on over the fire. Boiling eggs you didn't have to wait for the fire to slack, you could do it smoke and all.

"Peg," said Papa.

That was Mama's name, but Papa didn't say it in his Mama voice. He said it in his little-Peggy-you're-in-dutch voice, and little Peggy knew she was completely found out, and so she turned right around and yelled what she'd been planning to say all along.

"I forgot, Papa!"

Mama turned and looked at little Peggy in surprise. Papa wasn't surprised though. He just raised an eyebrow. He was holding his hand behind his back. Little Peggy knew there was an egg in that hand. Bloody Mary's nasty egg.

"What did you forget, little Peggy?" asked Papa, talking soft.

Right that minute little Peggy reckoned she was the stupidest girl ever born on the face of the earth. Here she was denying before anybody accused her of anything.

But she wasn't going to give up, not right off like that. She couldn't stand to have them mad at her and she just wanted them to let her go away and live in England. So she put on her innocent face and said, "I don't know, Papa."

She figgered England was the best place to go live, cause England had a Lord Protector. From the look in Papa's eye, a Lord Protector was pretty much what she needed just now.

"What did you forget?" Papa asked again.

"Just say it and be done, Horace," said Mama. "If she's done wrong then she's done wrong."

"I forgot one time, Papa," said little Peggy. "She's a mean old chicken and she hates me."

Papa answered soft and slow. "One time," he said.

Then he took his hand from behind him. Only it wasn't no single egg he held, it was a whole basket. And that basket was filled with a clot of straw—most likely all the straw from Bloody Mary's box—and that straw was mashed together and glued tight with dried-up raw egg and shell bits, mixed up with about three or four chewed-up baby chicken bodies.

"Did you have to bring that in the house before breakfast, Horace?" said Mama.

"I don't know what makes me madder," said Horace. "What she done wrong or her studying up to lie about it."

"I didn't study and I didn't lie!" shouted little Peggy. Or anyways she meant to shout. What came out sounded espiciously like crying even though little Peggy had decided only yesterday that she was done with crying for the rest of her life.

"See?" said Mama. "She already feels bad."

"She feels bad being caught," said Horace. "You're too slack on her, Peg. She's got a lying spirit. I don't want my daughter growing up wicked. I'd rather see her dead like her baby sisters before I see her grow up wicked."

Little Peggy saw Mama's heartfire flare up with memory, and in front of her eyes she could see a baby laid out pretty in a little box, and then another one only not so pretty cause it was the second baby Missy, the one what died of pox so nobody'd touch her but her own mama, who was still so feeble from the pox herself that she couldn't do much. Little Peggy saw that scene, and she knew Papa had made a mistake to say what he said cause Mama's face went cold even though her heartfire was hot.

"That's the wickedest thing anybody ever said in my presence," said Mama. Then she took up the basket of corruption from the table and carried it outside.

"Bloody Mary bites my hand," said little Peggy.

"We'll see what bites," said Papa. "For leaving the eggs I give you one whack, because I reckon that lunatic hen looks fearsome to a frog-size girl like you. But for telling lies I give you ten whacks."

Little Peggy cried in earnest at that news. Papa gave an honest count and full measure in everything, but most especially in whacks.

Papa took the hazel rod off the high shelf. He kept it up there ever since little Peggy put the old one in the fire and burnt it right up.

"I'd rather hear a thousand hard and bitter truths from you, Daughter, than one soft and easy lie," said he, and then he bent over and laid on with the rod across her thighs. Whick whick whick, she counted every one, they stung her to the heart, each one of them, they were so full of anger. Worst of all she knew it was all unfair because his heartfire raged for a different cause altogether, and it always did. Papa's hate for wickedness always came from his most secret memory. Little Peggy didn't understand it all, because it was twisted up and confused and Papa didn't remember it right well himself. All little Peggy ever saw plain was that it was a lady and it wasn't Mama. Papa thought of that lady whenever something went wrong. When baby Missy died of nothing at all, and then the next baby also named Missy died of pox, and then the barn burnt down once, and a cow died, everything that went wrong made him think of that lady and he began to talk about how much he hated wickedness and at those times the hazel rod flew hard and sharp.

I'd rather hear a thousand hard and bitter truths, that's what he said, but little Peggy knew that there was one truth he didn't ever want to hear, and so she kept it to herself. She'd never shout it at him, even if it made him break the hazel rod, cause whenever she thought of saying aught about that lady, she kept picturing her father dead, and that was a thing she never hoped to see for real. Besides, the lady that haunted his heartfire, she didn't have no clothes on, and little Peggy knew that she'd be whipped for sure if she talked about people being naked.

So she took the whacks and cried till she could taste that her nose was running. Papa left the room right away, and Mama came back to fix up breakfast for the blacksmith and the visitors and the hands, but neither one said boo to her, just as if they didn't even notice. She cried even harder and louder for a minute, but it didn't help. Finally she picked up her Bugy from the sewing basket and walked all stiff-legged out to Oldpappy's cabin and woke him right up.

He listened to her story like he always did.

"I know about Bloody Mary," he said, "and I told your papa fifty times if I told him once, wring that chicken's neck and be done. She's a crazy bird. Every week or so she gets crazy and breaks all her own eggs, even the ones ready to hatch. Kills her own chicks. It's a lunatic what kills its own."

"Papa like to killed *me*," said little Peggy.

"I reckon if you can walk somewhat it ain't so bad altogether."

"I can't walk *much*."

"No, I can see you're nigh crippled forever," said Oldpappy. "But I tell you what, the way I see it your mama and your papa's mostly mad at each other. So why don't you just disappear for a couple of hours?"

"I wish I could turn into a bird and fly."

"Next best thing, though," said Pappy, "is to have a secret place where nobody knows to look for you. Do you have a place like that? No, don't tell me—it wrecks it if you tell even a single other person. You just go to that place for a while. As long as it's a safe place, not out in the woods where a Red might take your pretty hair, and not a high place where you might fall off, and not a tiny place where you might get stuck."

"It's big and it's low and it ain't in the woods," said little Peggy.

"Then you go there, Maggie."

Little Peggy made the face she always made when

Oldpappy called her that. And she held up Bugy and in Bugy's squeaky high voice she said, "Her name is Peggy."

"You go there, *Piggy*, if you like that better—"

Little Peggy slapped Bugy right across Oldpappy's knee.

"Someday Bugy'll do that once too often and have a rupture and die," said Oldpappy.

But Bugy just danced right in his face and insisted, "Not piggy, *Peggy*!"

"That's right, Puggy, you go to that secret place and if anybody says, We got to go find that girl, I'll say, I know where she is and she'll come back when she's good and ready."

Little Peggy ran for the cabin door and then stopped and turned. "Oldpappy, you're the nicest grown-up in the whole world."

"Your papa has a different view of me, but that's all tied up with another hazel rod that I laid hand on much too often. Now run along."

She stopped again right before she closed the door. "You're the *only* nice grown-up!" She shouted it real loud, halfway hoping that they could hear it clear inside the house. Then she was gone, right across the garden, out past the cow pasture, up the hill into the woods, and along the path to the spring house.

✵ 2 ✵

Wagon People

THEY HAD ONE good wagon, these folks did, and two good horses pulling it. One might even suppose they was prosperous, considering they had six big boys, from mansize on down to twins that had wrestled each other into being a good deal stronger than their dozen years. Not to mention one big daughter and a whole passel of little girls. A big family. Right prosperous if you didn't know that not even a year ago they had owned a mill and lived in a big house on a streambank in west New Hampshire. Come down far in the world, they had, and this wagon was all they had left of everything. But they were hopeful, trekking west along the roads that crossed the Hio, heading for open land that was free for the taking. If you were a family with plenty of strong backs and clever hands, it'd be good land, too, as long as the weather was with them and the Reds didn't raid them and all the lawyers and bankers stayed in New England.

The father was a big man, a little run to fat, which was no surprise since millers mostly stood around all day. That softness in the belly wouldn't last a year on a deepwoods homestead. He didn't care much about that, anyway—he had no fear of hard work. What worried him today was his wife, Faith. It was her time for that baby, he knew it. Not that she'd ever talk about it direct. Women just don't speak about things like that with men. But he knew how big she was and how many months it had been. Besides, at the noon stop she murmured to him, "Alvin Miller, if there's a road house along this way, or even a little broken-down cabin, I reckon I could use a bit of rest." A man didn't have to be a philosopher to understand her. And after six sons and six daughters, he'd have to have the brains of a brick not to get the drift of how things stood with her.

So he sent off the oldest boy, Vigor, to run ahead on the road and see the lay of the land.

You could tell they were from New England, cause the boy didn't take no gun. If there'd been a bushwhacker the young man never would've made it back, and the fact he came back with all his hair was proof no Red had spotted him—the French up Detroit way were paying for English scalps with liquor and if a Red saw a White man alone in the woods with no musket he'd own that White man's scalp. So maybe a man could think that luck was with the family at last. But since these Yankees had no notion that the road wasn't safe, Alvin Miller didn't think for a minute of his good luck.

Vigor's word was of a road house three miles on. That was good news, except that between them and that road house was a river. Kind of a scrawny river, and the ford was shallow, but Alvin Miller had learned never to trust water. No matter how peaceful it looks, it'll reach and try to take you. He was halfway minded to tell Faith that they'd spend the night this side of the river, but she gave just the tiniest groan and at that moment he knew that there was no chance of that. Faith had borne him a dozen living children, but it was four years since the last one and a lot of women took it bad, having a baby so late. A lot of women died. A good road house meant women to help with the birthing, so they'd have to chance the river.

And Vigor did say the river wasn't much.

❋ 3 ❋

Spring House

THE AIR IN THE SPRING house was cool and heavy, dark and wet. Sometimes when little Peggy caught a nap here, she woke up gasping like as if the whole place was under water. She had dreams of water even when she wasn't here—that was one of the things that made some folks say she was a seeper instead of a torch. But when she dreamed outside, she always knew she was dreaming. Here the water was real.

Real in the drips that formed like sweat on the milkjars setting in the stream. Real in the cold damp clay of the spring house floor. Real in the swallowing sound of the stream as it hurried through the middle of the house.

Keeping it cool all summer long, cold water spilling right out of the hill and into this place, shaded all the way by trees so old the moon made a point of passing through their branches just to hear some good old tales. That was what little Peggy always came here for, even when Papa didn't hate her. Not the wetness of the air, she could do just fine without that. It was the way the fire went right out of her and she didn't have to be a torch. Didn't have to see into all the dark places where folks hid theirselfs.

From her they hid theirselfs as if it would do some good. Whatever they didn't like most about theirself they tried to tuck away in some dark corner but they didn't know how all them dark places burned in little Peggy's eyes. Even when she was so little that she spit out her corn mash cause

9

she was still hoping for a suck, she knew all the stories that the folks around her kept all hid. She saw the bits of their past that they most wished they could bury, and she saw the bits of their future that they most feared.

And that was why she took to coming up here to the spring house. Here she didn't have to see those things. Not even the lady in Papa's memory. There was nothing here but the heavy wet dark cool air to quench the fire and dim the light so she could be—just for a few minutes in the day—a little five-year-old girl with a straw poppet named Bugy and not even have to *think* about any of them grown-up secrets.

I'm not wicked, she told herself. Again and again, but it didn't work because she knew she was.

All right then, she said to herself, I *am* wicked. But I won't be wicked anymore. I'll tell the truth like Papa says, or I'll say nothing at all.

Even at five years old, little Peggy knew that if she kept *that* vow, she'd be better off saying nothing.

So she said nothing, not even to herself, just lay there on a mossy damp table with Bugy clenched tight enough to strangle in her fist.

Ching ching ching.

Little Peggy woke up and got mad for just a minute.

Ching ching ching.

Made her mad because nobody said to her, Little Peggy, you don't mind if we talk this young blacksmith feller into settling down here, do you?

Not at all, Papa, she would've said if they'd asked. She knew what it meant to have a smithy. It meant your village would thrive, and folks from other places would come, and when they came there'd be trade, and where there was trade then her father's big house could be a forest inn, and where there was a forest inn then all the roads would kind of bend a little just to pass the place, if it wasn't too far out of the way—little Peggy knew all that, as sure as the children of farmers knew the rhythms of the farm. A road house by a smithy was a road house that would prosper. So she would've said, Sure enough, let him stay, deed him land, brick his chimney, feed him free, let him have my bed so I have to double up with Cousin Peter who keeps trying to peek under my nightgown, I'll put up with all that—just as long as you don't put him near the spring house so that all the time, even when I want to be alone with the water, there's that whack thump hiss roar, noise all the time, and a fire burning up the sky to turn it black, and the smell of charcoal burning. It was enough to make a body wish to follow the stream right back into the mountain just to get some peace.

Of course the stream was the smart place to put the blacksmith. Except for water, he could've put his smithy anywheres at all. The iron came to him in the shipper's wagon clear from New Netherland, and the charcoal—well, there was plenty of farmers willing to trade charcoal for a good shoe. But water, that's what the smith needed that nobody'd bring him, so of course they put him right down the hill from the spring house where his ching ching ching could wake her up and put the fire back into her in the one place where she had used to be able to let it burn low and go almost to cold wet ash.

A roar of thunder.

She was at the door in a second. Had to see the lightning. Caught just the last shadow of the light but she knew that there'd be more. It wasn't much after noon, surely, or had she slept all day? What with all these blackbelly clouds she couldn't tell—it might as well be the last minutes of dusk. The air was all a-prickle with lightning just waiting to flash. She knew that feeling, knew that it meant the lightning'd hit close.

She looked down to see if the blacksmith's stable was still full of horses. It was. The shoeing wasn't done, the road would turn to muck, and so the farmer with his two sons from out West Fork way was stuck here. Not a chance they'd head home in *this*, with lightning ready to put a fire in the woods, or knock a tree down on them, or maybe just smack them a good one and lay them all out dead in a circle like them five Quakers they still was talking about and here it happened back in '90 when the first white folks came to settle here. People talked still about the Circle of Five and all that, some people wondering if God up and smashed them flat so as to shut the Quakers up, seeing how nothing else ever could, while other people was wondering if God took them up into heaven like the first Lord Protector Oliver Cromwell who was smote by lightning at the age of ninety-seven and just disappeared.

No, that farmer and his big old boys'd stay another night. Little Peggy was an innkeeper's daughter, wasn't she? Papooses learnt to hunt, pickaninnies learnt to tote, farmer children learnt the weather, and an innkeeper's daughter learnt which folks would stay the night, even before they knew it right theirselfs.

Their horses were champing in the stable, snorting and warning each other about the storm. In every group of horses, little Peggy figgered, there must be one that's remarkable dumb, so all the others have to tell him what all's going on. Bad storm, they were saying. We're going to get a soaking, if the lightning don't smack us first. And the dumb one kept nickering and saying, What's that noise, what's that noise?

Then the sky just opened right up and dumped water on the earth. Stripped leaves right off the trees, it came down so hard. Came down so thick, too, that little Peggy couldn't even see the smithy for a minute and she thought maybe it got washed right away into the stream. Oldpappy told her how that stream led right down to the Hatrack River, and the Hatrack poured right into the Hio, and the Hio shoved itself on through the woods to the Mizzipy, which went on down into the sea, and Oldpappy said how the sea drank so much water that it got indigestion and gave off the biggest old belches you ever heard, and what came up was clouds. Belches from the sea, and now the smithy would float all that way, get swallered up and belched out, and someday she'd just be minding her own business and some cloud would break up and plop that smithy down as neat as you please, old Makepeace Smith still ching ching chinging away.

Then the rain slacked off a mite and she looked down to see the smithy still there. But that wasn't what she saw at all. No, what she saw was sparks of fire way off in the forest, downstream toward the Hatrack, down where the ford was, only there wasn't a chance of taking the ford today, with this rain. Sparks, lots of sparks, and she knew every one of them was folks. She didn't hardly think of doing it anymore, she only had to see their heartfires and she was looking close. Maybe future, maybe past, all the visions lived together in the heartfire.

What she saw right now was the same in all their hearts. A wagon in the middle of the Hatrack, with the water rising and everything they owned in all the world in that wagon.

Little Peggy didn't talk much, but everybody knew she was a torch, so they listened whenever she spoke up about trouble. Specially this kind of trouble. Sure the settlements in these parts were pretty old now, a fair bit older than little Peggy herself, but they hadn't forgotten yet that anybody's wagon caught in a flood is everybody's loss.

She fair to flew down that grassy hill, jumping gopher holes and sliding the steep places, so it wasn't twenty seconds from seeing those far-off heartfires till she was speaking right up in the smithy's shop. That farmer from West Fork at first wanted to make her wait till he was done with telling stories about worse storms he'd seen. But Makepeace knew all about little Peggy. He just listened right up and then told those boys to saddle them horses, shoes or no shoes, there was folks caught in the Hatrack ford and there was no time for foolishness. Little Peggy didn't even get a chance to see them go—Makepeace already sent her off to the big house to fetch her father and all the hands and visitors there. Wasn't a one of them who hadn't once put all they owned in the world into a wagon and dragged it west across the mountain roads and down into this forest. Wasn't a one of them who hadn't felt a river sucking at that wagon, wanting to steal it away. They all got right to it. That's the way it was then, you see. Folks noticed other people's trouble every bit as quick as if it was their own.

✤ 4 ✤

Hatrack River

VIGOR LED THE BOYS in trying to push the wagon, while Eleanor hawed the horses. Alvin Miller spent his time carrying the little girls one by one to safety on the far shore. The current was a devil clawing at him, whispering, I'll have your babies, I'll have them all, but Alvin said no, with every muscle in his body as he strained shoreward he said no to that whisper, till his girls stood all bedraggled on the bank with rain streaming down their faces like the tears from all the grief in the world.

He would have carried Faith, too, baby in her belly and all, but she wouldn't budge. Just sat inside that wagon, bracing herself against the trunks and furniture as the wagon tipped and rocked. Lightning crashed and branches broke; one of them tore the canvas and the water poured into the wagon but Faith held on with white knuckles and her eyes staring out. Alvin knew from her eyes there wasn't a thing he could say to make her let go. There was only one way to get Faith and her unborn baby out of that river, and that was to get the wagon out.

"Horses can't get no purchase, Papa," Vigor shouted. "They're just stumbling and bound to break a leg."

"Well we can't pull out without the horses!"

"The horses are *something,* Papa. We leave 'em in here and we'll lose wagon and horses too!"

"Your mama won't leave that wagon."

15

He saw understanding in Vigor's eyes. The *things* in the wagon weren't worth a risk of death to save them. But Mama was.

"Still," Vigor said. "On shore the team could pull strong. Here in the water they can't do a thing."

"Set the boys to unhitching them. But first tie a line to a tree to hold that wagon!"

It wasn't two minutes before the twins Wastenot and Wantnot were on the shore making the rope fast to a stout tree. David and Measure made another line fast to the rig that held the horses, while Calm cut the strands that held them to the wagon. Good boys, doing their work just right, Vigor shouting directions while Alvin could only watch, helpless at the back of the wagon, looking now at Faith who was trying not to have the baby, now at the Hatrack River that was trying to push them all down to hell.

Not much of a river, Vigor had said, but then the clouds came up and the rain came down and the Hatrack became something after all. Even so it looked passable when they got to it. The horses strode in strong, and Alvin was just saying to Calm, who had the reins, "Well, we made it not a minute to spare," when the river went insane. It doubled in speed and strength all in a moment, and the horses got panicky and lost direction and started pulling against each other. The boys all hopped into the river and tried to lead them to shore but by then the wagon's momentum had been lost and the wheels were mired up and stuck fast. Almost as if the river knew they were coming and saved up its worst fury till they were already in it and couldn't get away.

"Look out! Look out!" screamed Measure from the shore.

Alvin looked upstream to see what devilment the river had in mind, and there was a whole tree floating down the river, endwise like a battering ram, the root end pointed at the center of the wagon, straight at the place where Faith was sitting, her baby on the verge of birth. Alvin couldn't think of anything to do, couldn't think at all, just screamed his wife's name with all his strength. Maybe in his heart he thought that by holding her name on his lips he could keep her alive, but there was no hope of that, no hope at all.

Except that Vigor didn't know there was no hope. Vigor leapt out when the tree was no more than a rod away, his body falling against it just above the root. The momentum of his leap turned it a little, then rolled it over, rolled it and turned it away from the wagon. Of course Vigor rolled with it, pulled right under the water—but it worked, the root end of the tree missed the wagon entirely, and the shaft of the trunk struck it a sidewise blow.

The tree bounded across the stream and smashed up against a boulder on the bank. Alvin was five rods off, but in his memory from then on, he always saw it like as if he'd been right there. The tree crashing into the boulder, and Vigor between them. Just a split second that lasted a lifetime, Vigor's eyes wide with surprise, blood already leaping out of his mouth, spattering out onto the tree that killed him. Then the Hatrack River swept the tree out into the current. Vigor slipped under the water, all except his arm, all tangled in the roots, which stuck up into the air for all the world like a neighbor waving good-bye after a visit.

Alvin was so intent on watching his dying son that he didn't even notice what was happening to his own self. The blow from the tree was enough to dislodge the mired wheels, and the current picked up the wagon, carried it downstream, Alvin clinging to the tailgate, Faith weeping inside, Eleanor screaming her lungs out from the driver's seat, and the boys on the bank shouting something. Shouting, "Hold! Hold! Hold!"

The rope held, one end tied to a strong tree, the other end tied to the wagon, it held. The river couldn't tumble the wagon downstream; instead it swung the wagon in to shore the way a boy swings a rock on a string, and when it came to a shuddering stop it was right against the bank, the front end facing upstream.

"It held!" cried the boys.

"Thank God!" shouted Eleanor.

"The baby's coming," whispered Faith.

But Alvin, all he could hear was the single faint cry that had been the last sound from the throat of his firstborn son, all he could see was the way his boy clung to the tree as it rolled and rolled in the water, and all he could say was a single word, a single command. "Live," he murmured. Vigor had always obeyed him before. Hard worker, willing companion, more a friend or brother than a son. But this time he knew his son would disobey. Still he whispered it. "Live."

"Are we safe?" said Faith, her voice trembling.

Alvin turned to face her, tried to strike the grief from his face. No sense her knowing the price that Vigor paid to save her and the baby. Time enough to learn of that after the baby was born. "Can you climb out of the wagon?"

"What's wrong?" asked Faith, looking at his face.

"I took a fright. Tree could have killed us. Can you climb out, now that we're up against the bank?"

Eleanor leaned in from the front of the wagon. "David and Calm are on the bank, they can help you up. The rope's holding, Mama, but who can say how long?"

"Go on, Mother, just a step," said Alvin. "We'll do better with the wagon if we know you're safe on shore."

"The baby's coming," said Faith.

"Better on shore than here," said Alvin sharply. "Go *now*."

Faith stood up, clambered awkwardly to the front. Alvin climbed through the wagon behind her, to help her if she should stumble. Even he could see how her belly had dropped. The baby must be grabbing for air already.

On the bank it wasn't just David and Calm, now. There were strangers, big men, and several horses. Even one small wagon, and that was a welcome sight. Alvin had no notion who these men were, or how they knew to come and help, but there wasn't a moment to waste on introductions. "You men! Is there a midwife in the road house?"

"Goody Guester does with birthing," said a man. A big man, with arms like oxlegs. A blacksmith, surely.

"Can you take my wife in that wagon? There's not a moment to spare." Alvin knew it was a shameful thing, for men to speak so openly of birthing, right in front of the woman who was set to bear. But Faith was no fool—she knew what mattered most, and getting her to a bed and a competent midwife was more important than pussyfooting around about it.

David and Calm were careful as they helped their mother toward the waiting wagon. Faith was staggering with pain. Women in labor shouldn't have to step from a wagon seat up onto a riverbank, that was sure. Eleanor was right behind her, taking charge as if she wasn't younger than all the boys except the twins. "Measure! Get the girls together. They're riding in the wagon with us. You too, Wastenot and Wantnot! I know you can help the big boys but I need you to watch the girls while I'm with Mother." Eleanor was never one to be trifled with, and the gravity of the situation was such that they didn't even call her Eleanor of Aquitaine as they obeyed. Even the little girls mostly gave over their squabbling and got right on.

Eleanor paused a moment on the bank and looked back to where her father stood on the wagon seat. She glanced downstream, then looked back at him. Alvin understood the question, and he shook his head no. Faith was not to know of Vigor's sacrifice. Tears came unwelcome to Alvin's eyes, but not to Eleanor's. Eleanor was only fourteen, but when she didn't want to cry, she didn't cry.

Wastenot hawed the horse and the little wagon lurched forward, Faith wincing as the girls patted her and the rain poured. Faith's gaze was somber as a cow's, and as mindless, looking back at her husband, back at the river. At times like birthing, Alvin thought, a woman becomes a beast, slack-minded as her body takes over and does its work. How else could she bear the pain? As if the soul of the earth possessed her the way it owns the souls of animals, making her part of the life of the whole world, unhitching her from family, from husband, from all the reins of the human race, leading her into the valley of ripeness and harvest and reaping and bloody death.

"She'll be safe now," the blacksmith said. "And we have horses here to pull your wagon out."

"It's slacking off," said Measure. "The rain is less, and the current's not so strong."

"As soon as your wife stepped ashore, it eased up,"

said the farmer-looking feller. "The rain's dying, that's sure."

"You took the worst of it in the water," said the blacksmith. "But you're all right now. Get hold of yourself, man, there's work to do."

Only then did Alvin come to himself enough to realize that he was crying. Work to do, that's right, get hold of yourself, Alvin Miller. You're no weakling, to bawl like a baby. Other men have lost a dozen children and still live their lives. You've had twelve, and Vigor lived to be a man, though he never did get to marry and have children of his own. Maybe Alvin had to weep because Vigor died so nobly; maybe he cried because it was so sudden.

David touched the blacksmith's arm. "Leave him be for a minute," he said softly. "Our oldest brother was carried off not ten minutes back. He got tangled in a tree floating down."

"It wasn't no *tangle,*" Alvin said sharply. "He jumped that tree and saved our wagon, and your mother inside it! That river paid him back, that's what it did, it punished him."

Calm spoke quietly to the local men. "It run him up against that boulder there." They all looked. There wasn't even a smear of blood on the rock, it seemed so innocent.

"The Hatrack has a mean streak in it," said the blacksmith, "but I never seen this river so riled up before. I'm sorry about your boy. There's a slow, flat place downstream where he's bound to fetch up. Everything the river catches ends up there. When the storm lets up, we can go down and bring back the—bring him back."

Alvin wiped his eyes on his sleeve, but since his sleeve was soaking wet it didn't do much good. "Give me a minute more and I can pull my weight," said Alvin.

They hitched two more horses and the four beasts had no trouble pulling the wagon out against the much weakened current. By the time the wagon was set to rights again on the road, the sun was even breaking through.

"Wouldn't you know," said the blacksmith. "If you ever don't like the weather hereabouts, you just set a spell, cause it'll change."

"Not this one," said Alvin. "This storm was laid in wait for us."

The blacksmith put his arm across Alvin's shoulder and spoke real gentle. "No offense, mister, but that's crazy talk."

Alvin shrugged him off. "That storm and that river wanted us."

"Papa," said David, "you're tired and grieving. Best be still till we get to the road house and see how Mama is."

"My baby is a boy," said Papa. "You'll see. He would have been the seventh son of a seventh son."

That got their attention, right enough, that blacksmith and the other men as well. Everybody knew a seventh son had certain gifts, but the seventh son of a seventh son was about as powerful a birth as you could have.

"That makes a difference," said the blacksmith. "He'd have been a born dowser, sure, and water hates that." The others nodded sagely.

"The water had its way," said Alvin. "Had its way, and all done. It would've killed Faith and the baby, if it could. But since it couldn't, why, it killed my boy Vigor. And now when the baby comes, he'll be the sixth son, cause I'll only have five living."

"Some says it makes no difference if the first six be alive or not," said a farmer.

Alvin said nothing, but he knew it made all the difference. He had thought this baby would be a miracle child, but the river had taken care of that. If water don't stop you one way, it stops you another. He shouldn't have hoped for a miracle child. The cost was too high. All his eyes could see, all the way home, was Vigor dangling in the grasp of the roots, tumbling through the current like a leaf caught up in a dust devil, with the blood seeping from his mouth to slake the Hatrack's murderous thirst.

❖ 5 ❖

Caul

LITTLE PEGGY STOOD IN THE WINDOW, looking out into the storm. She could see all those heartfires, especially one, one so bright it was like the sun when she looked at it. But there was a blackness all around them. No, not even black—a nothingness, like a part of the universe God hadn't finished making, and it swept around those lights as if to tear them from each other, sweep them away, swallow them up. Little Peggy knew what that nothingness was. Those times when her eyes saw the hot yellow heartfires, there were three other colors, too. The rich dark orange of the earth. The thin grey color of the air. And the deep black emptiness of water. It was the water that tore at them now. The river, only she had never seen it so black, so strong, so terrible. The heartfires were so tiny in the night.

"What do you see, child?" asked Oldpappy.

"The river's going to carry them away," said little Peggy.

"I hope not."

Little Peggy began to cry.

"There, child," said Oldpappy. "It ain't always such a grand thing to see afar off like that, is it."

She shook her head.

"But maybe it won't happen as bad as you think."

Just at that moment, she saw one of the heartfires break away and tumble off into the dark. "Oh!" she cried

23

out, reaching as if her hand could snatch the light and put it back. But of course she couldn't. Her vision was long and clear, but her reach was short.

"Are they lost?" asked Oldpappy.

"One," whispered little Peggy.

"Haven't Makepeace and the others got there yet?"

"Just now," she said. "The rope held. They're safe now."

Oldpappy didn't ask her how she knew, or what she saw. Just patted her shoulder. "Because you told them. Remember that, Margaret. One was lost, but if you hadn't seen and sent help, they might all have died."

She shook her head. "I should've seen them sooner, Oldpappy, but I fell asleep."

"And you blame yourself?" asked Oldpappy.

"I should've let Bloody Mary nip me, and then Father wouldn't've been mad, and then I wouldn't've been in the spring house, and then I wouldn't've been asleep, and then I would've sent help in time—"

"We can all make daisy chains of blame like that, Maggie. It don't mean a thing."

But she knew it meant something. You don't blame blind people cause they don't warn you you're about to step on a snake—but you sure blame somebody with eyes who doesn't say a word about it. She knew her duty ever since she first realized that other folks couldn't see all that she could see. God gave her special eyes, so she'd better see and give warning, or the devil would take her soul. The devil or the deep black sea.

"Don't mean a thing," Oldpappy murmured. Then, like he just been poked in the behind with a ramrod, he went all straight and said, "Spring house! Spring house, of course." He pulled her close. "Listen to me, little Peggy. It wasn't none of your fault, and that's the truth. The same water that runs in the Hatrack flows in the spring house brook, it's all the same water, all through the world. The same water that wanted them dead, it knew you could give warning and send help. So it sang to you and sent you off to sleep."

It made a kind of sense to her, it sure did. "How can that be, Oldpappy?"

"Oh, that's just in the nature of it. The whole universe is made of only four kinds of stuff, little Peggy, and each one wants to have its own way." Peggy thought of the four colors that she saw when the heartfires glowed, and she knew what all four were even as Oldpappy named them. "Fire makes things hot and bright and uses them up. Air makes things cool and sneaks in everywhere. Earth makes things solid and sturdy, so they'll last. But water, it tears things down, it falls from the sky and carries off everything it can, carries it off and down to the sea. If the water had its way, the whole world would be smooth, just a big ocean with nothing out of the water's reach. All dead and smooth. That's why you slept. The water wants to tear down these strangers, whoever they are, tear them down and kill them. It's a miracle you woke up at all."

"The blacksmith's hammer woke me," said little Peggy.

"That's it, then, you see? The blacksmith was working with iron, the hardest earth, and with a fierce blast of air from the bellows, and with a fire so hot it burns the grass outside the chimney. The water couldn't touch him to keep him still."

Little Peggy could hardly believe it, but it must be so. The blacksmith had drawn her from a watery sleep. The smith had *helped* her. Why, it was enough to make you laugh, to know the blacksmith was her friend this time.

There was shouting on the porch downstairs, and doors opened and closed. "Some folks is here already," said Oldpappy.

Little Peggy saw the heartfires downstairs, and found the one with the strongest fear and pain. "It's their mama," said little Peggy. "She's got a baby coming."

"Well, if that ain't the luck of it. Lose one, and here already is a baby to replace death with life." Oldpappy shambled on out to go downstairs and help.

Little Peggy, though, she just stood there, looking at what she saw in the distance. That lost heartfire wasn't lost at all, and that was sure. She could see it burning away far off, despite how the darkness of the river tried to cover it. He wasn't dead, just carried off, and maybe somebody could help him. She ran out then, passed Oldpappy all in a rush, clattered down the stairs.

Mama caught her by the arm as she was running into the great room. "There's a birthing," Mama said, "and we need you."

"But Mama, the one that went downriver, he's still alive!"

"Peggy, we got no time for—"

Two boys with the same face pushed their way into the conversation. "The one downriver!" cried one.

"Still alive!" cried the other.

"How do you know!"

"He can't be!"

They spoke so all on top of each other that Mama had to hush them up just to hear them. "It was Vigor, our big brother, he got swept away—"

"Well he's alive," said little Peggy, "but the river's got him."

The twins looked to Mama for confirmation. "She know what she's talking about, Goody Guester?"

Mama nodded, and the boys raced for the door, shouting, "He's alive! He's still alive!"

"Are you sure?" asked Mama fiercely. "It's a cruel thing, to put hope in their hearts like that, if it ain't so."

Mama's flashing eyes made little Peggy afraid, and she couldn't think what to say.

By then, though, Oldpappy had come up from behind. "Now Peg," he said, "how would she know one was taken by the river, lessun she saw?"

"I know," said Mama. "But this woman's been holding off birth too long, and I got a care for the baby, so come on now, little Peggy, I need you to tell me what you see."

She led little Peggy into the bedroom off the kitchen, the place where Papa and Mama slept whenever there were visitors. The woman lay on the bed, holding tight to the hand of a tall girl with deep and solemn eyes. Little Peggy didn't know their faces, but she recognized their fires, especially the mother's pain and fear.

"Someone was shouting," whispered the mother.

"Hush now," said Mama.

"About him still alive."

The solemn girl raised her eyebrows, looked at Mama. "Is that so, Goody Guester?"

"My daughter is a torch. That's why I brung her here in this room. To see the baby."

"Did she see my boy? Is he alive?"

"I thought you didn't tell her, Eleanor," said Mama.

The solemn girl shook her head.

"Saw from the wagon. Is he alive?"

"Tell her, Margaret," said Mama.

Little Peggy turned and looked for his heartfire. There were no walls when it came to this kind of seeing. His flame was still there, though she knew it was afar off. This time, though, she drew near in the way she had, took a close look. "He's in the water. He's all tangled in the roots."

"Vigor!" cried the mother on the bed.

"The river wants him. The river says, Die, die."

Mama touched the woman's arm. "The twins have gone off to tell the others. There'll be a search party."

"In the dark!" whispered the woman scornfully.

Little Peggy spoke again. "He's saying a prayer, I think. He's saying—seventh son."

"Seventh son," whispered Eleanor.

"What does that mean?" asked Mama.

"If this baby's a boy," said Eleanor, "and he's born while Vigor's still alive, then he's the seventh son of a seventh son, and all of them alive."

Mama gasped. "No wonder the river—" she said. No need to finish the thought. Instead she took little Peggy's hands and led her to the woman on the bed. "Look at this baby, and see what you see."

Little Peggy had done this before, of course. It was the chief use they had for torches, to have them look at an unborn baby just at the birthing time. Partly to see how it lay in the womb, but also because sometimes a torch could see who the baby was, what it would be, could tell stories of times to come. Even before she touched the woman's belly, she could see the baby's heartfire. It was the one that she had seen before, that burned so hot and bright that it was like the sun and the moon, to compare it to the mother's fire. "It's a boy," she said.

"Then let me bear this baby," said the mother. "Let him breathe while Vigor still breathes!"

"How's the baby set?" asked Mama.

"Just right," said little Peggy.

"Head first? Face down?"

Little Peggy nodded.

"Then why won't it come?" demanded Mama.

"She's been telling him not to," said little Peggy, looking at the mother.

"In the wagon," the mother said. "He was coming, and I did a beseeching."

"Well you should have told me right off," said Mama sharply. "Speck me to help you and you don't even tell me he's got a beseeching on him. You, girl!"

Several young ones were standing near the wall, wide-eyed, and they didn't know which one she meant.

"Any of you, I need that iron key from the ring on the wall."

The biggest of them took it clumsily from the hook and brought it, ring and all.

Mama dangled the large ring and the key over the mother's belly, chanting softly:

> *"Here's the circle, open wide,*
> *Here's the key to get outside,*
> *Earth be iron, flame be fair,*
> *Fall from water into air."*

The mother cried out in sudden agony. Mama tossed away the key, cast back the sheet, lifted the woman's knees, and ordered little Peggy fiercely to *see*.

Little Peggy touched the woman's womb. The boy's mind was empty, except for a feeling of pressure and gathering cold as he emerged into the air. But the very emptiness of his mind let her see things that would never be

plainly visible again. The billion billion paths of his life lay
open before him, waiting for his first choices, for the first
changes in the world around him to eliminate a million
futures every second. The future was there in everyone, a
flickering shadow that she could only sometimes see, and
never clearly, looking through the thoughts of the present
moment; but here, for a few precious moments, little Peggy
could see them sharp.

And what she saw was death down every path. Drowning, drowning, every path of his future led this child to a
watery death.

"Why do you hate him so!" cried little Peggy.

"What?" demanded Eleanor.

"Hush," said Mama. "Let her see what she sees."

Inside the unborn child, the dark blot of water that
surrounded his heartfire seemed so terribly strong that little
Peggy was afraid he would be swallowed up.

"Get him out to breathe!" shouted little Peggy.

Mama reached in, even though it tore the mother
something dreadful, and hooked the baby by the neck with
strong fingers, drawing him out.

In that moment, as the dark water retreated inside the
child's mind, and just before the first breath came, little
Peggy saw ten million deaths by water disappear. Now, for
the first time, there were some paths open, some paths
leading to a dazzling future. And all the paths that did not
end in early death had one thing in common. On all those
paths, little Peggy saw herself doing one simple thing.

So she did that thing. She took her hands from the
slackening belly and ducked under her mother's arm. The
baby's head had just emerged, and it was still covered with
a bloody caul, a scrap of the sac of soft skin in which he had
floated in his mother's womb. His mouth was open, sucking
inward on the caul, but it didn't break, and he couldn't
breathe.

Little Peggy did what she had seen herself do in the
baby's future. She reached out, took the caul from under
the baby's chin, and pulled it away from his face. It came
whole, in one moist piece, and in the moment it came away,

the baby's mouth cleared, he sucked in a great breath, and then gave that mewling cry that birthing mothers hear as the song of life.

Little Peggy folded the caul, her mind still full of the visions she had seen down the pathways of this baby's life. She did not know yet what the visions meant, but they made such clear pictures in her mind that she knew she would never forget them. They made her afraid, because so much would depend on her, and how she used the birth caul that was still warm in her hands.

"A boy," said Mama.

"Is he," whispered the mother. "Seventh son?"

Mama was tying the cord, so she couldn't spare a glance at little Peggy. "Look," she whispered.

Little Peggy looked for the single heartfire on the distant river. "Yes," she said, for the heartfire was still burning.

Even as she watched, it flickered, died.

"Now he's gone," said little Peggy.

The woman on the bed wept bitterly, her birth-wracked body shuddering.

"Grieving at the baby's birth," said Mama. "It's a dreadful thing."

"Hush," whispered Eleanor to her mother. "Be joyous, or it'll darken the baby all his life!"

"Vigor," murmured the woman.

"Better nothing at all than tears," said Mama. She held out the crying baby, and Eleanor took it in competent arms—she had cradled many a babe before, it was plain. Mama went to the table in the corner and took the scarf that had been blacked in the wool, so it was night-colored clear through. She dragged it slowly across the weeping woman's face, saying, "Sleep, Mother, sleep."

When the cloth came away, the weeping was done, and the woman slept, her strength spent.

"Take the baby from the room," said Mama.

"Don't he need to start his sucking?" asked Eleanor.

"She'll never nurse this babe," said Mama. "Not unless you want him to suck hate."

"She can't hate him," said Eleanor. "It ain't his fault."

"I reckon her milk don't know that," said Mama. "That right, little Peggy? What teat does the baby suck?"

"His mama's," said little Peggy.

Mama looked sharp at her. "You sure of that?"

She nodded.

"Well, then, we'll bring the baby in when she wakes up. He doesn't need to eat anything for the first night, anyway." So Eleanor carried the baby out into the great room, where the fire burned to dry the men, who stopped trading stories about rains and floods worse than this one long enough to look at the baby and admire.

Inside the room, though, Mama took little Peggy by the chin and stared hard into her eyes. "You tell me the truth, Margaret. It's a serious thing, for a baby to suck on its mama and drink up hate."

"She won't hate him, Mama," said little Peggy.

"What did you see?"

Little Peggy would have answered, but she didn't know words to tell most of the things she saw. So she looked at the floor. She could tell from Mama's quick draw of breath that she was ripe for a tongue-lashing. But Mama waited, and then her hand came soft, stroking across little Peggy's cheek. "Ah, child, what a day you've had. The baby might have died, except you told me to pull it out. You even reached in and opened up its mouth—that's what you did, isn't it?"

Little Peggy nodded.

"Enough for a little girl, enough for one day." Mama turned to the other girls, the ones in wet dresses, leaning against the wall. "And you, too, you've had enough of a day. Come out of here, let your mama sleep, come out and get dry by the fire. I'll start a supper for you, I will."

But Oldpappy was already in the kitchen, fussing around, and refused to hear of Mama doing a thing. Soon enough she was out with the baby, shooing the men away so she could rock it to sleep, letting it suck her finger.

Little Peggy figured after a while that she wouldn't be missed, so she snuck up the stairs to the attic ladder and up the ladder into the lightless, musty space. The spiders didn't bother her much, and the cats mostly kept the mice away, so she wasn't afraid. She crawled right to her secret hiding place and took out the carven box that Oldpappy gave her, the one he said his own papa brought from Ulster when he came to the colonies. It was full of the precious scraps of childhood—stones, strings, buttons—but now she knew that these were nothing compared to the work before her all the rest of her life. She dumped them right out, and blew into the box to clear away the dust. Then she laid the folded caul inside and closed the lid.

She knew that in the future she would open that box a dozen dozen times. That it would call to her, wake her from her sleep, tear her from her friends, and steal from her all her dreams. All because a baby boy downstairs had no future at all but death from the dark water, excepting if she used that caul to keep him safe, the way it once protected him in the womb.

For a moment she was angry, to have her own life so changed. Worse than the blacksmith coming, it was, worse than Papa and the hazel wand he whupped her with, worse than Mama when her eyes were angry. Everything would be different forever and it wasn't fair. Just for a baby she never invited, never asked to come here, what did she care about any old baby?

She reached out and opened the box, planning to take the caul and cast it into a dark corner of the attic. But even in the darkness, she could see a place where it was darker still: near her heartfire, where the emptiness of the deep black river was all set to make a murderer out of her.

Not me, she said to the water. You ain't part of me.

Yes I am, whispered the water. I'm all through you, and you'd dry up and die without me.

You ain't the boss of me, anyway, she retorted.

She closed the lid on the box and skidded her way down the ladder. Papa always said that she'd get splinters in her butt doing that. This time he was right. It stung something fierce, so she walked kind of sideways into the kitchen where Oldpappy was. Sure enough, he stopped his cooking long enough to pry the splinters out.

"My eyes ain't sharp enough for this, Maggie," he complained.

"You got the eyes of an eagle. Papa says so."

Oldpappy chuckled. "Does he now."

"What's for dinner?"

"Oh, you'll like this dinner, Maggie."

Little Peggy wrinkled up her nose. "Smells like chicken."

"That's right."

"I don't like chicken soup."

"Not just soup, Maggie. This one's a-roasting, except the neck and wings."

"I hate *roast* chicken, too."

"Does your Oldpappy ever lie to you?"

"Nope."

"Then you best believe me when I tell you this is one chicken dinner that'll make you *glad.* Can't you think of any way that a partickler chicken dinner could make you glad?"

Little Peggy thought and thought, and then she smiled. "Bloody Mary?"

Oldpappy winked. "I always said that was a hen born to make gravy."

Little Peggy hugged him so tight that he made choking sounds, and then they laughed and laughed.

Later that night, long after little Peggy was in bed, they brought Vigor's body home, and Papa and Makepeace set to making a box for him. Alvin Miller hardly looked alive, even when Eleanor showed him the baby. Until she said, "That torch girl. She says that this baby is the seventh son of a seventh son."

Alvin looked around for someone to tell him if it was true.

"Oh, you can trust her," said Mama.

Tears came fresh to Alvin's eyes. "That boy hung on," he said. "There in the water, he hung on long enough."

"He knowed what store you set by that," said Eleanor.

Then Alvin reached for the baby, held him tight, looked down into his eyes. "Nobody named him yet, did they?" he asked.

"Course not," said Eleanor. "Mama named all the other boys, but you always said the seventh son'd have—"

"My own name. Alvin. Seventh son of a seventh son, with the same name as his father. Alvin Junior." He looked around him, then turned to face toward the river, way off in the nighttime forest. "Hear that, you Hatrack River? His name is Alvin, and you didn't kill him after all."

Soon they brought in the box and laid out Vigor's body with candles, to stand for the fire of life that had left him. Alvin held up the baby, over the coffin. "Look on your brother," he whispered to the infant.

"That baby can't see nothing yet, Papa," said David.

"That ain't so, David," said Alvin. "He don't *know* what he's seeing, but his eyes can see. And when he gets old enough to hear the story of his birth, I'm going to tell him that his own eyes saw his brother Vigor, who gave his life for this baby's sake."

It was two weeks before Faith was well enough to travel. But Alvin saw to it that he and his boys worked hard for their keep. They cleared a good spot of land, chopped the winter's firewood, set some charcoal heaps for Makepeace Smith, and widened the road. They also felled four big trees and made a strong bridge across the Hatrack River, a covered bridge so that even in a rainstorm people could cross that river without a drop of water touching them.

Vigor's grave was the third one there, beside little Peggy's two dead sisters. The family paid respects and prayed there on the morning that they left. Then they got in their wagon and rode off westward. "But we leave a part of ourselves here always," said Faith, and Alvin nodded.

Little Peggy watched them go, then ran up into the attic, opened the box, and held little Alvin's caul in her hand. No danger—for now, at least. Safe for now. She put the caul away and closed the lid. You better be something, baby Alvin, she said, or else you caused a powerful lot of trouble for nothing.

✤ 6 ✤

Ridgebeam

AXES RANG, STRONG MEN sang hymns at their labor, and
Reverend Philadelphia Thrower's new church building rose
tall over the meadow commons of Vigor Township. It was
all happening so much faster than Reverend Thrower ever
expected. The first wall of the meetinghouse had hardly
been erected a day or so ago, when that drunken one-eyed
Red wandered in and was baptized, as if the mere sight of
the churchhouse had been the fulcrum on which he could
be levered upward to civilization and Christianity. If a Red
as benighted as Lolla-Wossiky could come unto Jesus, what
other miracles of conversion might not be wrought in this
wilderness when his meetinghouse was finished and his
ministry firmly under way?

Reverend Thrower was not altogether happy, however,
for there were enemies of civilization far stronger than the
barbarity of the heathen Reds, and the signs were not all so
hopeful as when Lolla-Wossiky donned White man's clothing for the first time. In particular what somewhat darkened
this bright day was the fact that Alvin Miller was not among
the workers. And his wife's excuses for him had run out.
The trip to find a proper millstone quarry had ended, he
had rested for a day, and by rights he should be here.

"What, is he ill?" asked Thrower.

Faith tightened her lips. "When I say he *won't* come,
Reverend Thrower, it's not to say he *can't* come."

It confirmed Thrower's gathering suspicions. "Have I offended him somewise?"

Faith sighed and looked away from him, toward the posts and beams of the meetinghouse. "Not you yourself, sir, not the way a man treads on another, as they say." Abruptly she became alert. "Now what is that?"

Right up against the building, most of the men were tying ropes to the north half of the ridgebeam, so they could lift it into place. It was a tricky job, and all the harder because of the little boys wrestling each other in the dust and getting underfoot. It was the wrestlers that had caught her eye. "Al!" cried Faith. "Alvin Junior, you let him up this minute!" She took two strides toward the cloud of dust that marked the heroic struggles of the six-year-olds.

Reverend Thrower was not inclined to let her end the conversation so easily. "Mistress Faith," said Reverend Thrower sharply. "Alvin Miller is the first settler in these parts, and people hold him in high regard. If he's against me for some reason, it will greatly harm my ministry. At least you can tell me what I did to give offense."

Faith looked him in the eye, as if to calculate whether he could stand to hear the truth. "It was your foolish sermon, sir," she said.

"Foolish?"

"You couldn't know any better, being from England, and—"

"From Scotland, Mistress Faith."

"And being how you're educated in schools where they don't know much about—"

"The University of Edinburgh! Don't know much indeed, I—"

"About hexes and doodles and charms and beseechings and suchlike."

"I know that claiming to use such dark and invisible powers is a burning offense in the lands that obey the Lord Protector, Mistress Faith, though in his mercy he merely banishes those who—"

"Well looky there, that's my point," she said triumphantly. "They're not likely to teach you about that in university, now, are they? But it's the way we live here, and calling it a superstition—"

"I called it hysteria—"

"That don't change the fact that it works."

"I understand that you *believe* that it works," said Thrower patiently. "But everything in the world is either science or miracles. Miracles came from God in ancient times, but those times are over. Today if we wish to change the world, it is not magic but science that will give us our tools."

From the set of her face, Thrower could see that he wasn't making much impression on her.

"Science," she said. "Like feeling head bumps?"

He doubted she had tried very hard to hide her scorn. "Phrenology is an infant science," he said coldly, "and there are many flaws, but I am seeking to discover—"

She laughed—a girlish laugh, that made her seem much younger than a woman who had borne fourteen children. "Sorry, Reverend Thrower, but I just remembered how Measure called it 'dowsing for brains,' and he allowed as how you'd have slim luck in these parts."

True words, thought Reverend Thrower, but he was wise enough not to say so. "Mistress Faith, I spoke as I did to let people understand that there are superior ways of thought in the world today, and we need no longer be bound by the delusions of—"

It was no use. Her patience had quite run out. "My boy looks about to get himself smacked with a spare joist if he don't let up on them other boys, Reverend, so you'll just have to excuse me." And off she went, to fall on six-year-old Alvin and three-year-old Calvin like the vengeance of the Lord. She was a champion tongue-lasher. He could hear the scolding from where he stood, and that with the breeze blowing the other way, too.

Such ignorance, said Thrower to himself. I am needed here, not only as a man of God among near heathens, but also as a man of science among superstitious fools. Somebody whispers a curse and then, six months later, something bad happens to the person cursed—it always does, something bad happens to everybody at least twice a year—and it makes them quite certain that their curse had malefic effect. Post hoc ergo propter hoc.

In Britain, students learned to discard such elementary logic errors while yet studying the trivium. Here it was a way of life. The Lord Protector was quite right to punish practitioners of magic arts in Britain, though Thrower would prefer that he do it on grounds of stupidity rather than heresy. Treating it as heresy gave it too much dignity, as if it were something to be feared rather than despised.

Three years ago, right after he earned his Doctor of Divinity degree, it had dawned on Thrower what harm the Lord Protector was actually doing. He remembered it as the turning point of his life; wasn't it also the first time the Visitor had come to him? It was in his small room in the rectory of St. James Church in Belfast, where he was junior assistant pastor, his first assignment after ordination. He was looking at a map of the world when his eye strayed to America, to where Pennsylvania was clearly marked, stretching from the Dutch and Swedish colonies westward until the lines faded in the obscure country beyond the Mizzipy. It was as if the map then came alive, and he saw the flood of people arriving in the New World. Good Puritans, loyal churchmen, and sound businessmen all went to New England; Papists, Royalists, and scoundrels all went to the rebellious slave country of Virginia, Carolina, and Jacobia, the so-called Crown Colonies. The sort of people who, once they found their place, stayed in it forever.

But it was another kind of people went to Pennsylvania. Germans, Dutchmen, Swedes, and Huguenots fled their countries and turned Pennsylvania Colony into a slop pot, filled with the worst human rubbish of the continent. Worse yet, they would *not* stay put. These dimwitted country people would debark in Philadelphia, discover that the settled—Thrower did not call them "civilized"—portions of Pennsylvania were too crowded for them, and immediately head westward into the Red country to hew out a farm among the trees. Never mind that the Lord Protector specifically forbade them to settle there. What did such pagans care for law? Land was what they wanted, as if the mere ownership of dirt could turn a peasant into a squire.

Then Thrower's vision of America turned from bleak to black indeed. He saw that war was coming to America with the new century. In his vision, he foresaw that the King of France would send that obnoxious Corsican colonel, Bonaparte, to Canada, and his people would stir up the Reds from the French fortress town in Detroit. The Reds would fall upon the settlers and destroy them; scum they might be, but they were mostly English scum, and the vision of the Reds' savagery made Thrower's skin crawl.

Yet even if the English won, the overall result would be the same. America west of the Appalachees would never be a Christian land. Either the damned Papist French and Spanish would have it, or the equally damned heathen Reds would keep it, or else the most depraved sort of Englishmen would thrive and thumb their noses at Christ and the Lord Protector alike. Another whole continent would be lost to the knowledge of the Lord Jesus. It was such a fearsome vision that Thrower cried out, thinking none would hear him in the confines of his little room.

But someone did hear him. "There's a life's work for a man of God," said someone behind him. Thrower turned at once, startled; but the voice was gentle and warm, the face old and kindly, and Thrower was not afraid for more than a moment, despite the fact that the door and window were both locked tight, and no natural man could have come inside his little room.

Thinking that this man was surely a part of the manifestation he had just seen, Thrower addressed him reverently. "Sir, whoever you are, I have seen the future of North America, and it looks like the victory of the devil to me."

"The devil takes his victories," the man replied, "wherever men of God lose heart, and leave the field to him."

Then the man simply was not there.

Thrower had known in that moment what the work of his life would be. To come to the wilds of America, build a country church, and fight the devil in his own country. It had taken him three years to get the money and the permission of his superiors in the Scottish Church, but now he was here, the posts and beams of his church were rising, their white and naked wood a bright rebuke to the dark forest of barbarism from which they had been hewn.

Of course, with such a magnificent work under way, the devil was bound to take notice. And it was obvious that the devil's chief disciple in Vigor Township was Alvin Miller. Even though all his sons were here, helping to build the churchhouse, Thrower knew that this was Faith's doing. The woman had even allowed as how she was probably Church of Scotland in her heart, even though she was born in Massachusetts; her membership would mean that Thrower could look forward to having a congregation —provided Alvin Miller could be kept from wrecking everything.

And wreck it he would. It was one thing if Alvin had been offended by something Thrower had inadvertently said and done. But to have the quarrel be about belief in sorcery, right from the start—well, there was no hiding from this conflict. The battle lines were laid. Thrower stood on the side of science and Christianity, and on the other side stood all the powers of darkness and superstition; the bestial, carnal nature of man was on the other side, with Alvin Miller as its champion. I am only at the beginning of my tournament for the Lord, thought Thrower. If I can't vanquish this first opponent, then no victory will ever be possible for me.

"Pastor Thrower!" shouted Alvin's oldest boy, David. "We're ready to raise the ridgebeam!"

Thrower started toward them at a trot, then remembered his dignity and walked the rest of the way. There was nothing in the gospels to imply that the Lord ever ran —only walked, as befitted his high station. Of course, Paul had his comments about running a good race, but that was allegory. A minister was supposed to be a shadow of Jesus Christ, walking in His way and representing Him to the people. It was the closest these people would ever come to beholding the majesty of God. It was Reverend Thrower's duty to deny the vitality of his youth and walk at the reverent pace of an old man, though he was only twenty-four.

"You mean to bless the ridgebeam, don't you?" asked one of the farmers. It was Ole, a Swedish fellow from the banks of the Delaware, and so a Lutheran at heart; but he was willing enough to help build a Presbyterian Church here in the Wobbish valley, seeing how the nearest church besides that was the Papist Cathedral in Detroit.

"I do indeed," said Thrower. He laid his hand on the heavy, axehewn beam.

"Reverend Thrower." It was a child's voice behind him, piercing and loud as only a child's voice can be. "Ain't it a kind of a charm, to give a blessing to a piece of wood?"

Thrower turned around to see Faith Miller already hushing the boy. Only six years old, but Alvin Junior was obviously going to grow up to be just as much trouble as his father. Maybe more—Alvin Senior had at least had the good grace to stay away from the church-raising.

"You go on," said Faith. "Never mind him. I haven't learned him yet when to speak and when to keep silence."

Even though his mother's hand was tight-clamped over his mouth, the boy's eyes were steady, looking right at him. And when Thrower turned back around, he found that all the grown men were looking at him expectantly. The child's question was a challenge that he had to answer, or he'd be branded a hypocrite or fool before the very men he had come to convert.

"I suppose that if you think my blessing actually does something to change the nature of the ridgebeam," he said, "that might be akin to ensorcelment. But the truth is that the ridgebeam itself is just the *occasion*. Whom I'm really blessing is the congregation of Christians who'll gather under this roof. And there's nothing magic about that. It's the power and love of God we're asking for, not a cure for warts or a charm against the evil eye."

"Too bad," murmured a man. "I could use a cure for warts."

They all laughed, but the danger was over. When the ridgebeam went up, it would be a Christian act to raise it, not a pagan one.

He blessed the ridgebeam, taking care to change the usual prayer to one that specifically did *not* confer any special properties upon the beam itself. Then the men tugged on the rope, and Thrower sang out "O Lord Who on the Mighty Sea" at the top of his magnificent baritone voice, to give them the rhythm and inspiration for their labors.

All the time, however, he was acutely aware of the boy Alvin Junior. It was not just because of the boy's embarrassing challenge a moment ago. The child was as simple-minded as most children—Thrower doubted he had any dire purpose in mind. What drew him to the child was something else entirely. Not any property in the boy himself, but rather something about the people near him. They always seemed to keep him in attention. Not that they always *looked* at him—that would be a full-time occupation, he ran about so much. It was as if they were always aware of him, the way the college cook had always been aware of the dog in the kitchen, never speaking to it, but stepping over and around it without so much as pausing in his work.

It wasn't just the boy's family, either, that was so careful of him. Everyone acted the same way—the Germans, the Scandinavians, the English, newcomers and old-timers alike. As if the raising of this boy were a community project, like the raising of a church or the bridging of a river.

"Easy, easy, easy!" shouted Wastenot, who was perched near the east ridgepole to guide the heavy beam into place. It had to be just so, for the rafters to lean evenly against it and make a sturdy roof.

"Too far your way!" shouted Measure. He was standing on scaffolding above the crossbeam on which rested the short pole that would support the two ridgebeams where they butted ends in the middle. This was the most crucial point of the whole roof, and the trickiest to get right; they had to lay the ends of two heavy beams onto a pole top that was barely two palms wide. That was why Measure stood there, for he had grown into his name, keen-eyed and careful.

"Right!" shouted Measure. "More!"

"My way again!" shouted Wastenot.

"Steady!" shouted Measure.

"Set!" shouted Wastenot.

Then "Set!" from Measure, too, and the men on the ground relaxed the tension on the ropes. As the lines went slack, they let out a cheer, for the ridgebeam now went half the length of the church. It was no cathedral, but it was still a mighty thing to achieve in this benighted place, the largest structure anyone had dared to think of for a hundred miles around. The mere fact of building it was a declaration that the settlers were here to stay, and not French, not Spanish, not Cavaliers, not Yankees, not even the savage Reds with their fire arrows, no man would get these folks to leave this place.

So of course Reverend Thrower went inside, and so did all the others, to see the sky blocked for the first time by a ridgebeam no less than forty feet in length—and that only half of what it would finally be. My church, thought Thrower, and already finer than most I saw in Philadelphia itself.

Up on the flimsy scaffolding, Measure was driving a wooden pin through the notch in the end of the ridgebeam and down into the hole in the top of the ridgepole. Wastenot was doing the same at his end, of course. The pins would hold the beam in place until the rafters could be laid. When that was done, the ridgebeam would be so strong that they could almost remove the crossbeam, if it weren't needed for the chandelier that would light the church at night. At night, so that the stained glass would shine out against the darkness. That's how grandiose a place Reverend Thrower had in mind. Let their simple minds stand in awe when they see this place, and so reflect upon the majesty of God.

Those were his thoughts when, suddenly, Measure let out a shout of fear, and all saw in horror that the center ridgepole had split and shivered at the blow of Measure's mallet against the wooden pin, bouncing the great heavy ridgebeam some six feet into the air. It pulled the beam out of Wastenot's hands at the other end, and broke the scaffolding like tinderwood. The ridgebeam seemed to hover in the air a moment, level as you please, then rushed downward as if the Lord's own foot were stomping it.

And Reverend Thrower knew without looking that there would be someone directly under that beam, right under the midpoint of it when it landed. He knew because he was *aware* of the boy, of how he was running just exactly the wrong direction, of how his own shout of "Alvin!" brought the boy to a stop in just exactly the wrong place.

And when he looked, it was exactly as he knew it would be—little Al standing there, looking up at the shaven tree that would grind him into the floor of the church. Nothing else would be damaged—because the beam was level, its impact would be spread across the whole floor. The boy was too small even to slow the ridgebeam's fall. He would be broken, crushed, his blood spattering the white wood of the church floor. I'll never get that stain out, thought Thrower —insanely, but one could not control one's own thoughts in the moment of death.

Thrower saw the impact as if it were a blinding flash of light. He heard the crash of wood on wood. He heard the screams. Then his eyes cleared and he saw the ridgebeam lying there, the one end exactly where it should be, the other too, but in the middle, the beam split in two parts, and between the two parts little Alvin standing, his face white with terror.

Untouched. The boy was untouched.

Thrower didn't understand German or Swedish, but he knew what the muttering near him meant, well enough. Let them blaspheme—I must understand what has happened here, thought Thrower. He strode to the boy, placed his hands on the child's head, searching for injury. Not a hair out of place, but the boy's head felt warm, very warm, as if he had been standing near a fire. Then Thrower knelt and looked at the wood of the ridgebeam. It was cut as smooth as if the wood had grown that way, just exactly wide enough to miss the boy entirely.

Al's mother was there only a moment later, scooping up her boy, sobbing and babbling with relief. Little Alvin also cried. But Thrower had other things on his mind. He *was* a man of science, after all, and what he had seen was not possible. He made the men step off the length of the ridgebeam, measuring it again. It lay exactly its original length along the floor—the east end just as far from the west end as it should be. The boy-sized chunk in the middle had simply disappeared. Vanished in a momentary flash of fire that left Alvin's head and the butt ends of the wood as hot as coals, yet not marked or seared in any way.

Then Measure began yelling from the crossbeam, where he dangled by his arms, having caught himself after the collapse of the scaffolding. Wantnot and Calm climbed up and got him down safely. Reverend Thrower had no thought for that. All he could think about was a six-year-old boy who could stand under a falling ridgebeam, and the beam would break and make room for him. Like the Red Sea parting for Moses, on the right hand and the left.

"Seventh son," murmured Wastenot. The boy sat astride the fallen ridgebeam, just west of the break.

"What?" asked Reverend Thrower.

"Nothing," said the young man.

"You said 'Seventh son,'" said Thrower. "But it's little Calvin who's the seventh."

Wastenot shook his head. "We had another brother. He died a couple minutes after Al was born." Wastenot shook his head again. "Seventh son of a seventh son."

"But that makes him devil's spawn," said Thrower, aghast.

Wastenot looked at him with contempt. "Maybe in England you think so, but around here we look on such to be a healer, maybe, or a doodlebug, and a right good one of whatever he is." Then Wastenot thought of something and grinned. "'Devil's spawn,'" he repeated, maliciously savoring the words. "Sounds like hysteria to me."

Furious, Thrower stalked out of the church.

He found Mistress Faith sitting on a stool, holding Alvin Junior on her lap and rocking him as he continued to whimper. She was scolding him gently. "Told you not to run without looking, always underfoot, can't never hold still, makes a body go plumb lunatic looking after you—" Then she saw Thrower standing before her, and fell silent.

"Don't worry," she said. "I'll not bring him back here."

"For his safety, I'm glad," said Thrower. "If I thought my churchhouse had to be built at the cost of a child's life, I'd sooner preach in the open air all the days of my life."

She looked close at him and knew that he meant it with his whole heart. "It's no fault of yourn," she said. "He's always been a clumsy boy. Seems to live through scrapes that'd kill an ordinary child."

"I'd like—I'd like to understand what happened in there."

"Ridgepole shivered, of course," she said. "It happens sometimes."

"I mean—how it happened to miss him. The beam split—before it touched his head. I want to feel his head, if I may—"

"Not a mark on him," she said.

"I know. I want to feel it to see if—"

She rolled her eyes upward and muttered, "Dowsing for brains," but she also moved her hands away so he could feel the child's head. Slowly now, and carefully, trying to understand the map of the boy's skull, to read the ridges and bumps, the troughs and depressions. He had no need to consult a book. The books were nonsense, anyway. He had found that out quite quickly—they all spouted idiotic generalities, such as, "The Red will always have a bump just over the ear, indicating savagery and cannibalism," when of course Reds had just as much variety in their heads as Whites. No, Thrower had no faith in those books—but he *had* learned a few things about people with particular skills, and head bumps they had in common. He had developed a knack of understanding, a map of the shapes of the human skull; he knew as his hands passed over Al's head what it was he found there.

Nothing remarkable, that's what he found. No one trait that stood out above all others. Average. As average as can be. So utterly average that it could be a virtual textbook example of normality, if only there were any textbook worth reading.

He lifted his fingers away, and the boy—who had stopped crying under his hands—twisted on his mother's lap to look at him. "Reverend Thrower," he said, "your hands are so cold I like to froze." Then he squirmed off his mother's lap and ran off, shouting for one of the German boys, the one he had been wrestling so savagely before.

Faith laughed ruefully. "You see how quickly they forget?"

"And you, too," he said.

She shook her head. "Not me," she said. "I don't forget a thing."

"You're already smiling."

"I *go on,* Reverend Thrower. I just go on. That's not the same as forgetting."

He nodded.

"So—tell me what you found," she said.

"Found?"

"Feeling his bumps. Brain-dowsing. Does he got any?"

"Normal. Absolutely normal. Not a single thing unusual about his head."

She grunted. "*Nothing* unusual?"

"That's right."

"Well, if you ask me, that's pretty unusual right there, if a body was smart enough to notice it." She picked up the stool and carried it off, calling to Al and Cally as she went.

After a moment, Reverend Thrower realized she was right. Nobody was so perfectly average. Everybody had *some* trait that was stronger than the others. It wasn't normal for Al to be so well balanced. To have every possible skill that could be marked by the skull, and to have it in exactly even proportions. Far from being average, the child was extraordinary, though Thrower had no notion what it would mean in the child's life. Jack of all trades and master of none? Or master of all?

Superstition or not, Thrower found himself wondering. A seventh son of a seventh son, a startling shape to the head, and the miracle—he could think of no other word —of the ridgebeam. An ordinary child would have died this day. Natural law demanded it. But someone or something was protecting this child, and natural law had been overruled.

Once the talk had subsided, the men resumed work on the roof. The original beam was useless, of course, and they carried the two sections of it outside. After what had happened, they had no intention of using the beams for anything at all. Instead they set to work and completed another beam by midafternoon, rebuilt the scaffolding, and by nightfall the whole roof ridge was set in place. No one spoke of the incident with the ridgebeam, at least not in Thrower's presence. And when he went to look for the shivered ridgepole, he couldn't find it anywhere.

7

Altar

ALVIN JUNIOR WASN'T SCARED when he saw the beam falling, and he wasn't scared when it crashed to the floor on either side. But when all the grown-ups started carrying on like the Day of Rapture, a-hugging him and talking in whispers, *then* he got scared. Grown-ups had a way of doing things for no reason at all.

Like the way Papa was setting on the floor by the fire, just studying the split pieces of the shivered ridgepole, the piece of wood that sprung under the weight of the ridge-beam and sent it all crashing down. When Mama was being herself, not Papa or nobody could bring big old pieces of split and dirty wood into her house. But today Mama was as crazy as Papa, and when he showed up toting them big old splinters of wood, she just bent over, rolled up the rug, and got herself out of Papa's way.

Well, anybody who didn't know to get out of Papa's way when he had that look on his face was too dumb to live. David and Calm was lucky, they could go off to their own houses on their own cleared land, where their own wives had their own suppers cooking and they could decide whether to be crazy or not. The rest of them weren't so lucky. With Papa and Mama being crazy, the rest of them had to be crazy, too. Not one of the girls fought with any of the others, and they all helped fix supper and clean up after without a word of complaint. Wastenot and Wantnot went
49

out and chopped wood and did the evening milking without so much as punching each other in the arm, let alone getting in a wrestling match, which was right disappointing to Alvin Junior, seeing as how he always got to wrestle the loser, which was the best wrestling he ever got to do, them being eighteen years old and a real challenge, not like the boys he usually hunkered down with. And Measure, he just sat there by the fire, whittling out a big old spoon for Mama's cooking pot, never so much as looking up—but he was waiting, just like the others, for Papa to come back to his right self and yell at somebody.

The only normal person in the house was Calvin, the three-year-old. The trouble was that normal for him meant tagging along after Alvin Junior like a kitten on a mouse's trail. He never came close enough to *play* with Alvin Junior, or to touch him or talk to him or anything useful. He was just there, always there at the edge of things, so Alvin would look up just as Calvin looked away, or catch a glimpse of his shirt as he ducked behind a door, or sometimes in the dark of night just hear a faint breathing that was closer than it ought to be, which told him Calvin wasn't lying on his cot, he was standing right there by Alvin's bed, *watching*. Nobody ever seemed to notice it. It had been more than a year since Alvin gave up trying to get him to stop. If Alvin Junior ever said, "Ma, Cally's pestering me," Mama would just say, "Al Junior, he didn't say a thing, he didn't touch you, and if you don't like him just standing quiet as a body could ask, well, that's just too bad for you, because it suits me fine. I wish certain other of my children could learn to be as still." Alvin figured that it wasn't that Calvin was *normal* today, it's that the rest of the family had just come up to his regular level of craziness.

Papa just stared and stared at the split wood. Now and then he'd fit it together the way it was. Once he spoke, real quiet. "Measure, you sure you got all them pieces?"

Measure said, "Ever single bit, Pa, I couldn't've got more with a broom. I couldn't've got more if I'd bent down and lapped it up like a dog."

Ma was listening, of course. Papa once said that when Ma was paying attention, she could hear a squirrel fart in the woods a half mile away in the middle of a storm with the girls rattling dishes and the boys all chopping wood. Alvin Junior wondered sometimes if that meant Ma knew more witchery than she let on, since one time he sat in the woods not three yards away from a squirrel for more than an hour, and he never heard it so much as belch.

Anyway, she was right there in the house tonight, so of course she heard what Papa asked, and she heard what Measure answered, and her being as crazy as Papa, she lashed out like as if Measure had just taken the name of the Lord. "You mind your tongue, young man, because the Lord said unto Moses on the mount, honor your father and mother that your days may be long on the land which the Lord your God has given you, and when you speak fresh to your father then you are taking days and weeks and even *years* off your own life, and your soul is not in such a condition that you should welcome an early visit to the judgment bar to meet your Savior and hear him say your eternal fate!"

Measure wasn't half so worried about his eternal fate as he was worried about Mama being riled at him. He didn't try to argue that he wasn't talking smart or being sassy—only a fool would do that when Mama was already hot. He just started in looking humble and begging her pardon, not to mention the forgiveness of Papa and the sweet mercy of the Lord. By the time she was done with ragging him, poor Measure had already apologized a half a dozen times, so that she finally just grumped and went back to her sewing.

Then Measure looked up at Alvin Junior and winked.

"I saw that," said Mama, "and if you don't go to hell, Measure, I'll get up a petition to Saint Peter to send you there."

"I'd sign that petition myself," said Measure, looking meek as a puppy dog that just piddled on a big man's boot.

"That's right you would," said Mama, "and you'd sign it in blood, too, because by the time I'm through with you there'll be enough open wounds to keep ten clerks in bright red ink for a year."

Alvin Junior couldn't help himself. Her dire threat just

struck him funny. And even though he knew he was taking his life in his hands, he opened up his mouth to laugh. He knew that if he laughed he'd have Mama's thimble hard on his head, or maybe her hand clapped hard on his ear, or even her hard little foot smashed right down on his bare foot, which she did once to David the time he told her she should have learnt the word *no* sometime before she had thirteen mouths to cook for.

This was a matter of life and death. This was more frightening than the ridgebeam, which after all never hit him, which was more than he could say for Mama. So he caught that laugh before it got loose, and he turned it into the first thing he could think of to say.

"Mama," he said, "Measure can't sign no petition in blood, cause he'd already be dead, and dead people don't bleed."

Mama looked him in the eye and spoke slow and careful. "They do when I tell them to."

Well, that did it. Alvin Junior just laughed out loud. And that set half the girls to laughing. Which made Measure laugh. And finally Mama laughed, too. They all just laughed and laughed till they were mostly crying and Mama started sending people upstairs to bed, including Alvin Junior.

All the excitement had Alvin Junior feeling pretty spunky, and he hadn't figured out yet that sometimes he ought to keep all that jumpiness locked up tight. It happened that Matilda, who was sixteen and fancied herself a lady, was walking up the stairs right in front of him. Everybody hated walking anywhere behind Matilda, she took such delicate, ladylike steps. Measure always said he'd rather walk in line behind the moon, cause it moved faster. Now Matilda's backside was right in Al Junior's face, swaying back and forth, and he thought of what Measure said about the moon, and reckoned how Matilda's backside was just about as round as the moon, and then he got to wondering what it would be like to *touch* the moon, and whether it would be hard like a beetle's back or squishy as a slug. And when a boy six years old who's already feeling spunky gets a thought like that in his head, it's not even half a second till his finger is two inches deep in delicate flesh.

Matilda was a real good screamer.

Al might have got slapped right then, except Wastenot and Wantnot were right behind him, saw the whole thing, and laughed so hard at Matilda that she started crying and fled on up the stairs two steps at a time, not ladylike at all. Wastenot and Wantnot carried Alvin up the stairs between them, so high up he got a little dizzy, singing that old song about St. George killing the dragon, only they sang it about St. Alvin, and where the song usually said something about poking the old dragon a thousand times and his sword didn't melt in the fire, they changed *sword* to *finger* and made even Measure laugh.

"That's a filthy filthy song!" shouted ten-year-old Mary, who stood guard outside the big girls' door.

"Better stop singing that song," said Measure, "before Mama hears you."

Alvin Junior could never understand why Mama didn't like that song, but it was true that the boys never sang it where she could hear. The twins stopped singing and clambered up the ladder to the loft. At that moment the door to the big girls' room was flung open and Matilda, her eyes all red from crying, stuck her head out and shouted, "You'll be sorry!"

"Ooh, I'm sorry, I'm sorry," Wantnot said in a squeaky voice.

Only then did Alvin remember that when the girls set out to get even, he would be the main victim. Calvin was still considered the baby, so he was safe enough, and the twins were older and bigger and there was always two of them. So when the girls got riled, Alvin was first in line for their deadly wrath. Matilda was sixteen, Beatrice was fifteen, Elizabeth was fourteen, Anne was twelve, Mary was ten, and they all preferred picking on Alvin to practically any other recreation that the Bible would permit. One time when Alvin was tormented past endurance and only Measure's strong arms held him back from hot-blooded murder with a hayfork, Measure allowed as how the punishments of hell would most likely consist of living in the same house with five women who were all about twice a man's size.

Ever since then, Alvin wondered what sin he committed before he was born to make him deserve to grow up half-damned to start with.

Alvin went into the little room he shared with Calvin and just set there, waiting for Matilda to come and kill him. But she didn't come and didn't come, and he realized that she was probably waiting till after the candles were all out, so that no one would know which of his sisters snuck in and snuffed him out. Heaven knew he'd given them all ample reason to want him dead in the last two months alone. He was trying to guess whether they'd stifle him with Matilda's goosedown pillow—which would be the first time he was ever allowed to touch it—or if he'd die with Beatrice's precious sewing scissors in his heart, when all of a sudden he realized that if he didn't get outside to the privy in about twenty-five seconds he'd embarrass himself right in his trousers.

Somebody was in the privy, of course, and Alvin stood outside jumping and yelling for three minutes and still they wouldn't come out. It occurred to him that it was probably one of the girls, in which case this was the most devilish plan they'd ever come up with, keeping him out of the privy when they knew he was scared to go into the woods after dark. It was a terrible vengeance. If he messed himself he'd be so ashamed he'd probably have to change his name and run away, and that was a whole lot worse than a poke in the behind. It made him mad as a constipated buffalo, it was so unfair.

Finally he was mad enough to make the ultimate threat. "If you don't come out I'll do it right in front of the door so you'll step in it when you come out!"

He waited, but whoever was in there *didn't* say, "If you do I'll make you lick it off my shoe," and since that was the customary response, Al realized for the first time that the person inside the privy might not be one of his sisters after all. It was certainly not one of the boys. Which left only two possibilities, each one worse than the other. Al was so mad at himself he smacked his own head with his fist, but it didn't make him feel no better. Papa would probably give him a lick, but even worse would be Mama. She might give him a tongue-lashing, which was bad enough, but if she was in a real vile temper, she'd get that cold look on her face and say real soft, "Alvin Junior, I used to hope that at least one of my boys would be a born gentleman, but now I see my life was wasted," which always made him feel about as low as he knew how to feel without dying.

So he was almost relieved when the door opened and Papa stood there, still buttoning his trousers and looking none too happy. "Is it safe for me to step out this door?" he asked coldly.

"Yup," said Alvin Junior.

"What?"

"Yes sir."

"Are you sure? There's some wild animals around here that think it's smart to leave their do on the ground outside privy doors. I tell you that if there's any such animal I'll lay a trap and catch it by the back end one of these nights. And when I find it in the morning, I'll stitch up its bung hole and turn it loose to bloat up and die in the woods."

"Sorry, Papa."

Papa shook his head and started walking toward the house. "I don't know what's wrong with your bowel, boy. One minute you don't need to go and the next minute you're about to die."

"Well if you'd just build another outhouse I'd be fine," Al Junior muttered. Papa didn't hear him, though, because Alvin didn't actually say it till the privy door was closed and Papa'd gone back to the house, and even then he didn't say it very loud.

Alvin rinsed his hands at the pump a long time, because he feared what was waiting for him back in the house. But then, alone outside in the darkness, he began to be afraid for another reason. Everybody said that a White man never could hear when a Red man was walking through the woods, and his big brothers got some fun out of telling Alvin that whenever he was alone outside, especially at night, there was Reds in the forest, watching him, playing with their flint-bladed tommy-hawks and itching to have his scalp. In broad daylight, Al didn't believe them, but at night, his hands cold with the water, a chill ran through him, and he thought he even knew where the Red was standing. Just over his shoulder, back over near the pigsty, moving so quiet that the pigs didn't even grunt and the dogs didn't bark or nothing. And they'd find Al's body, all hairless and bloody, and *then* it'd be too late. Bad as his sisters were—and they were *bad*—Al figured they'd be better than dying from a Red man's flint in his head. He fair to flew from the pump to the house, and he *didn't* look back to see if the Red was really there.

As soon as the door was closed, he forgot his fears of silent invisible Reds. Things were right quiet in the house, which was pretty suspicious to start with. The girls were never quiet till Papa shouted at them at least three times each night. So Alvin walked up real careful, looking before every step, checking over his shoulder so often he started getting a crick in his neck. By the time he was inside his room with the door closed he was so jittery that he almost hoped they'd do whatever they were planning to do and get it over with.

But they didn't do it and they didn't do it. He looked around the room by candlelight, turned down his bed, looked into every corner, but there was nothing there. Calvin was asleep with his thumb in his mouth, which meant that if they *had* prowled around his room, it had been a while ago. He began to wonder if maybe, just this once, the girls had decided to leave him be or even do their dirty tricks to the twins. It would be a whole new life for him, if the girls started being nice. Like as if an angel came down and lifted him right out of hell.

He stripped off his clothes quick as he could, folded them, and put them on the stool by his bed so they wouldn't be full of roaches in the morning. He had kind of an agreement with the roaches. They could get into anything they wanted if it was on the floor, but they didn't climb into Calvin's bed or Alvin's neither, and they didn't climb onto his stool. In return, Alvin never stomped them. As a result Alvin's room was pretty much the roach sanctuary of the house, but since they kept the treaty, he and Calvin were the only ones who never woke up screaming about roaches in the bed.

He took his nightgown off its peg and pulled it on over his head.

Something bit him under the arm. He cried out from the sharp pain. Something else bit him on the shoulder. Whatever it was, it was all over inside his nightgown, and as he yanked it off, it kept right on nipping him everywhere. Finally it was off, and he stood there stark naked slapping and brushing with his hands to try to get the bugs or whatever they were off him.

Then he reached down and carefully picked up his nightgown. He couldn't see anything scurrying away from it, and even when he shook it and shook it, nary a bug fell off. Something else fell off. It glinted for a moment in the candlelight and made a tiny twinking sound when it hit the floor.

Only then did Alvin Junior notice the stifled giggling from the room next door. Oh, they got him, they got him sure. He sat on the edge of his bed, picking pins out of his nightgown and poking them into the bottom corner of his quilt. He never thought they'd be so mad they'd risk losing one of Mama's precious steel pins, just to get even with him. But he should have known. Girls never did have any bounds of fair play, the way boys did. When a boy knocked you down in a wrestling match, why, he'd either jump on you or wait for you to get back up, and either way you'd be even—both up or both down. But Al knew from painful experience that girls'd kick you when you were down and gang up on you whenever they had the chance. When they fought, they fought in order to end the fight as quick as they could. Took all the fun out of it.

Just like tonight. It wasn't a fair punishment, him poking her with his finger, and them getting him all jabbed up with pins. A couple of those places were bleeding, they stabbed so deep. And Alvin didn't reckon Matilda had so much as a bruise, though he wished she did.

Alvin Junior wasn't mean, no sir. But sitting there on the edge of the bed, taking pins out of his nightgown, he couldn't help but notice the roaches going about their business in the cracks of the floor, and he couldn't help imagining what it would be like if all those roaches just happened to go a-calling in a certain room full of giggles.

So he knelt down on the floor and set the candle right there, and he began whispering to the roaches, just the way he did the day he made his peace treaty with them. He started telling them all about nice smooth sheets and soft squishy skin they could scamper on, and most of all about Matilda's satin pillowcase on her goosedown pillow. But they didn't seem to care about that. Hungry, that's all they are, thought Alvin. All they care about is food, food and fear. So he started telling them about food, the most perfectly delicious food they ever ate in their life. The roaches perked right up and came close to listen, though nary one of them climbed on him, which was right in keeping with the treaty. All the food you ever wanted, all over that soft pink skin. And it's safe, too, not a speck of danger, nothing to worry about, you just go on in there and find the food on that soft pink squishy smooth skin.

Sure enough, a few of the roaches started skittering under Alvin's door, and then more and more of them, and finally the whole troop went off in a single great cavalry charge under the door, through the wall, their bodies shiny and glowing in the candlelight, guided by their eternal insatiable hunger, fearless because Al had told them there wasn't nothing to fear.

It wasn't ten seconds before he heard the first whoop from the room next door. And within a minute the whole house was in such an uproar you'd've thought it was on fire. Girls screaming, boys shouting, and big old boots stomping as Papa rushed up the stairs and squashed roaches. Al was about as happy as a pig in mud.

Finally things started calming down in the next room. In a minute they'd come in to check on him and Calvin, so he blew out the candle, ducked under the covers, and whispered for the roaches to hide. Sure enough, here came Mama's footsteps in the hall outside. Just at the last moment, Alvin Junior remembered that he wasn't wearing his nightgown. He snaked out his hand, snatched the nightgown, and pulled it under the covers just as the door opened. Then he concentrated on breathing easy and regular.

Mama and Papa came in, holding up candles. He heard them pull down Calvin's covers to check for roaches, and he feared they might pull down his as well. That would be such a shameful thing, to sleep like an animal without a stitch on. But the girls, who knew he couldn't possibly be asleep so soon after getting stuck with so many pins, they were naturally afraid of what Alvin might tell Mama and Papa, so they made sure to hustle them out of the room before they could do more than shine a candle in Alvin's face to make sure he was asleep. Alvin held his face absolutely still, not even twitching his eyelids. The candle went away, the door softly closed.

Still he waited, and sure enough, the door opened again. He could hear the padding of bare feet across the floor. Then he felt Anne's breath against his face and heard her whisper in his ear. "We don't know how you did it, Alvin Junior, but we know you set those roaches onto us."

Alvin pretended not to hear anything. He even snored a little.

"You don't fool me, Alvin Junior. You better not go to sleep tonight, because if you do, you'll never wake up, you hear me?"

Outside the room, Papa was saying, "Where's Anne got to?"

She's in here, Papa, threatening to kill me, thought Alvin. But of course he didn't say it out loud. Anyway, she was just trying to scare him.

"We'll make it look like an accident," said Anne. "You always have accidents, nobody will think it's murder."

Alvin was beginning to believe her, more and more.

"We'll carry your body out and stuff it down the privy hole, and they'll all think you went to relieve yourself and fell in."

That would work, thought Alvin. Anne was just the one to think of something so devilish clever, since she was the very best at secretly pinching people and being a good ten feet away before they screamed. That was why she always kept her fingernails so long and sharp. Even now, Alvin could feel one of those sharp nails scraping along his cheek.

The door opened wider. "Anne," whispered Mama, "you come out of there this instant."

The fingernail quit scratching. "I was just making sure little Alvin was all right." Her bare feet padded back out of the room.

Soon all the doors were closed, and he heard Papa's and Mama's shoes clattering down the stairs.

He knew that by rights he should still be scared to death by Anne's threats, but it wasn't so. He had won the battle. He pictured the roaches crawling all over the girls, and he started to laugh. Well, that wouldn't do. He had to stifle that, breathe calm as could be. His whole body shook from trying to hold in the laughter.

There was somebody in the room.

He couldn't hear anything, and when he opened his eyes he couldn't see anybody. But he knew somebody was there. Hadn't come in the door, so they must've come in the open window. That's plain silly, Alvin told himself, there isn't a soul in here. But he lay still, all laughter gone out of him, because he could *feel* it, somebody standing there. No, it's a nightmare, that's all, I'm still spooked from thinking about Reds watching me outside, or maybe from Anne's threat, something like that, if I just lie here with my eyes closed it'll go away.

The blackness inside Al's eyelids turned pink. There was a light in his room. A light as bright as daylight. There wasn't no candle in the world, no, not even a lantern that could burn so bright as that. Al opened his eyes, and all his dread turned into terror, for now he saw that what he feared was real.

There was a man standing at the foot of his bed, a man shining as if he was made of sunlight. The light in the room was coming from his skin, from his chest where his shirt was tore open, from his face, and from his hands. And in one of those hands, a knife, a sharp steel knife. I am going to die, thought Al. Just like Anne promised me, only there wasn't no way his sisters could conjure up such an awful apparition as this one. This bright Shining Man had come on his own, that was sure, and planned to kill Alvin Junior

for his own sins and not cause somebody else had set him
on.

Then it was like as if the light from the man pushed
right through Alvin's skin and came inside him, and the
fear just went right out of him. The Shining Man might
have him a knife, and he might've snuck on into the room
without so much as opening a door, but he didn't mean no
harm to Alvin. So Alvin relaxed a little and wriggled up in
his bed till he was mostly sitting, leaning up against the
wall, watching the Shining Man, waiting to see what all he'd
do.

The Shining Man took his bright steel knife and
brought the blade against his other palm—and cut. Alvin
saw the gleaming crimson blood flow from the wound in the
Shining Man's hand, stream down his forearm, and drip
from his elbow onto the floor. He hadn't seen four drops,
though, before he came to see a vision in his mind. He
could see his sisters' room, he knew the place, but it was
different. The beds were up high, and his sisters were giants,
so all he could see clear was big old feet and legs. Then he
realized he was seeing a little creature's view of the room. A
roach's view. In his vision he was scurrying, filled with
hunger, absolutely fearless, knowing that if he could get up
onto those feet, those legs, there'd be food, all the food he'd
ever want. So he rushed, he climbed, he scurried, searching.
But there wasn't no food, not a speck of it, and now huge
hands reached and swept him off, and then a great huge
shadow loomed over him, and he felt the hard sharp
crushing agony of death.

Not once, but many times, dozens of times, the hope of
food, the confidence that no harm would come; then
disappointment—nothing to eat, nothing at all—and after
disappointment, terror and injury and death. Each small
trusting life, betrayed, crushed, battered.

And then in his vision he was one who lived, one who
got away from the looming, stomping boots, under the beds,
into the cracks in the walls. He fled from the room of death,
but not into the old place, not into the safe room, because
now that was no longer safe. That was where the lies came

from. That was the place of the betrayer, the liar, the killer who had sent them into this place to die. There were no words in this vision, of course. There could be no words, no clarity of thought in a roach's brain. But Al had words and thoughts, and he knew more than any roach what the roaches had learned. They had been promised something about the world, they had been made *sure* of it, and then it was a lie. Death was a fearful thing, yes, flee that room; but in the other room, there was worse than death—there the world had gone crazy, it was a place where anything could happen, where nothing could be trusted, where nothing was certain. A terrible place. The worst place.

Then the vision ended. Alvin sat there, his hands pressed against his eyes, sobbing desperately. They suffered, he cried out silently, they suffered, and I did it to them, I betrayed them. That's what the Shining Man came to show me. I made the roaches trust me, but then I cheated them and sent them to die. I've done murder.

No, not murder! Who ever heard of roach-killing being murder? Nobody in the whole world would call it that.

But it didn't matter what other folks thought of it, Al knew that. The Shining Man had come to show him that murder was murder.

And now the Shining Man was gone. The light was gone from the room, and when Al opened his eyes, there was no one in the room but Cally, fast asleep. Too late even to beg forgiveness. In pure misery Al Junior closed his eyes and cried some more.

How long was it? A few seconds? Or did Alvin doze off and not notice the passage of a much longer time? Never mind how long—the light came back. Once again it came into him, not just through his eyes, but piercing clear to his heart, whispering to him, calming him. Again Alvin opened his eyes and looked at the face of the Shining Man, waiting for him to speak. When he said nothing, Alvin thought it was *his* turn, and so he stammered out the words, so weak compared to the feelings in his heart. "I'm sorry, I'll never do it again, I'll—"

He was babbling, he knew it, couldn't even hear himself speak he was so upset. But the light grew brighter for a moment, and he felt a question in his mind. Not a word was spoke, mind you, but he knew that the Shining Man wanted him to say what it was he was sorry *for*.

And when he thought about it, Alvin wasn't altogether sure what all was wrong. Sure it wasn't the killing itself —you could starve to death if you didn't slaughter a pig now and then, and it wasn't hardly murder when a weasel killed himself a mouse, was it?

Then the light pushed at him again, and he saw another vision. Not roaches this time. Now he saw the image of a Red man, kneeling before a deer, calling it to come and die; the deer came, all trembling and its eyes wide, the way they are when they're scared. It knew it was coming to die. The Red loosed him an arrow, and there it stood, quivering in the doe's flank. Her legs wobbled. She fell. And Alvin knew that in this vision there wasn't no sin at all, because dying and killing, they were both just a part of life. The Red was doing right, and so was the deer, both acting according to their natural law.

So if the evil he done wasn't the death of the roaches, what was it? The power he had? His knack for making things go just where he wanted, making them break just in the right place, understanding how things ought to be and helping them get that way? He'd found that right useful, as he made and fixed the things a boy makes and fixes in a rough country household. He could fit the two pieces of a broken hoe handle, fit them so tight that they joined forever without glue or tack. Or two pieces of torn leather, he didn't even have to stitch them; and when he tied a knot in string or rope, it stayed tied. It was the same knack he used with the roaches. Making them understand how things was supposed to be, and then they did what he wanted. Was that his sin, that knack of his?

The Shining Man heard his question before he even found words for it. Here came the push of light, and another vision. This time he saw himself pressing his hands against a stone, and the stone melted like butter under his hands, came out in just the shape he wanted, smooth and whole, fell from the side of the mountain and rolled away, a perfect ball, a perfect sphere, growing and growing until it was a whole world, shaped just the way his hands had made it, with trees and grass springing up on its face, and animals running and leaping and flying and swimming and crawling and burrowing on and above and within the ball of stone that he had made. No, it wasn't a terrible power, it was a glorious one, if he only knew how to use it.

Well if it ain't the dying and it ain't the knack, what did I do wrong?

This time the Shining Man didn't show him a thing. This time Alvin didn't see no burst of light, there wasn't a vision at all. Instead the answer just came, not from the Shining Man but from inside his own self. One second he felt too stupid ever to understand his own wickedness, and then the next second he saw it all as clear as could be.

It wasn't the roaches dying, and it wasn't the fact he made them do it. It was the fact that he made them do it just to suit his own pleasure. He told them it was for their own good, but it wasn't so, it was for Alvin's benefit alone. Harming his sisters, more than harming the roaches, and all so Alvin could lie in his bed shaking with laughter because he got *even*—

The Shining Man heard the thoughts of Alvin's heart, yes sir, and Al Junior saw a fire leap from his gleaming eye and strike him in the heart. He had guessed it. He was right.

So Alvin made the most solemn promise of his whole life, right then and there. He had a knack, and he'd use it, but there was rules in things like that, rules that he would follow even if it killed him. "I'll never use it for myself again," said Alvin Junior. And when he said the words he felt like his heart was on fire, it burned so hot inside.

The Shining Man disappeared again.

Alvin lay back, slid down under the blanket, exhausted from weeping, weary with relief. He'd done a bad thing, that was so. But as long as he kept this oath he made, as long as he only used his knack to help other people and never ever used it to help himself, why then he would be a good boy and didn't need to be ashamed. He felt light-headed the way you do coming out of a fever, and that was about right, he had been healed of the wickedness that grew inside him for a spell. He thought of himself laughing when he'd just caused death for his own pleasure, and he was ashamed, but that shame was tempered, it was softened, cause he knew that it would never happen again.

As he lay there, Alvin once again felt the light grow in the room. But this time it didn't come from a single source. Not from the Shining Man at all. This time when he opened his eyes he realized the light was coming from himself. His own hands were shining, his own face must be glowing the way the Shining Man had. He threw off his covers and saw that his whole body glowed with light so dazzling he couldn't hardly bear to look at himself, except that he also couldn't bear to look anywhere else. Is this me? he thought.

No, not me. I'm shining like this because I've also got to do something. Just like the Shining Man did something for me, I've got something to do, too. But who am I supposed to do it for?

There was the Shining Man, visible again at the foot of his bed, but not shining no more. Now Al Junior realized that he knew this man. It was Lolla-Wossiky, that one-eyed whisky-Red who got himself baptized a few days ago, still wearing the White man's clothes they gave him when he turned Christian. With the light inside him now, Alvin saw clearer than he ever did before. He saw that it wasn't likker that poisoned this poor Red man, and it wasn't losing one eye that crippled him. It was something much darker, something growing like a mold inside his head.

The Red man took three steps and knelt beside the bed, his face only a little way from Alvin's eyes. What do you want from me? What am I supposed to do?

For the first time, the man opened his eyes and spoke. "Make all things whole," he said. A second later, Al Junior realized that the man had said it in his Red language —Shaw-Nee, he remembered, from what the grown-ups said when he was baptized. But Al had understood it plain as if it was the Lord Protector's own English. Make all things whole.

Well, that was Al's knack, wasn't it? Fixing things, making things go the way they were supposed to. Trouble was, he didn't even half understand how he did it, and he surely had no idea how to fix something that was alive.

Maybe, though, he didn't have to understand. Maybe he just had to *act*. So he lifted his hand, reached out as careful as he could, and touched Lolla-Wossiky's cheek, under the broken eye. No, that wasn't right. He raised his finger until it touched the slack eyelid where the Red man's other eye was supposed to be. Yes, he thought. Be whole.

The air crackled. Light sparked. Al gasped and pulled his hand away.

All the light was gone from the room. Just the moonlight now coming in the window. Not even a glimmer of the brightness was left. Like as if he just woke up from a dream, the strongest dream he ever had in his life.

It took a minute for Alvin's eyes to change so he could see. It wasn't no dream, that was sure. Cause there was the Red man, who had once been the Shining Man. You ain't dreaming when you got a Red man kneeling by your bed, tears coming out of his one good eye, and the other eye, where you just touched him—

That eyelid was still loose, hanging over nothing. The eye wasn't healed. "It didn't work," whispered Alvin. "I'm sorry."

It was a shameful thing, that the Shining Man had saved him from awful wickedness, and he hadn't done a thing for him in return. But the Red man said nary a word of reproach. Instead he reached out and took Alvin's naked shoulders in both his large strong hands and pulled him close, kissed him on the forehead, hard and strong, like a father to a son, like brothers, like true friends the day before they die. That kiss and all it held—hope, forgiveness, love—let me never forget that, Alvin said silently.

Lolla-Wossiky sprang to his feet. Lithe as a boy he was, not staggering drunk at all. Changed, he *was* changed, and it occurred to Alvin that maybe he *had* healed something, set something right, something deeper than his eyes. Cured him of the whisky-lust, maybe.

But if that was so, Al knew it wasn't himself that done it, it was the light that was in him for a time. The fire that had warmed him without burning.

The Red man rushed to the window, swung over the

sill, hung for a moment by his hands, then disappeared. Alvin didn't even hear his feet touch the ground outside, he was that quiet. Like the cats in the barn.

How long had it been? Hours and hours? Would it be daylight soon? Or had it taken only a few seconds since Anne had whispered in his ear and the family had quieted down?

Didn't matter much. Alvin couldn't sleep, not now, not with all that had just happened. Why had this Red man come to him? What did it all mean, the light that filled Lolla-Wossiky and then came to fill him? He couldn't just lie here in bed, all full of wonder. So he got up, slithered into his nightgown as fast as he could, and slipped out of his door.

Now that he was in the hall, he heard talking from downstairs. Mama and Papa were still up. At first he wanted to rush down and tell them what all happened to him. But then he heard the tone of their voices. Anger, fear, all upset. Not a good time to come to them with a tale of a dream. Even if Alvin knew it wasn't a dream at all, that it was real, *they'd* treat it like a dream. And now that he was thinking straight, he couldn't tell them at all. What, that he sent the roaches into his sisters' room? The pins, the pokes, the threats? All of that would come out too, even though it felt like months, *years* ago to Alvin. None of it mattered now, compared to the vow he had taken and the future he thought might be in store for him—but it would matter to Mama and Papa.

So he tiptoed down the hall and down the stairs, just close enough to hear, just far enough to be around the corner and out of sight.

After just a few minutes, he forgot about being out of sight, too. He crept farther down, until he could see into the big room. Papa sat on the floor, surrounded with wood. It surprised Al Junior that Papa was still doing that, even after coming upstairs to kill roaches, even after so much time had passed. He was bent over now, his face buried in his hands. Mama knelt in front of him, the biggest hunks of wood between them.

"He's alive, Alvin," said Mama. "All the rest ain't worth never mind."

Papa lifted his head and looked at her. "It was water that seeped into the tree and froze and thawed, long before we even cut it down. And we happened to cut it in just such a way that the flaw never showed on the surface. But it was split three ways inside, just waiting for the weight of the ridgebeam. It was water done it."

"Water," said Mama, and there was derision in her voice.

"This is fourteen times the water's tried to kill him."

"Children always get in scrapes."

"The time you slipped on a wet floor when you were holding him. The time David knocked down the boiling cauldron. Three times when he was lost and we found him on the bank of the river. Last winter when the ice broke on the Tippy-Canoe River—"

"You think he's the first child to fall into the water?"

"The poison water that made him throw up blood. The mud-covered buffalo that charged him in that meadow—"

"Mud-covered. Everybody knows that buffaloes wallow like pigs. It had nothing to *do* with water."

Papa slapped his hand down hard on the floor. The sound rang like a gunshot through the house. It startled Mama, and of course she started to look toward the stairs to where the children would be sleeping. Alvin Junior scampered right back up the stairs and waited out of sight for her to order him back to bed. But she must not have seen him, cause she didn't shout anything and nobody came up after him.

When he tiptoed back down, they were still going at it, only a little quieter.

Papa whispered, but there was fire in his eyes. "If you think this *doesn't* have to do with water, then *you're* the one that's a lunatic."

Mama was icy now. Alvin Junior knew that look—it was the maddest Mama knew how to get. No slaps then, no tongue-lashings. Just coldness and silence, and any child who got that treatment from her began to long for death and the tortures of hell, because at least it would be warmer.

With Papa she wasn't silent, but her voice was terrible cold. "The Savior himself drank water from the Samaritan well."

"I don't recollect that Jesus fell down that well, neither," said Papa.

Alvin Junior thought of hanging onto the well bucket, falling down into the darkness, until the rope bound up on the windlass and the bucket stopped just above the water, where he would have drowned for certain. They told him he wasn't yet two years old when that happened, but he still dreamed sometimes about the stones that lined the inside of the well, getting darker and darker as he went down. In his dreams the well was ten miles deep and he fell forever before waking up.

"Then think of this, Alvin Miller, since you think you know scripture."

Papa started to protest that he didn't think nothing of the kind—

"The devil hisself said to the Lord in the desert that the angels would bear Jesus up lest he dash his foot against a stone."

"I don't know what that has to do with water—"

"It's plain that if I married you for brains I was plumb cheated."

Papa's face turned red. "Don't you call me no simpleton, Faith. I know what I know and—"

"He has a guardian angel, Alvin Miller. He has someone watching out for him."

"You and your scriptures. You and your angels."

"You tell me why else he had those fourteen accidents and not one of them so much as gave him a scrape on his arm. How many other boys get to six years old without no injury?"

Papa's face looked strange then, twisted up a little, as if it was hard for him to speak at all. "I tell you that there's something wants him dead. I *know* it."

"You don't know any such thing."

Papa spoke even slower, biting out the words as if each one caused him pain. "I *know*."

He had such a hard time talking that Mama just went on and talked right over him. "If there's some devil plot to kill him—which I ain't saying, Alvin—then there's an even stronger heavenly plan to preserve him."

Then, suddenly, Papa didn't have no trouble talking at all. Papa just gave up saying the hard thing, and Alvin Junior felt let down, like when somebody said uncle before they even got throwed. But he knew, the minute he thought about it, that his papa wouldn't give up like that lessen it was some terrible force stopping him from speaking up. Papa was a strong man, not a bit cowardly. And seeing Papa beat down like that, well, it made the boy afraid. Little Alvin knew that Mama and Papa were talking about him, and even though he didn't understand half what they said, he knew that Papa was saying somebody wanted Alvin Junior dead, and when Papa tried to tell his real proof, the thing that made him *know*, something stopped his mouth and kept him still.

Alvin Junior knew without a word being said that whatever it was stopped Papa's mouth, it was the plain opposite of the shining light that had filled Alvin and the Shining Man tonight. There was something that wanted Alvin to be strong and good. And there was something else that wanted Alvin dead. Whatever the good thing was, it could bring visions, it could show him his terrible sin and teach him how to be shut of it forever. But the bad thing, it had the power to shut Papa's mouth, to beat down the strongest, best man Al Junior ever knew or heard of. And that made Al afraid.

When Papa went on with his arguments, his seventh son knew that he wasn't using the proof that counted. "Not devils, not angels," said Papa, "it's the elements of the universe, don't you see that he's an offense against nature? There's power in him like you nor I can't even guess. So much power that one part of nature itself can't bear it—so much power that he protects hisself even when he don't know he's doing it."

"If there's so much power in being seventh son of a seventh son, then where's *your* power, Alvin Miller? You're a seventh son—that ain't nothing, supposedly, but I don't see you doodlebugging or—"

"You don't know what I do—"

"I know what you *don't* do. I know that you don't believe—"

"I believe in every true thing—"

"I know that every other man is down at the commons building that fine church, except for you—"

"That preacher is a fool—"

"Don't you ever think that maybe God is using your precious seventh son to try to wake you up and call you to repentance?"

"Oh, is that the kind of God you believe in? The kind what tries to kill little boys so their papas will go to meeting?"

"The Lord has *saved* your boy, as a sign to you of his loving and compassionate nature—"

"The love and compassion that let my Vigor die—"

"But someday his patience will run out—"

"And then he'll murder another of my sons."

She slapped his face. Alvin Junior saw it with his own eyes. And it wasn't the offhand kind of cuffing she gave her sons when they lipped or loafed around. It was a slap that like to took his face off, and he fell over to sprawl on the floor.

"I'll tell you this, Alvin Miller." Her voice was so cold it burned. "If that church is finished, and there's none of your handiwork in it, then you will cease to be my husband and I will cease to be your wife."

If there were more words, Alvin Junior didn't hear them. He was up in his bed a-trembling that such a terrible thought could be thought, not to mention being spoke out loud. He had been afraid so many times tonight, afraid of pain, afraid of dying when Anne whispered murder in his ear, and most of all afraid when the Shining Man came to him and named his sin. But this was something else. This was the end of the whole universe, the end of the one sure thing, to hear Mama talk about not being with Papa anymore. He lay there in his bed, all kinds of thoughts dancing in his head so fast he couldn't lay hold of any one of them, and finally in all that confusion there wasn't nothing for it but to sleep.

In the morning he thought maybe it was all a dream, it had to be a dream. But there were new stains on the floor at the foot of his bed, where the blood of the Shining Man had dripped, so that wasn't a dream. And his parents' quarrel, that wasn't no dream neither. Papa stopped him after breakfast and told him, "You stay up here with me today, Al."

The look on Mama's face told him plain as day that what was said last night was still meant today.

"I want to help on the church," Alvin Junior said. "I ain't afraid of no ridgebeams."

"You're going to stay here with me, today. You're going to help me build something." Papa swallowed, and stopped himself from looking at Mama. "That church is going to need an altar, and I figure we can build a right nice one that can go inside that church as soon as the roof is on and the walls are up." Papa looked at Mama and smiled a smile that sent a shiver up Alvin Junior's back. "You think that preacher'll like it?"

That took Mama back, it was plain. But she wasn't the kind to back off from a wrestling match just because the other guy got one throw, Alvin Junior knew that much. "What can the boy do?" she asked. "He ain't no carpenter."

"He's got a good eye," said Papa. "If he can patch and tool leather, he can put some crosses onto the altar. Make it look good."

"Measure's a better whittler," said Mama.

"Then I'll have the boy *burn* the crosses in." Papa put his hand on Alvin Junior's head. "Even if he sits here all day and reads in the Bible, this boy ain't going down to that church till the last pew is in."

Papa's voice sounded hard enough to carve his words in stone. Mama looked at Alvin Junior and then at Alvin

Senior. Finally she turned her back and started filling the basket with dinner for them as was going to the church.

Alvin Junior went outside to where Measure was hitching the team and Wastenot and Wantnot were loading roof shakes onto the wagon for the church.

"You aim to stand inside the church again?" asked Wantnot.

"We can drop logs down on you, and you can split them into shakes with your head," said Wastenot.

"Ain't going," said Alvin Junior.

Wastenot and Wantnot exchanged identical knowing looks.

"Well, too bad," said Measure. "But when Mama and Papa get cold, the whole Wobbish Valley has a snowstorm." He winked at Alvin Junior, just the way he had last night, when it got him in so much trouble.

That wink made Alvin figure he could ask Measure a question that he wouldn't normally speak right out. He walked over closer, so his voice wouldn't carry to the others. Measure caught on to what Alvin wanted, and he squatted down right there by the wagon wheel, to hear what Alvin had to say.

"Measure, if Mama believes in God and Papa doesn't, how do I know which one is right?"

"I think Pa believes in God," said Measure.

"But if he don't. That's what I'm asking. How do I know about things like that, when Mama says one thing and Papa says another?"

Measure started to answer something easy, but he stopped himself—Alvin could see in his face how he made up his mind to say something serious. Something true, instead of something easy. "Al, I got to tell you, I wisht I knew. Sometimes I figure ain't nobody knows nothing."

"Papa says you know what you see with your eyes. Mama says you know what you feel in your heart."

"What do *you* say?"

"How do *I* know, Measure? I'm only six."

"I'm twenty-two, Alvin, I'm a growed man, and I still don't know. I reckon Ma and Pa don't know, neither."

"Well, if they don't *know*, how come they get so mad about it?"

"Oh, that's what it means to be married. You fight all the time, but you never fight about what you think you're fighting about."

"What are they really fighting about?"

Alvin could see just the opposite thing this time. Measure thought of telling the truth, but he changed his mind. Stood up tall and tousled Alvin's hair. That was a sure sign to Alvin Junior that a grown-up was going to lie to him, the way they always lied to children, as if children weren't reliable enough to be trusted with the truth. "Oh, I reckon they just quarrel to hear theirselfs talk."

Most times Alvin just listened to grown-ups lie and didn't say nothing about it, but this time it was Measure, and he especially didn't like having Measure lie to him.

"How old will I have to be before you tell me straight?" asked Alvin.

Measure's eyes flashed with anger for just a second —nobody likes being called a liar—but then he grinned, and his eyes were sharp with understanding. "Old enough that you already guess the answer for yourself," he said, "but young enough that it'll still do you some good."

"When's that?" Alvin demanded. "I want you to tell me the truth now, all the time."

Measure squatted down again. "I can't always do that, Al, cause sometimes it'd just be too hard. Sometimes I'd have to explain things that I just don't know how to explain. Sometimes there's things that you have to figure out by living long enough."

Alvin was mad and he knew his face showed it.

"Don't you be so mad at me, little brother. I can't tell you some things because I just don't know myself, and that's not lying. But you can count on this. If I *can* tell you, I will, and if I can't, I'll just say so, and won't pretend."

That was the most fair thing a grown-up ever said, and it made Alvin's eyes fill up. "You keep that promise, Measure."

"I'll keep it or die, you can count on that."

"I won't forget, you know." Alvin remembered the vow he had made to the Shining Man last night. "I know how to keep a promise, too."

Measure laughed and pulled Alvin to him, hugged him right against his shoulder. "You're as bad as Mama," he said. "You just don't let up."

"I can't help it," said Alvin. "If I start believing you, then how'll I know when to stop?"

"Never stop," said Measure.

Calm rode up on his old mare about then, and Mama came out with the dinner basket, and everybody that was going, went. Papa took Alvin Junior out to the barn and in no time at all Alvin was helping notch the boards, and his pieces fit together just as good as Papa's. Truth to tell they fit even better, cause Al could use his knack for *this,* couldn't he? This altar was for everybody, so he could make the wood fit so snug that it wouldn't ever come apart, not at the joints or nowhere. Alvin even thought of making Papa's joints fit just as tight, but when he tried, he saw that Papa had something of a knack at this himself. The wood didn't join together to make one continuous piece, like Alvin's did—but it fit good enough, yes sir, so there wasn't no need to fiddle.

Papa didn't say much. Didn't have to. They both knew Alvin Junior had a knack for making things fit right, just like his Papa did. By nightfall the whole altar was put together and stained. They left it to dry, and as they walked into the house Papa's hand was firm on Alvin's shoulder. They walked together just as smooth and easy as if they were both parts of the same body, as if Papa's hand just growed there right out of Alvin's neck. Alvin could feel the pulse in Papa's fingers, and it was beating right in time with the blood pounding in his throat.

Mama was working by the fire when they came in. She turned and looked at them. "How is it?" she asked.

"It's the smoothest box I ever seen," said Alvin Junior.

"There wasn't a single accident at the church today," said Mama.

"Everything went real good here, too," said Papa.

For the life of him Alvin Junior couldn't figure out why Mama's words sounded like "I ain't going nowhere," and why Papa's words sounded like "Stay with me forever." But he knew he wasn't crazy to think so, cause right then Measure looked up from where he lay all sprawled out afore the fire and winked so only Alvin Junior could see.

❖ 8 ❖

Visitor

REVEREND THROWER ALLOWED himself few vices, but one
was to eat Friday supper with the Weavers. Friday *dinner*
was more accurate, since the Weavers were shopkeepers and
manufacturers, and didn't stop work for more than a snack
at noon. It wasn't the quantity so much as the quality that
brought Thrower back every Friday. It was said that
Eleanor Weaver could take an old tree stump and make it
taste like sweet rabbit stew. And it wasn't just the food,
either, because Armor-of-God Weaver was a churchgoing
man who knew his Bible, and conversation was on a higher
plane. Not so elevated as conversation with highly educated
churchmen, of course, but the best that could be had in this
benighted wilderness.

They would eat in the room back of the Weavers' store,
which was part kitchen, part workshop, and part library.
Eleanor stirred the pot from time to time, and the smell of
boiled venison and the day's bread baking mingled with the
odors from the soapmaking shed out back and the tallow
they used in candlemaking right here. "Oh, we're some of
everything," said Armor, the first time Reverend Thrower
visited. "We do things that every farmer hereabouts can do
for himself—but we do it better, and when they buy it from
us it saves them hours of work, which gives them time to
clear and plow and plant more land."

The store itself, out front, was shelved to the ceiling,

and the shelves were filled with dry goods brought in by wagon from points east. Cotton cloth from the spinning jennies and steam looms of Irrakwa, pewter dishes and iron pots and stoves from the foundries of Pennsylvania and Suskwahenny, fine pottery and small cabinets and boxes from the carpenters of New England, and even a few precious bags of spices shipped into New Amsterdam from the Orient. Armor Weaver had confessed once that it took all his life savings to buy his stock, and it was no sure bet that he'd prosper out here in this thinly settled land. But Reverend Thrower had noticed the steady stream of wagons coming up from the lower Wobbish and down the Tippy-Canoe, and even a few from out west in the Noisy River country.

Now, as they waited for Eleanor to announce that the venison stew was ready, Reverend Thrower asked him a question that had bothered him for some time.

"I've seen what they haul away," said Reverend Thrower, "and I can't begin to guess what they use to pay you. Nobody makes cash money around here, and not much they can trade that'll sell back east."

"They pay with lard and charcoal, ash and fine lumber, and of course food for Eleanor and me and—whoever else might come." Only a fool wouldn't notice that Eleanor was thickening enough to be about halfway to a baby. "But mostly," said Armor, "they pay with credit."

"Credit! To farmers whose scalps might well be traded for muskets or liquor in Fort Detroit next winter?"

"There's a lot more talk of scalping than there is scalping going on," said Armor. "The Reds around here aren't stupid. They know about the Irrakwa, and how they have seats in Congress in Philadelphia right along with White men, and how they have muskets, horses, farms, fields, and towns just like they do in Pennsylvania or Suskwahenny or New Orange. They know about the Cherriky people of Appalachee, and how they're farming and fighting right alongside Tom Jefferson's White rebels to keep their country independent from the King and the Cavaliers."

"They might also have noticed the steady stream of

flatboats coming down the Hio and wagons coming west, and the trees falling down and the log houses going up."

"I reckon you're half right, Reverend," said Armor. "I reckon the Reds might go either way. Might try to kill us all, or might try to settle down and live among us. Living with us wouldn't be exactly easy for them—they aren't much used to town living, whereas it's the most natural way for White folks to live. But fighting us has got to be worse, cause if they do that they'll end up dead. They may think that killing White folks might scare the others into staying away. They don't know how it is in Europe, how the dream of owning land will bring people five thousand mile to work harder than they ever did in their lives and bury children who might have lived in the home country and risk having a tommyhock mashed into their brains cause it's better to be your own man than to serve any lord. Except the Lord God."

"And that's how it is with you, too?" asked Thrower. "Risk everything, for land?"

Armor looked at his wife Eleanor and smiled. She didn't smile back, Thrower noticed, but he also noticed that her eyes were beautiful and deep, as if she knew secrets that made her solemn even though she was joyful in her heart.

"Not land the way farmers own it, I'm no farmer, I'll tell you that," said Armor. "There's other ways to own land. You see, Reverend Thrower, I give them credit now because I believe in this country. When they come to trade with me, I make them tell me the names of all their neighbors, and make rough maps of the farms and streams where they live, and the roads and rivers along their way here. I make them carry letters that other folks writ, and I write their letters for them and ship them on back east to folks they left behind. I know where everything and everybody in the whole upper Wobbish and Noisy River country is and how to get there."

Reverend Thrower squinted and smiled. "In other words, Brother Armor, you're the government."

"Let's just say that if there comes a time when a government would come in handy, I'll be ready to serve," said Armor. "And in two years, three years, when more folks come through, and some more start making things, like bricks and pots and blackware, cabinets and kegs, beer and cheese and fodder, well, where do you think they'll come to sell it or to buy? To the store that gave them credit when their wives were longing for the cloth to make a bright-colored dress, or they needed an iron pot or a stove to keep out the winter cold."

Philadelphia Thrower chose not to mention that he had somewhat less confidence in the likelihood of grateful people staying loyal to Armor-of-God Weaver. Besides, thought Thrower, I might be wrong. Didn't the Savior say that we should cast our bread upon the waters? And even if Armor doesn't achieve all he dreams of, he will have done a good work, and helped to open this land to civilization.

The food was ready. Eleanor dished out the stew. When she set a fine white bowl in front of him, Reverend Thrower had to smile. "You must be right proud of your husband, and all that's he's doing."

Instead of smiling demurely, as Thrower expected that she would, Eleanor almost laughed aloud. Armor-of-God wasn't half so delicate. He just plain guffawed. "Reverend Thrower, you're a caution," said Armor. "When I'm up to my elbows in candle tallow, Eleanor's up to hers in soap. When I'm writing up folks' letters and having them delivered, Eleanor's drawing up maps and taking down names for our little census book. There ain't a thing I do that Eleanor isn't beside me, and not a thing she does that I'm not beside her. Except maybe her herb garden, which she cares for more than me. And Bible reading, which I care for more than her."

"Well, it's good she's a righteous helpmeet for her husband," said Reverend Thrower.

"We're helpmeets for each other," said Armor-of-God, "and don't you forget it."

He said it with a smile, and Thrower smiled back, but the minister was a little disappointed that Armor was so henpecked that he had to admit right out in the open that he wasn't in charge of his own business or his own home. But what could one expect, considering that Eleanor had grown up in that strange Miller family? The oldest daughter of Alvin and Faith Miller could hardly be expected to bend to her husband as the Lord intended.

The venison, however, was the best that Thrower had ever tasted. "Not gamy a bit," he said. "I didn't think wild deer could taste like this."

"She cuts off the fat," said Armor, "and throws in some chicken."

"Now you mention it," said Thrower, "I can taste it in the broth."

"And the deer fat goes into the soap," said Armor. "We never throw anything away, if we can think of any use for it."

"Just as the Lord intended," said Thrower. Then he fell to eating. He was well into his second bowl of stew and his third slice of bread when he made a comment that he thought was a jesting compliment. "Mrs. Weaver, your cooking is so good that it almost makes me believe in sorcery."

Thrower was expecting a chuckle, at the most. Instead, Eleanor looked down at the table just as ashamed as if he had accused her of adultery. And Armor-of-God sat up stiff and straight. "I'll thank you not to mention that subject in this house," he said.

Reverend Thrower tried to apologize. "I wasn't serious about it," he said. "Among rational Christians that sort of thing is a joke, isn't it? A lot of superstition, and I—"

Eleanor got up from the table and left the room.

"What did I say?" Thrower asked.

Armor sighed. "Oh, there's no way you could know," he said. "It's a quarrel that goes back to before we were married, when I first come out to this land. I met her when she came with her brothers to help build my first cabin —the soapmaking shed, now. She started to scatter spearmint on my floor and say some kind of rhyme, and I shouted for her to stop it and get out of my house. I quoted the Bible, where it says, You shall not suffer a witch to live. It made for a right testy half hour, you may be sure."

"You called her a witch, and she married you?"

"We had a few conversations in between."

"She doesn't believe in that sort of thing anymore, does she?"

Armor knitted his brows. "It ain't a matter of believing, it's a matter of doing, Reverend. She doesn't do it anymore. Not here, not anywhere. And when you sort of halfway accused her of it, well, it made her upset. Because it's a promise to me, you see."

"But when I apologized, why did she—"

"Well, there you are. You have your way of thinking, but you can't tell her that come-hithers and herbs and incantations got no power, because she's seen some things herself that you can't just explain away."

"Surely a man like you, well read in the scripture and acquainted with the world, surely you can convince your wife to give up the superstitions of her childhood."

Armor gently laid his hand on Reverend Thrower's wrist. "Reverend, I got to tell you something that I didn't think I'd ever have to tell a grown man. A good Christian refuses to allow that stuff in his life because the only proper way to bring the hidden powers into your life is through prayer and the grace of the Lord Jesus. It ain't because it doesn't *work*."

"But it *doesn't*," said Thrower. "The powers of heaven are real, and the visions and visitations of angels, and all the miracles attested in the scripture. But the powers of heaven have nothing at all to do with young couples falling in love, or curing the croup, or getting chickens to lay, or all the other silly little things that the ignorant common people do with their so-called hidden wisdom. There's not a thing that's done by doodlebugging or hexing or whatever that can't be explained by simple scientific investigation."

Armor didn't answer for the longest while. The silence made Thrower quite uncomfortable, but he had no idea what more he could say. It hadn't occurred to him before that Armor could possibly *believe* in such things. It was a startling perspective. It was one thing to abstain from witchery because it was nonsense, and quite another to believe in it and abstain because it was unrighteous. It occurred to Thrower that this latter view was actually more ennobling: for Thrower to disdain witching was a matter of mere common sense, while for Armor and Eleanor it was quite a sacrifice.

Before he could find a way to express this thought, however, Armor leaned back on his chair and changed the subject entirely.

"Reckon your church is just about done."

With relief, Reverend Thrower followed Armor onto safer ground. "The roof was finished yesterday, and today they were able to clap all the boards on the walls. It'll be watertight tomorrow, with shutters on the windows, and when we get them glazed and the doors hung it'll be tight as a drum."

"I've got the glass coming by boat," said Armor. Then he winked. "I solved the problem of shipping on Lake Erie."

"How did you manage that? The French are sinking every third boat, even from Irrakwa."

"Simple. I ordered the glass from Montreal."

"French glass in the windows of a British church!"

"An American church," said Armor. "And Montreal's a city in America, too. Anyway, the French may be trying to get rid of us, but in the meantime we're a market for their manufactured goods, so the Governor, the Marquis de la Fayette, he doesn't mind letting his people turn a profit from our trade as long as we're here. They're going to ship it clear around and down into Lake Michigan, and then barge it up the St. Joseph and down the Tippy-Canoe."

"Will they make it before the bad weather?"

"I reckon so," said Armor, "or they won't get paid."

"You're an amazing man," said Thrower. "But I wonder that you have so little loyalty to the British Protectorate."

"Well, you see, that's how it is," said Armor. "You grew up under the Protectorate, and so you still think like an Englishman."

"I'm a Scot, sir."

"A Brit, anyway. In your country, everybody who was even rumored to be practicing the hidden arts got exiled, right away, hardly even bothered with a trial, did they?"

"We try to be just—but the ecclesiastical courts are swift, and there is no appeal."

"Well, now, think about it. If everybody who had any gift for the hidden arts got shipped off to the American colonies, how would you ever see a lick of witchery while you were growing up?"

"I didn't see it because there's no such thing."

"There's no such thing *in Britain*. But it's the curse of good Christians in America, because we're up to our armpits in torches, doodlebugs, bog-stompers and hexifiers, and a child can't hardly grow to be four feet tall without bumping headlong into somebody's go-away or getting caught up in some prankster's speak-all spell, so he says everything that comes to mind and offends everybody for ten miles around."

"A speak-all spell! Now, Brother Armor, surely you can see that a touch of liquor does as much."

"Not to a twelve-year-old boy who never touched a drop of liquor in his life."

It was plain that Armor was talking from his own experience, but that didn't change the facts. "There is always another explanation."

"There's a powerful lot of explanations you can think up for anything that happens," said Armor. "But I tell you this. You can preach against conjuring, and you'll still have a congregation. But if you keep on saying that conjuring don't *work*, well, I reckon most folks'll wonder why they should come all the way to church to hear the preaching of a plumb fool."

"I have to tell the truth as I see it," said Thrower.

"You may see that a man cheats in his business, but you don't have to name his name from the pulpit, do you? No sir, you just keep giving sermons about honesty and hope it soaks in."

"You're saying that I should use an indirect approach."

"That's a right fine church building, Reverend Thrower, and it wouldn't be half so fine if it wasn't for your dream of how it ought to be. But the folks here figure it's *their* church. They cut the wood, they built it, it's on common land. And it'd be a crying shame if you were so stubborn that they up and gave your pulpit to another preacher."

Reverend Thrower looked at the remnants of dinner for a long time. He thought of the church, not unpainted raw lumber the way it was right now, but finished, pews in place, the pulpit standing high, and the room bright with sunlight through clean-glazed windows. It isn't just the place, he told himself, but what I can accomplish here. I'd be failing in my Christian duty if I let this place fall under the control of superstitious fools like Alvin Miller and, apparently, his whole family. If my mission is to destroy evil and superstition, then I must dwell among the ignorant and superstitious. Gradually I will bring them to knowledge of the truth. And if I can't convince the parents, then in time I can convert the children. It is the work of a lifetime, my ministry, so why should I throw it away for the sake of speaking the truth for a few moments only?

"You're a wise man, Brother Armor."

"So are you, Reverend Thrower. In the long run, even if we disagree here and there, I think we both want the same thing. We want this whole country to be civilized and Christian. And neither one of us would mind if Vigor Church became Vigor City, and Vigor City became the capital of the whole Wobbish territory. There's even talk back in Philadelphia about inviting Hio to become a state and join right in, and certainly they'll make such an offer to Appalachee. Why not Wobbish someday? Why not a country that stretches from sea to sea, White man and Red, every soul of us free to vote the government we want to make the laws we'll be glad to obey?"

It was a good dream. And Thrower could see himself within it. The man who had the pulpit of the greatest church in the greatest city of the territory would become the spiritual leader of a whole people. For a few minutes he believed so intensely in his dream that when he thanked Armor kindly for the meal and stepped outside, it made him gasp to see that right now Vigor Township consisted entirely of Armor's big store and its outbuildings, a fenced common with a dozen sheep grazing on it, and the raw wood shell of a big new church.

Still, the church was real enough. It was almost ready,

the walls were *there,* the roof was on. He was a rational man. He had to see something solid before he could believe in a dream, but that church was solid enough now, and between him and Armor they could make the rest of the dream come true. Bring people to this place, make this the center of the territory. This church was big enough for town meetings, not just church meetings. And what about during the week? He'd be wasting his education if he didn't start a school for the children hereabouts. Teach them to read, to write, to cipher, and, above all, to *think,* to expunge all superstition from their minds, and leave behind nothing but pure knowledge and faith in the Savior.

He was so caught up in these thoughts that he didn't even realize he wasn't heading for Peter McCoy's farm downriver, where his bed would be waiting for him in the old log cabin. He was walking back up the slope to the meetinghouse. Not till he lit a couple of candles did he realize that he actually meant to spend the night here. It was his home, these bare wooden walls, as no other place in the world had ever been home to him. The sappish smell was like a madness in his nostrils, it made him want to sing hymns he'd never even heard before, and he sat there humming, thumbing through the pages of the Old Testament without so much as noticing that there were words on the paper.

He didn't hear them until they stepped onto the wooden floor. Then he looked up and saw, to his surprise, Mistress Faith carrying a lantern, followed by the eighteen-year-old twins, Wastenot and Wantnot. They were carrying a large wooden box between them. It took a moment before he realized that the box was meant to be an altar. That in fact it was a rather fine altar, the wood was tightly fitted as any master cabinetmaker could manage, beautifully stained. And burnt into the boards surrounding the top of the altar were two rows of crosses.

"Where do you want it?" asked Wastenot.

"Father said we had to bring it down tonight, now that the roof and walls were done."

"Father?" asked Thrower.

"He made it for you special," said Wastenot. "And

little Al burnt in the crosses hisself, seeing how he wasn't allowed down here no more."

By now Thrower was standing with them, and he could see that the altar had been lovingly built. It was the last thing he expected from Alvin Miller. And the perfectly even crosses hardly looked like the work of a six-year-old child.

"Here," he said, leading them to the place where he had imagined his altar would stand. It was the only thing in the meetinghouse besides the walls and the floor, and being stained, it was darker than the new-wood floor and walls. It was perfect, and tears came to Thrower's eyes. "Tell them that it's beautiful."

Faith and the boys smiled as broad as could be. "You see he ain't your enemy," said Faith, and Thrower could only agree.

"I'm not his enemy, either," he said. And he didn't say: I will win him over with love and patience, but I *will* win, and this altar is a sure sign that in his heart he secretly longs for me to set him free from the darkness of ignorance.

They didn't linger, but headed home briskly through the night. Thrower set his candlestick on the floor near the altar—never *on* it, since that would smack of Papistry —and knelt in a prayer of thanksgiving. The church mostly built, and a beautiful altar already inside it, built by the man he had most feared, the crosses burnt into it by the strange child who most symbolized the compelling superstitions of these ignorant people.

"You're so full of pride," said a voice behind him.

He turned, already smiling, for he was always glad when the Visitor appeared.

But the Visitor was not smiling. "So full of pride."

"Forgive me," said Thrower. "I repent of it already. Still, can I help it if I rejoice in the great work that is begun here?"

The Visitor gently touched the altar, his fingers seeking out the crosses. "*He* made this, didn't he?"

"Alvin Miller."

"And the boy?"

"The crosses. I was so afraid they were servants of the devil—"

The Visitor looked at him sharply. "And because they built an altar, you think that proves they're not?"

A thrill of dread ran through him, and Thrower whispered, "I didn't think the devil could use the sign of the cross—"

"You're as superstitious as any of the others," said the Visitor coldly. "Papists cross themselves all the time. Do you think it's a hex against the devil?"

"How can I know anything, then?" asked Thrower. "If the devil can make an altar and draw a cross—"

"No, no. Thrower, my dear son, they aren't devils, either of them. You'll know the devil when you see him. Where other men have hair on their heads, the devil has the horns of a bull. Where other men have feet, the devil has the cloven hooves of a goat. Where other men have hands, the devil has the great paws of a bear. And be sure of this: he'll make no altars for you when he comes." Then the Visitor laid both his hands on the altar. "This is *my* altar now," he said. "No matter who made it, I can turn it to my purpose."

Thrower wept in relief. "Consecrated now, you've made it holy." And he reached out a hand to touch the altar.

"Stop!" whispered the Visitor. Even voiceless, though, his word had the power to set the walls a-trembling. "Hear me first," he said.

"I always listen to you," said Thrower. "Though I can't guess why you should have chosen such a lowly worm as me."

"Even a worm can be made great by a touch from the finger of God," said the Visitor. "No, don't misunderstand me—I am not the Lord of Hosts. Don't worship me."

But Thrower could not help himself, and he wept in devotion, kneeling before this wise and powerful angel. Yes, angel, Thrower had no doubt of it, though the Visitor had no wings and wore a suit of clothes one might expect to see in Parliament.

"The man who built this is confused, but there is murder in his soul, and if he is provoked enough, it will come forth. And the child who made the crosses—he is as remarkable as you suppose. But he is not yet ordained to a life of good or evil. Both paths are set before him, and he is open to influence. Do you understand me?"

"Is this my work?" asked Thrower. "Should I forget all else, and devote myself to turning the child to righteousness?"

"If you seem too devoted, his parents will reject you. Rather you should conduct your ministry as you have planned. But in your heart, you'll bend everything toward this remarkable child, to win him to my cause. Because if he does not serve me by the time he's fourteen years of age, then I'll destroy him."

The mere thought of Alvin Junior being hurt or killed was unbearable to Thrower. It filled him with such a sense of loss that he could not imagine a father or even a mother feeling more. "All that a weak man can do to save the child, I will do," he cried, his voice wrung almost to a scream by his anguish.

The Visitor nodded, smiled his beautiful and loving smile, and reached out his hand to Thrower. "I trust you," he said softly. His voice was like healing water on a burning wound. "I know you will do well. And as for the devil, you must feel no fear of *him*."

Thrower reached for the proffered hand, to cover it with kisses; but when he should have touched flesh, there was nothing there, and in that moment the Visitor was gone.

* 9 *

Taleswapper

THERE WAS ONCE A TIME, Taleswapper well remembered, when he could climb a tree in these parts and look out over a hundred square miles of undisturbed forest. A time when oaks lived a century or more, with ever-thickening trunks making mountains out of wood. A time when leaves were so thick overhead that there were places where the forest ground was bare from lack of light.

That world of eternal dusk was slipping away now. There still were reaches of primeval wood, where Red men wandered more quietly than deer and Taleswapper felt himself to be in the cathedral of the most well-worshipped God. But such places were so rare that in this last year of wandering, Taleswapper had not journeyed a single day in which he could climb a tree and see no interruption in the forest roof. All the country between the Hio and the Wobbish was being settled, sparsely but evenly, and even now, from his perch atop a willow at the crest of a rise, Taleswapper could see three dozen cookfires sending pillars of smoke straight up into the cold autumn air. And in every direction, great swatches of forest had been cleared, the land plowed, crops planted, tended, harvested, so that where once great trees had shielded the earth from the sky's eye, now the stubbled soil was naked, waiting for winter to cover its shame.

Taleswapper remembered his vision of drunken Noah.

He had engraved it for an edition of Genesis for Scottish rite Sunday schools. Noah, nude, his mouth lolling open, a cup half-spilled still dangling from his curled fingers; Ham, not far off, laughing derisively; and Japheth and Shem, walking backward to draw a robe over their father, so they would not see what their father had exposed in his stupefaction. With an electric excitement, Taleswapper realized that this, now, is what that prophetic moment foreshadowed. That he, Taleswapper, perched atop a tree, was seeing the naked land in its stupor, awaiting the modest covering of winter. It was prophecy fulfilled, a thing which one hoped for but could not expect in one's own life.

Or, then again, the story of drunken Noah might not be a figure of this moment at all. Why not the other way around? Why not cleared land as a figure for drunken Noah?

Taleswapper was in a foul mood by the time he reached the ground. He thought and thought, trying to open his mind to see visions, to be a good prophet. Yet every time he thought he had got something firm and tight, it shifted, it changed. He thought one thought too many, and the whole fabric came undone, and he was left as uncertain as ever before.

At the base of the tree he opened his pack. From it he took the Book of Tales that he had first made for Old Ben back in '85. Carefully he unbuckled the sealed portion, then closed his eyes and riffled the pages. He opened his eyes and found his fingers resting among the Proverbs of Hell. Of course, at a time like this. His finger touched two proverbs, both written by his own hand. One meant nothing, but the other seemed appropriate. "A fool sees not the same tree that a wise man sees."

Yet the more he tried to study out the meaning of that proverb at this moment, the less connection he saw, except that it included mention of trees. So he tried the first proverb after all. "If the fool would persist in his folly he would become wise."

Ah. This was speaking to him, after all. This was the voice of prophecy, recorded when he lived in Philadelphia, before he ever began his journey, on a night when the Book of Proverbs came alive for him and he saw as if in letters of flame the words that should have been included. That night he had stayed up until dawn's light killed the fires of the page. When Old Ben came thumping down the stairs to grouch his way in for breakfast, he stopped and sniffed the air. "Smoke," he said. "You haven't been trying to burn down the house, have you, Bill?"

"No sir," answered Taleswapper. "But I saw a vision of what God meant the Book of Proverbs to say, and wrote them down."

"You are obsessed with visions," said Old Ben. "The only true vision comes not from God but from the inmost recesses of the human mind. Write that down as a proverb, if you want. It's far too agnostic for me to use it in Poor Richard's Almanac."

"Look," said Taleswapper.

Old Ben looked, and saw the last flames as they died. "Well, now, if that's not the most remarkable trick to do with letters. And you told me you weren't a wizard."

"I'm not. God gave this to me."

"God or the devil? When you're surrounded by light, Bill, how do you know whether it's the glory of God or the flames of hell?"

"I don't know," said Taleswapper, growing confused. Being young then, not yet thirty, he was easily confused in the presence of the great man.

"Or perhaps you, wanting truth so badly, gave it to yourself." Old Ben tilted his head to examine the pages of Proverbs through the lower lenses of his bifocals. "The letters have been burned right in. Funny, isn't it, that I'm called a wizard, who am not, and you, who are, refuse to admit it."

"I'm a prophet. Or—want to be."

"If one of your prophecies comes true, Bill Blake, then I'll believe it, but not until."

In the years since then, Taleswapper had searched for the fulfilment of even one prophecy. Yet whenever he thought he had found such a fulfilment, he could hear Old Ben's voice in the back of his mind, providing an alternate explanation, scoffing at him for thinking that any connection between prophecy and reality could be true.

"Never *true*," Old Ben would say. "Useful—now, there's something. Your mind might make a connection that is useful. But *true* is another matter. True implies that you have found a connection that exists independent of your apprehension of it, that would exist whether you noticed it or not. And I must say that I have never seen such a connection in my life. There are times when I suspect that there are no such connections, that all links, bonds, ties, and similarities are creatures of thought and have no substance."

"Then why doesn't the ground dissolve beneath our feet?" asked Taleswapper.

"Because we have managed to persuade it not to let our bodies by. Perhaps it was Sir Isaac Newton. He was such a persuasive fellow. Even if human beings doubt him, the ground does not, and so it endures." Old Ben laughed. It was all a lark to him. He never could bring himself to believe even his own skepticism.

Now, sitting at the base of the tree, his eyes closed, Taleswapper connected again: The tale of Noah with Old Ben. Old Ben was Ham, who saw the naked truth, limp and shameful, and laughed at it, while all the loyal sons of church and university walked backward to cover it up again, so the silly truth would not be seen. Thus the world continued to think of the truth as firm and proud, never having seen it in a slack moment.

That is a true connection, thought Taleswapper. That is the meaning of the story. That is the fulfilment of the prophecy. The truth when we see it is ridiculous, and if we wish to worship it, we must never allow ourselves to see it.

In that moment of discovery, Taleswapper sprang to his feet. He must find someone at once, to tell of this great discovery while he still believed it. As his own proverb said, "The cistern contains: the fountain overflows." If he did not speak his tale, it grew dank and musty, it shrank inside him, while with the telling the tale stayed fresh and virtuous.

Which way? The forest road, not three rods off, led toward a large white church with an oak-high steeple—he had seen it, not a mile away, while up the tree. It was the largest building Taleswapper had seen since he last visited in Philadelphia. Such a large building for people to gather in implied that folks in this part of the land felt they had plenty of room for newcomers. A good sign for an itinerant teller of tales, since he lived by the trust of strangers, who might take him in and feed him when he brought nothing with him to pay with, except his book, his memory, two strong arms, and sturdy legs that had carried him ten thousand miles and were good for at least five thousand more.

The road was rutted with wagon tracks, which meant it was often used, and in the low places it was firmed up with rails, making a good strong corduroy so that wagons wouldn't mire in rain-soaked soil. So this was on its way to being a town, was it? The large church might not mean openness at all—it might speak more of ambition. That's the danger of judging anything, thought Taleswapper: There are a hundred possible causes for every effect, and a hundred possible effects from every cause. He thought of writing down that thought, but decided against it. It had no traces on it save the prints of his own soul—neither the marks of heaven nor of hell. By this he knew that it hadn't been given to him. He had forced the thought himself. So it couldn't be prophecy, and couldn't be true.

The road ended in a commons not far from a river. Taleswapper knew that from the smell of rushing water —he had a good nose. Around the commons were scattered several buildings, but the largest of all was a whitewashed clapboard two-story building with a small sign that said "Weaver's."

Now when a house has a sign on it, Taleswapper knew, that generally means the owners want people to recognize the place though they've never been shown the way, which is the same as to say that the house is open to strangers. So Taleswapper went right up and knocked.

"Minute!" came a shout from inside. Taleswapper waited on the porch. Toward one end were several hanging baskets, with the long leaves of various herbs dangling. Taleswapper recognized many of them as being useful in various arts, such as healing, finding, sealing, and reminding. He also recognized that the baskets were arranged so that, seen from a spot near the base of the door, they would form a perfect hex. In fact, this was so pronounced an effect that Taleswapper squatted and finally lay prone on the porch to see it properly. The colors daubed on the baskets at exactly the correct points proved that it was no accident. It was an exquisite hex of protection, oriented toward the doorway.

Taleswapper tried to think of why someone would put up such a powerful hex, and yet seek to conceal it. Why, Taleswapper was probably the only person around likely to feel the whiff of power from something as passive as a hex, and so be drawn to notice it. He was still lying there on the floor, puzzling about it, when the door opened and a man said, "Are you so tired, then, stranger?"

Taleswapper leapt to his feet. "Admiring your arrangement of herbs. Quite an aerial garden, sir."

"My wife's," said the man. "She fusses over them all the time. Has to have them just so."

Was the man a liar? No, Taleswapper decided. He wasn't trying to hide the fact that the baskets made a hex and the trailing leaves intertwined to bind them together. He simply didn't know. Someone—his wife, probably, if it was her garden—had set up a protection on his house, and the husband didn't have a clue.

"They look just right to me," said Taleswapper.

"I wondered how someone could arrive here, and me not hear the wagon nor the horse. But from the looks of you, I'd guess you came afoot."

"That I did, sir," said Taleswapper.

"And your pack doesn't look full enough to hold many articles to trade."

"I don't trade in *things,* sir," said Taleswapper.

"What, then? What but things can be traded?"

"Work, for one thing," said Taleswapper. "I work for food and shelter."

"You're an old man, to be a vagrant."

"I was born in fifty-seven, so I still have a good

seventeen years until I've used up my three-score and ten. Besides, I have a few knacks."

At once the man seemed to shrink away. It wasn't in his body. It was his eyes that got more distant, as he said, "My wife and I do our own work here, seeing how our sons are right small yet. We've no need of help."

There was a woman behind him now, a girl still young enough that her face hadn't grown hard and weathered, though she was solemn. She held a baby in her arms. She spoke to her husband. "We have enough to spare another place for dinner tonight, Armor—"

At that the husband's face went firm and set. "My wife is more generous than I am, stranger. I'll tell you straight out. You spoke of having a few knacks, and in my experience that means you make some claim to hidden powers. I'll have no such workings in a Christian house."

Taleswapper looked hard at him, and then looked a bit softer at the wife. So that was the way of it here: she working such hexes and spells as she could hide from her husband, and he flat rejecting any sign of it. If her husband ever realized the truth, Taleswapper wondered what would happen to the wife. The man—Armor?—seemed not to be the murdering kind, but then, there was no telling what violence would flow in a man's veins when the flood of rage came undammed.

"I understand your caution, sir," said Taleswapper.

"I know you have protections on you," said Armor. "A lone man, afoot in the wild for all this way? The fact that your hair is still on your head says that you must have warded off the Reds."

Taleswapper grinned and swept his cap off his head, letting his bald crown show. "Is it a true warding, to blind them with the reflected glory of the sun?" he asked. "They'd get no bounty for *my* scalp."

"Truth to tell," said Armor, "the Reds in these parts are more peaceable than most. The one-eyed Prophet has built him a city on the other side of the Wobbish, where he teaches Reds not to drink likker."

"That's good advice for any man," said Taleswapper.

And he thought: A Red man who calls himself a prophet. "Before I leave this place I'll have to meet that man and have words with him."

"He won't talk to *you*," said Armor. "Not unless you can change the color of your skin. He hasn't spoke to a White man since he had his first vision a few years back."

"Will he kill me if I try?"

"Not likely. He teaches his people not to kill White men."

"That's also good advice," said Taleswapper.

"Good for White men, but it may not have the best result for Reds. There's folks like so-called Governor Harrison down in Carthage City who mean naught but harm for all Reds, peaceable or not." The truculence had not left Armor's face, but he was talking anyway, and from his heart, too. Taleswapper put a great deal of trust in the sort of man who spoke his mind to all men, even strangers, even enemies. "Anyway," Armor went on, "not all Reds are believers in the Prophet's peaceable words. Them as follow Ta-Kumsaw are stirring up trouble down by the Hio, and a lot of folks are moving north to the upper Wobbish country. So you won't lack for houses willing to take a beggar in—you can thank the Reds for that, too."

"I'm no beggar, sir," said Taleswapper. "As I told you, I'm willing to work."

"With knacks and hidden shiftiness, no doubt."

The man's hostility was the plain opposite of his wife's gentle welcoming air. "What *is* your knack, sir?" asked the wife. "From your speech you're an educated man. You'd not be a teacher, would you?"

"My knack is spoken with my name," he said. "Taleswapper. I have a knack for stories."

"For making them up? We call that lying, hereabouts." The more the wife tried to befriend Taleswapper, the colder her husband became.

"I have a knack for remembering stories. But I tell only those that I believe are true, sir. And I'm a hard man to convince. If you tell me your stories, I'll tell you mine, and we'll both be richer for the trade, since neither one of us loses what we started with."

"I've got no stories," said Armor, even though he had already told a tale of the Prophet and another of Ta-Kumsaw.

"That's sad news, and if it's so, then I've come to the wrong house indeed." Taleswapper could see that this truly wasn't the house for him. Even if Armor relented and let him in, he would be surrounded by suspicion, and Taleswapper couldn't live where people looked sharp at him all the time. "Good day to you."

But Armor wasn't letting him go so easily. He took Taleswapper's words as a challenge. "Why should it be sad? I live a quiet, ordinary life."

"No man's life is ordinary to himself," said Taleswapper, "and if he says it is, then that's a story of the kind that I never tell."

"You calling me a liar?" demanded Armor.

"I'm asking if you know a place where my knack might be welcome."

Taleswapper saw, though Armor didn't, how the wife did a calming with the fingers of her right hand, and held her husband's wrist with her left. It was smoothly done, and the husband must have become quite attuned to it, because he visibly relaxed as she stepped a bit forward to reply. "Friend," she said, "if you take the track behind that hill yonder, and follow it to the end, over two brooks, both with bridges, you'll reach the house of Alvin Miller, and I know he'll take you in."

"Ha," said Armor.

"Thank you," said Taleswapper. "But how can you know such a thing?"

"They'll take you in for as long as you want to stay, and never turn you away, as long as you show willingness to help out."

"Willing I always am, milady," said Taleswapper.

"*Always* willing?" said Armor. "Nobody's *always* willing. I thought you always spoke true."

"I always tell what I believe. Whether it's true, I'm no more sure than any man."

"Then how do you call me 'sir,' when I'm no knight, and call her 'milady,' when she's as common as myself?"

"Why, I don't believe in the King's knightings, that's why. He calls a man a knight because he owes him a favor, whether he's a true knight or not. And all his mistresses are called 'ladies' for what they do between the royal sheets. That's how the words are used among the Cavaliers—lies half the time. But your wife, sir, acted like a true lady, gracious and hospitable. And you, sir, like a true knight, protecting your household against the dangers you most fear."

Armor laughed aloud. "You talk so sweet I bet you have to suck on salt for half an hour to get the taste of sugar out of your mouth."

"It's my knack," said Taleswapper. "But I have other ways to talk, and not sweetly, when the time is right. Good afternoon to you, and your wife, and your children, and your Christian house."

Taleswapper walked out onto the grass of the commons. The cows paid him no mind, because he *did* have a warding, though not of the sort that Armor would ever see. Taleswapper sat in the sunlight for a little while, to let his brain get warm and see if it could come up with a thought. But it didn't work. Almost never had a thought worth having, after noon. As the proverb said, "Think in the morning, Act in the noon, Eat in the evening, Sleep in the night." Too late for thinking now. Too early for eating.

He headed up the pathway to the church, which stood well back from the commons, atop a good-sized hill. If I were a true prophet, he thought, I'd know things now. I'd know whether I'd stay here for a day or a week or a month. I'd know whether Armor would be my friend, as I hope, or my enemy, as I fear. I'd know whether his wife would someday win herself free to use her powers in the open. I'd know whether I'd ever meet this Red Prophet face to face.

But that was nonsense, he knew. That was the sort of seeing that a torch would do—he'd seen them doing it before, more than a few of them, and it filled him with dread, because it wasn't good, he knew, for a man to know too much of the path of his own life ahead. No, for him the knack he wanted was prophecy, to see, not the small doings of men and women in their little corners of the world, but rather the great sweep of events as directed by God. Or by Satan—Taleswapper wasn't particular, since both of them had a good idea of what they planned to do in the world, and so either one was likely to know a few things about the future. Of course, it was likely to be more *pleasant* to hear from God. What traces of the devil he had touched so far in his life had all been painful, each in its own way.

The church door stood open, this being a warmish day for autumn, and Taleswapper buzzed right in along with the flies. It was as fine a church inside as out—obviously Scottish rite, so it was plain—but all the more cheerful for that, a bright and airy place, with whited walls and glass-paned windows. Even the pews and pulpit were of light wood. The only thing dark in the whole place was the altar. So naturally his eye was drawn to it. And, because he had a knack for this sort of thing, he saw traces of a liquid touch upon the surface of it.

He walked slowly toward the altar. Toward it, because he had to know for sure; slowly, because this sort of thing ought not to be in a Christian church. Up close, though, there was no mistaking. It was the same trace he had seen on the face of the man in DeKane who tortured his own children to death and blamed it on the Reds. The same trace he had seen lingering on the sword that beheaded George Washington. It was like a thin film of filthy water, invisible unless you looked at a certain angle, in a certain light. But to Taleswapper it was always visible now—he had an eye for it.

He reached out his hand and set his forefinger carefully on the clearest trace. It took all his strength just to hold it there for a moment, it burned so, setting his whole arm to trembling and aching, right to the shoulder.

"You're welcome in God's house," said a voice.

Taleswapper, sucking on his burnt finger, turned to face the speaker. He was robed as a Scottish Rite preacher —Presbyterian, they called them here in America.

"You didn't get a splinter, did you?" asked the preacher.

It would have been easier just to say Yes, I got a splinter. But Taleswapper only told stories he believed.

"Preacher," said Taleswapper, "the devil has set his hand upon this altar."

At once the preacher's lugubrious smile disappeared. "How do you know the devil's handprint?"

"It's a gift of God," said Taleswapper. "To see."

The preacher looked at him closely, unsure whether or not to believe. "Then can you also tell where angels have touched?"

"I could see traces, I think, if goodly spirits had intervened. I've seen such marks before."

The preacher paused, as if he wanted to ask a very important question but was afraid of the answer. Then he shuddered, the desire to learn plainly fled from him, and the preacher spoke now with contempt. "Nonsense. You can fool the common people, but I was educated in England, and I am not deluded by talk of hidden powers."

"Oh," said Taleswapper. "You're an educated man."

"And so are you, by your speech," said the preacher. "The south of England, I would say."

"The Lord Protector's Academy of Art," said Taleswapper. "I was trained as an engraver. Since you're Scottish rite, I daresay you've seen my work in your Sunday school book."

"I never notice such things," said the preacher. "Engravings are a waste of paper that could be given over to words of truth. Unless they illustrate matters that the artist's eye has actually seen, like anatomies. But what the artist conceives in his imagination has no better claim on my eyes than what I imagine for myself."

Taleswapper followed that notion to its root. "What if the artist were also a prophet?"

The preacher half-closed his eyes. "The day of prophets is over. Like that apostate heathen one-eyed drunken Red man across the river, all who claim to be prophets now are charlatans. And I have no doubt that if God granted the gift of prophecy even to one artist, we would soon have a surplus of sketchers and daubers wishing to be taken for prophets, especially if it would bring them better pay."

Taleswapper answered mildly, but he did not let the preacher's implicit accusation stand. "A man who preaches the word of God for a salary ought not to criticize others who seek to earn a living by revealing the truth."

"I was ordained," said the preacher. "No one ordains artists. They ordain themselves."

Just as Taleswapper had expected. The preacher retreated to authority as soon as he feared his ideas could not stand on their own merit. Reasonable argument was impossible when authority became the arbiter; Taleswapper returned to the immediate matter. "The devil laid his fingers on this altar," said Taleswapper. "It burned my finger to touch the place."

"It never burned mine," said the preacher.

"I expect not," said Taleswapper. "*You* were ordained."

Taleswapper made no effort to hide the scorn in his voice, and it plainly irked the preacher, who lashed back. It did not bother Taleswapper when people got angry at him. It meant they were listening, and at least half believing him. "Tell me, then, if you have such keen eyes," said the preacher. "Tell me if a messenger from God has ever touched the altar."

Plainly the preacher regarded this question as a test. Taleswapper had no idea which answer the preacher thought was correct. It hardly mattered; Taleswapper would answer truthfully, no matter what. "No," he said.

It was the wrong answer. The preacher smirked. "Just like that? You can say that he has not?"

Taleswapper thought for a moment that the preacher might believe his own ordained hands had left the marks of God's will. He would lay that notion to rest at once. "Most preachers don't leave tracks of light on things they touch. Only a few are ever holy enough."

But it wasn't himself the preacher had in mind. "You've said enough now," said the preacher. "I know that you're a fraud. Get out of my church."

"I'm no fraud," said Taleswapper. "I may be mistaken, but I never lie."

"And I never believe a man who says he never lies."

"A man always assumes that others are as virtuous as himself," said Taleswapper.

The preacher's face flushed with anger. "Get out of here, or I'll throw you out."

"I'll go gladly," said Taleswapper. He walked briskly to the door. "I never hope to return to a church whose preacher is not surprised to learn that Satan has touched his altar."

"I wasn't surprised because I don't believe you."

"You believed me," said Taleswapper. "You also believe an angel has touched it. That's the story you think is true. But I tell you that no angel could touch it without leaving a trace that I could see. And I see but one trace there."

"Liar! You yourself are sent by the devil, trying to do your necromancy here in the house of God! Begone! Out! I conjure you to leave!"

"I thought churchmen like you didn't practice conjurings."

"Out!" The preacher screamed the last word, the veins standing out in his neck. Taleswapper put his hat back on and strode away. He heard the door slam closed behind him. He walked across a hilly meadow of dried-out autumn grass until he struck the track that led up toward the house that the woman had spoken of. Where she was sure they'd take him in.

Taleswapper wasn't so sure. He never made more than three visits in a place—if he hadn't found a house to take him in by the third try, it was best to move on. This time, the first stop had been unusually bad, and the second had gone even worse.

Yet his uneasiness wasn't just that things were going badly. Even if at this last place they fell on their faces and kissed his feet, Taleswapper felt peculiar about staying around here. Here was a town so Christian that the leading citizen wouldn't allow hidden powers in his house—yet the altar in the church had the devil's mark on it. Even worse was the pattern of deception. The hidden powers were being used right under Armor's nose, and by the person he loved and trusted most; while in the church, the preacher was convinced that God, not the devil, had claimed his altar. What could Taleswapper expect, in this place up the hill, but more madness, more deception? Twisted people entwined each other, Taleswapper knew that much from the evidence of his own past.

The woman was right—the brooks were bridged. Even this, though, wasn't a good sign. To bridge a river was a necessity; to bridge a broad stream, a kindness to travelers. But why did they build such elaborate bridges over brooks so narrow that even a man as old as Taleswapper could leap them without wetting a foot? The bridges were sturdy, anchored into the earth far to either side of the stream, and both had roofs, well thatched. People pay money to stay in inns that aren't as tight and dry as these bridges, thought Taleswapper.

Surely this meant that the people at the end of the track were at least as strange as those he had met so far. Surely he ought to turn away. Prudence demanded that he leave.

But prudence was not strong in Taleswapper's character. It was as Old Ben told him, years before. "You'll go into the mouth of hell someday, Bill, just to find out why the devil has such bad teeth." There was a reason for the bridges, and Taleswapper sensed that it would mean a story worth remembering in his book.

It was only a mile, after all. Just when it seemed the track was about to wander into impenetrable wood, it took a sharp northward turn and opened into as pretty a holding as Taleswapper had seen, even in the placid settled lands of New Orange and Pennsylvania. The house was large and fine, with shaped logs, to show that they meant it to last, and there were barns and sheds and pens and coops that made it almost a village in itself. A wisp of smoke rising a half mile on up the track told him that his guess wasn't all wrong. There was another household nearby, sharing the road, which meant it was probably kin. Married children, no doubt, and all farming together, for the better prosperity of all. That was a good thing, Taleswapper knew, when brothers could grow up liking each other well enough to plow each other's fields.

Taleswapper always headed for the house—best to announce himself at once, rather than skulking about and being taken for a robber. Yet this time, when he meant to walk toward the house, he felt himself become stupid all at once, unable to remember what it was he was about to do. It was a warding so powerful that he did not realize he had been pushed away until he was halfway down the hill toward a stone building beside a brook. He stopped abruptly, frightened, for no one had power enough, he thought, to back him off without him realizing what was happening. This place was as strange as the other two, and he wanted no part of it.

Yet as he tried to turn back the way he had come, the same thing happened again. He found himself going down the hill toward the stone-walled building.

Again he stopped, and this time muttered, "Whoever you are, and whatever you want, I'll go of my own free will or I'll not go at all."

All at once it was like a breeze behind him, pushing him toward the building. But he knew he could go back if he wanted. Against the breeze, yes, but he could do it. That eased his mind considerably. Whatever constraints had been placed upon him, they were not meant to enslave him. And that, he knew, was one of the marks of a goodly spell—not the hidden chains of a tormentor.

The path rounded to the left a bit, along the brook, and now he could see that the building was a mill, for it had a millrace and the frame of a tall wheel standing where the water would flow. But no water flowed in the race today, and as he came close enough to see through the large barn-size door, he discovered why. It wasn't just closed up for the winter. It had never been used as a mill. The gears were in place, but the great round millstone wasn't there. Just a foundation of rammed cobbles, level and ready and waiting.

Waiting a long time. This construction was at least five years old, from the vines and the mosses on the building. It had been a lot of work to build this millhouse, and yet it was being used as a common haybarn.

Just inside the large door, a wagon was rocking back and forth as two boys grappled together atop a half-load of hay. It was a friendly bout; the boys were obviously brothers, the one about twelve years old, the other perhaps nine, and the only reason the young one wasn't thrown off the wagon and out the door was because the older boy couldn't keep himself from laughing. They didn't notice Taleswapper, of course.

They also didn't notice the man standing at the edge of the loft, pitchfork in hand, looking down at them. Taleswapper thought at first that the man was watching in pride, like a father. Then he came close enough to see how he held the fork. Like a javelin, ready to cast. For a single moment, Taleswapper saw in his mind's eye just what would happen —the fork thrown, burying itself in the flesh of one of the boys, surely killing him, if not immediately, then soon enough, with gangrene or belly bleeding. It was murder that Taleswapper saw.

"No!" he shouted. He ran through the doorway, fetching up alongside the wagon, looking up at the man in the loft.

The man plunged the pitchfork into the hay beside him and heaved the hay over the edge onto the wagon, half-burying the two boys. "I brought you here to work, you two bearcubs, not to tie each other in knots." The man was smiling, teasing. He winked at Taleswapper. Just as if there hadn't been death in his eyes a moment before.

"Howdy, young feller," said the man.

"Not so young," said Taleswapper. He doffed his hat, letting his bare pate give away his age.

The boys dug themselves out of the hay. "What were you shouting at, Mister?" asked the younger one.

"I was afraid someone might come to harm," said Taleswapper.

"Oh, we wrassle like that all the time," said the older boy. "Put her there, friend. My name's Alvin, same as my pa." The boy's grin was contagious. Scared as he'd been, with so much dark dealing going on today, Taleswapper had no choice but to smile back and take the proffered hand. Alvin Junior had a handshake like a grown man, he was that strong. Taleswapper commented on it.

"Oh, he gave you his fish hand. When he gets to wringing and wrenching on you, he like to pops your palm like a razzleberry." The younger boy shook hands, too.

"I'm seven years old, and Al Junior, he's ten." Younger than they looked. They both had that nasty bitter body stench that young boys get when they've been playing hard. But Taleswapper never minded that. It was the father who puzzled him. Was it just a fancy in his own mind, that Taleswapper thought he meant to kill the boys? What man could take a murderous hand to boys as sweet and fine as these?

The man had left the pitchfork in the loft, clambered down the ladder, and now strode toward Taleswapper with his arms out as if to hug him. "Welcome here, stranger," said the man. "I'm Alvin Miller, and these are my two youngest sons, Alvin Junior and Calvin."

"Cally," corrected the younger boy.

"He doesn't like the way our names rhyme," said Alvin Junior. "Alvin and Calvin. See, they named him like me hoping he'd grow up to be as fine a specimen of manhood as I am. Too bad it ain't working."

Calvin gave him a shove of mock anger. "Near as I can tell, he was the first try, and when I came along they finally got it right!"

"Mostly we call them Al and Cally," said the father.

"Mostly you call us 'shutup' and 'get over here,'" said Cally.

Al Junior gave him a whack on the shoulder and sent him sprawling in the dirt. Whereupon his father placed a boot on his backside and sent him head over heels out the door. All in fun. Nobody was hurt. How could I have thought there was murder going on here?

"You come with a message? A letter?" asked Alvin Miller. Now that the boys were outside, yelling at each other across the meadow, the grown men could get a word in.

"Sorry," said Taleswapper. "Just a traveler. A young lady in town said I might find a place to sleep up here. In exchange for whatever good hard work you might have for my arms."

Alvin Miller grinned. "Let me see how much work those arms can do." He thrust out an arm, but it wasn't to shake hands. He gripped Taleswapper by the forearm and braced his right foot against Taleswapper's right foot. "Think you can throw me?" asked Alvin Miller.

"Just tell me before we start," said Taleswapper, "whether I'll get a better supper if I throw you, or if I don't throw you."

Alvin Miller leaned back his head and whooped like a Red. "What's your name, stranger?"

"Taleswapper."

"Well, Mr. Taleswapper, I hope you like the taste of dirt, cause that's what you'll eat before you eat anything else here!"

Taleswapper felt the grip on his forearm tighten. His own arms were strong, but not like this man's grip. Still, a game of throws wasn't all strength. It was also wit, and Taleswapper had a bit of that. He let himself slowly flinch under Alvin Miller's pressure, long before he had forced the man to use his full strength. Then, suddenly, he pulled with all his might in the direction Miller was pushing. Usually that was enough to topple the bigger man, using his own weight against him—but Alvin Miller was ready, pulled the other way, and flung Taleswapper so far that he landed right among the stones that formed the foundation for the missing millstone.

There had been no malice in it, though, just the love of the contest. No sooner was Taleswapper down than Miller was helping him up, asking him if anything was broken.

"I'm just glad your millstone wasn't in place yet," said Taleswapper, "or you'd be stuffing brains back into my head."

"What? You're in Wobbish country, man! There ain't no need for brains out *here*."

"Well, you threw me," said Taleswapper. "Does that mean you won't let me earn a bed and a meal?"

"Earn it? No sir. I won't allow such a thing." But the grin on his face denied the harshness of his words. "No, no, you can work if you like, because a man likes to feel that he pays his way in the world. But truth is I'd let you stay even if you had two legs broke and couldn't help a lick. We've got a bed all ready for you, just off the kitchen, and I'll bet a hog against a huckleberry that them boys already told Faith to set another bowl for supper."

"That's kind of you, sir."

"Not at all," said Alvin Miller. "You sure nothing got broke? You hit them stones awful hard."

"Then I imagine you ought to check to make sure none of those stones got split, sir."

Alvin laughed again, slapped him on the back, and led him up to the house.

Such a house it was. There couldn't be more screeching and shouting in hell. Miller tried to sort out all the children for him. The four older girls were his daughters, busy as could be at half a dozen jobs, each one carrying on separate arguments with each of her sisters, at the top of her voice, passing from quarrel to quarrel as her work took her from room to room. The screaming baby was a grandchild, as were the five toddlers playing Roundheads and Cavaliers on and under the dining table. The mother, Faith, seemed oblivious to it all as she labored in the kitchen. Occasionally she'd reach out to cuff a nearby child, but otherwise she didn't let them interrupt her work—or her steady stream of orders, rebukes, threats, and complaints. "How do you keep your wits together, in all this?" Taleswapper asked her.

"Wits?" she asked him sharply. "Do you think anyone with wits would put up with this?"

Miller showed him to his room. That's what he called it, "your room, as long as you care to stay." It had a large bed and a feather pillow, and blankets, too, and half of one wall was the back of the chimney, so it was warm. Taleswapper hadn't been offered a bed like this in all his wandering. "Promise me that your name isn't really Procrustes," he said.

Miller didn't understand the allusion, but it didn't matter, he knew the look on Taleswapper's face. No doubt he'd seen it before. "We don't put our guests in the worst room, Taleswapper, we put them in the best. And no more talk about *that*."

"You have to let me work for you tomorrow, then."

"Oh, there's jobs to do, if you're good with your hands. And if you ain't ashamed of women's work, my wife could use a help or two. We'll see what happens." At that, Miller left the room and closed the door behind him.

The noise of the house was only partly dampened by the closed door, but it was a music that Taleswapper didn't mind hearing. It was only afternoon, but he couldn't help himself. He swung off his pack and pried off his boots and eased himself down on the mattress. It rustled like a straw tick, but there was a feather mattress on top of that, so it was deep and soft. And the straw was fresh, and dried herbs hung by the hearthstones to give it the smell of thyme and rosemary. Did I ever lie upon so soft a bed in Philadelphia? Or before that, in England? Not since I left my mother's womb, he thought.

There was nothing shy about the use of powers in this house; the hex was right in the open, painted above the door. But he recognized the pattern. It wasn't a peacemaker, designed to quell any violence in the soul that slept here. It wasn't a warning, and it wasn't a fending. Not a bit of it was designed to protect the house from the guest, or the guest from the house. It was for comfort, pure and simple. And it was perfectly, exquisitely drawn, exactly the right proportions. An exact hex wasn't easy to draw, being made of threes. Taleswapper couldn't remember seeing a more perfect one.

So it didn't surprise him, as he lay on the bed, to feel the muscles of his body unknotting, as if this bed and this room were undoing the weariness of twenty-five years of wandering. It occurred to him that when he died, he hoped the grave was as comfortable as this bed.

When Alvin Junior rocked him awake, the whole house smelled of sage and pepper and simmered beef. "You've just got time to use the privy, wash up, and come eat," said the boy.

"I must have fallen asleep," said Taleswapper.

"That's what I made that hex to do," said the boy. "Works good, don't it?" Then he charged out of the room. Almost immediately Taleswapper heard one of the girls yelling the most alarming series of threats at the boy. The quarrel continued at top volume as Taleswapper went out to the privy, and when he came back inside, the yelling was still going on—though Taleswapper thought perhaps now it was a different sister yelling.

"I swear tonight in your sleep Al Junior I'll sew a skunk to the soles of your feet!" Al's answer was muffled by distance, but it caused another bout of screaming. Taleswapper had heard yelling before. Sometimes it was love and sometimes it was hate. When it was hate, he got out as quickly as he could. In this house, he could stay.

Hands and face washed, he was clean enough that Goody Faith allowed him to carry the loaves of bread to the table—"as long as you don't let the bread touch that gamy shirt of yours." Then Taleswapper took his place in line, bowl in hand, as the whole family trooped into the kitchen and emerged with the majority of a hog parceled out among them.

It was Faith, not Miller himself, who called on one of the girls to pray, and Taleswapper took note that Miller didn't so much as close his eyes, though all the children had bowed heads and clasped hands. It was as if prayer was a thing he tolerated, but didn't encourage. Without having to ask, Taleswapper knew that Alvin Miller and the preacher down in that fine white church did not get along at all. Taleswapper decided Miller might even appreciate a proverb from his book: "As the caterpillar chooses the fairest leaves to lay her eggs on, so the priest lays his curse on the fairest joys."

The meal was not a time of chaos, to Taleswapper's surprise. Each child in turn reported what he did that day, and all listened, sometimes giving advice or praise. Finally, when the stew was gone and Taleswapper was dabbing at the last traces in his bowl with a sop of bread, Miller turned to him, just like he had to everyone else in the family.

"And your day, Taleswapper. Was it well spent?"

"I walked some miles before noon, and climbed a tree," said Taleswapper. "There I saw a steeple, which led me to a town. There a Christian man feared my hidden powers, though he saw none of them, and so did a preacher, though he said he didn't believe I had any. Still, I was looking for a meal and a bed, and a chance to work to earn them, and a woman said that the folks at the end of a particular wagon track would take me in."

"That would be our daughter Eleanor," said Faith.

"Yes," said Taleswapper. "I see now that she has her mother's eyes, which are always calm no matter what is happening."

"No, friend," said Faith. "It's just that these eyes have seen such times that since then it hasn't been easy to alarm me."

"I hope before I leave to hear the story of such times," Taleswapper said.

Faith looked away as she put another slab of cheese on a grandchild's bread.

Taleswapper went right on with his account of the day, however, not wishing to show that she might have embarrassed him by not answering. "That wagon track was most peculiar," he said. "There were covered bridges over brooks that a child could wade in, and a man could step over. I hope to hear the story of those bridges before I go."

Again, no one would meet his gaze.

"And when I came out of the woods, I found a mill with no millstone, and two boys wrestling on a wagon, and a miller who gave me the worst throw of my life, and a family that took me in and gave me the best room in the house even though I was a stranger, and they didn't know me to be good or evil."

"Of course you're good," said Al Junior.

"Do you mind my asking? I've met many hospitable people in my time, and stayed in many a happy home, but not one happier than this, and no one quite so glad to see me."

All were still around the table. Finally, Faith raised her head and smiled at him. "I'm glad you found us to be happy," she said. "But we all remember other times as well, and perhaps our present happiness is sweeter, from the memory of grief."

"But why do you take in a man like me?"

Miller himself answered. "Because once we were strangers, and good folk took us in."

"I lived in Philadelphia for a time, and it strikes me to ask you, are you of the Society of Friends?"

Faith shook her head. "I'm Presbyterian. So are many of the children."

Taleswapper looked at Miller.

"I'm nothing," he said.

"A Christian isn't nothing," said Taleswapper.

"I'm no Christian, either."

"Ah," said Taleswapper. "A Deist, then, like Tom Jefferson." The children murmured at his mention of the great man's name.

"Taleswapper, I'm a father who loves his children, a husband who loves his wife, a farmer who pays his debts, and a miller without a millstone." Then the man stood up from the table and walked away. They heard a door close. He was gone away outside.

Taleswapper turned to Faith. "Oh, milady, I'm afraid you must regret my coming to your house."

"You ask a powerful lot of questions," she said.

"I told you my name, and my name is what I do. Whenever I sense that there's a story, one that matters, one that's true, I hunger for it. And if I hear it, and believe it, then I remember it forever, and tell it again wherever I go."

"That's how you earn your way?" asked one of the girls.

"I earn my way by helping mend wagons and dig ditches and spin thread and anything else that needs doing. But my life work is tales, and I swap them one for one. You may think right now that you don't want to tell me any of your stories, and that's fine with me, because I never took a story that wasn't willingly told. I'm no thief. But you see, I've already got a story—the things that happened to me today. The kindest people and the softest bed between the Mizzipy and the Alph."

"Where's the Alph? Is that a river?" asked Cally.

"What, you want a story?" asked Taleswapper.

Yes, clamored the children.

"But not about the river Alph," said Al Junior. "That's not a real place."

Taleswapper looked at him in genuine surprise. "How did you know? Have you read Lord Byron's collection of Coleridge's poetry?"

Al Junior looked around in bafflement.

"We don't get much bookstuff here," said Faith. "The preacher gives them Bible lessons, so they can learn to read."

"Then how did you know the river Alph isn't real?"

Al Junior scrunched his face, as if to say, Don't ask me questions when I don't even know the answer myself. "The story I want is about Jefferson. You said his name like you met him."

"Oh, I did. And Tom Paine, and Patrick Henry before they hanged him, and I saw the sword that cut off George Washington's head. I even saw King Robert the Second, before the French sank his ship back in naught one and took him to the bottom of the sea."

"Where he belonged," murmured Faith.

"If not deeper," said one of the older girls.

"I'll say amen to that. They say in Appalachee that he had so much blood on his hands that even his bones are stained brown with it, and even the most indiscriminate fish won't gnaw at them."

The children laughed.

"Even more than Tom Jefferson," said Al Junior, "I want a tale of the greatest American wizard. I bet you knew Ben Franklin."

Again, the child had startled him. How did he guess that of all tales, those about Ben Franklin were the ones he best loved to tell? "Know him? Oh, a little," said Taleswapper, knowing that the way he said it promised them all the stories they could hope for. "I lived with him only half a dozen years, and there were eight hours every night that I wasn't with him—so I can't say I know *much.*"

Al Junior leaned over the table, his eyes bright and unblinking. "Was he truly a maker?"

"All those stories, each in its own time," said Taleswapper. "As long as your father and mother are willing to have me around, and as long as I believe I'm being useful, I'll stay and tell stories night and day."

"Starting with Ben Franklin," insisted Alvin Junior. "Did he really pull lightning out of the sky?"

❧ 10 ❧

Visions

ALVIN JUNIOR WOKE UP sweating from the nightmare. It was so real, and he was panting just as if he had been trying to run away. But there was no running away, he knew that. He lay there with his eyes closed, afraid to open them for a while, knowing that when he did, it would still be there. A long time ago, when he was still little, he used to cry out when this nightmare came. But when he tried to explain it to Pa and Mama, they always said the same thing. "Why, that's just *nothing*, son. You're telling me you're so a-scared of *nothing*?" So he learned himself to stifle and never cry when the dream came.

He opened his eyes, and it fled away to the corners of the room, where he didn't have to look right at it. That was good enough. Stay there and let me be, he said silently.

Then he realized that it was full daylight, and Mama had laid out his black broadcloth pants and jacket and a clean shirt. His Sunday go-to-meeting clothes. He'd almost rather go back to the nightmare than wake up to this.

Alvin Junior hated Sunday mornings. He hated getting all dressed up, so he couldn't set on the ground or kneel in the grass or even bend over without something getting messed up and Mama telling him to have some respect for the Lord's day. He hated having to tiptoe around the house all morning because it was the Sabbath and there wasn't to be no playing or making noise on the Sabbath. Worst of all he hated the thought of sitting on a hard bench down front, with Reverend Thrower looking him in the eye while he preached about the fires of hell that were waiting for the ungodly who despised the true religion and put their faith in the feeble understanding of man. Every Sunday, it seemed like.

And it wasn't that Alvin really despised religion. He just despised Reverend Thrower. It was all those hours in school, now that harvest was over. Alvin Junior was a good reader, and he got right answers most of the time in his ciphering. But that wasn't enough for old Thrower. He also had to teach religion right along with it. The other children —the Swedes and Knickerbockers from upriver, the Scotch and English from down—only got a licking when they sassed or got three wrong answers in a row. But Thrower took his cane to Alvin Junior every chance he got, it seemed like, and it wasn't over book-learning, it was always about religion.

Of course it didn't help much that the Bible kept striking Alvin funny at all the wrong times. That's what Measure said, the time that Alvin ran away from school and hid in David's house till Measure found him nigh onto suppertime. "If you just didn't laugh when he reads from the Bible, you wouldn't get whupped so much."

But it was *funny*. When Jonathan shot all those arrows in the sky and they missed. When Jeroboam didn't shoot enough arrows out his window. When Pharaoh kept finding tricky ways to keep the Israelites from leaving. When Samson was so dumb he told his secret to Delilah after she already betrayed him twice. "How can I keep from laughing?"

"Just think about getting blisters on your butt," said Measure. "That ought to take the smile off your face."

"But I never remember till after I already laughed."

"Then you'll probably never need a chair till you're fifteen years old," said Measure. "Cause Mama won't ever let you out of that school, and Thrower won't ever let up on you, and you can't hide in David's house forever."

"Why not?"

"Because hiding from your enemy is the same as letting him win."

So Measure wouldn't keep him safe, and he had to go back—and take a licking from Pa, too, for scaring everybody by running away and hiding so long. Still, Measure *had* helped him. It was a comfort to know that somebody else was willing to say that Thrower was his enemy. All the others were so full of how wonderful and godly and educated Thrower was, and how *kind* he was to teach the children from his fount of wisdom, that it like to made Alvin puke.

Even though Alvin mostly kept his face under control during school, and so got less lickings, Sunday was the most terrible struggle of all, because he sat there on that hard bench listening to Thrower, half the time wanting to bust out laughing till he fell on the floor, and half the time wanting to stand up and shout, "That's just about the stupidest thing I ever heard a growed man say!" He even had a feeling Pa wouldn't lick him very hard for saying that to Thrower, since Pa never had much of an opinion of the man. But Mama—she'd never forgive him for doing blasphemy in the house of the Lord.

Sunday morning, he decided, is designed to let sinners have a sample of the first day of eternity in hell.

Probably Mama wouldn't even let Taleswapper tell so much as the tiniest story today, lessen it came from the Bible. And since Taleswapper never seemed to tell stories from the Bible, Alvin Junior guessed that nothing good would come today.

Mama's voice blasted up the stairs. "Alvin Junior, I'm so sick and tired of you taking three hours to get dressed on Sunday morning that I'm about to take you to church naked!"

"I ain't naked!" Alvin shouted down. But since what he was wearing was his nightgown, it was probably *worse* than being naked. He shucked off the flannel nightgown, hung it on a peg, and started dressing as fast as he could.

It was funny. On any other day, he only had to reach out for his clothes without even thinking, and they'd be there, just the piece he wanted. Shirt, trousers, stockings, shoes. Always there in his hand when he reached. But on Sunday morning, it was like the clothes ran away from his hand. He'd go for his shirt and come back with his pants. He'd reach for a sock and come up with a shoe, time after time. It was like as if the clothes didn't want to get put on his body any more than he wanted them there.

So when Mama banged open the door, it wasn't altogether Alvin's fault that he didn't even have his pants on yet.

"You've missed breakfast! You're still half-naked! If you think I'm going to make the whole family parade into church late on account of you, you've got—"

"Another think coming," said Alvin.

It wasn't *his* fault that she always said the same thing. But she got mad at him as if he should have pretended to be *surprised* to hear her say it for the ninetieth time since summer. Oh, she was all set to give him a licking, all right, or call for Pa to do it even worse, when there was Taleswapper, come to save him.

"Goody Faith," said Taleswapper, "I'd be glad to see to it he comes to church, if you want to go on ahead with the others."

The minute Taleswapper spoke, Mama whirled around and tried to hide how mad she'd been. Alvin right away started doing a calming on her—with his right hand, where she couldn't see it, since if she saw him doing a spell on her, she'd break his arm, and that was one threat Alvin Junior truly believed. A calming didn't work so well without touching, but since she was trying so hard to *look* calm in front of Taleswapper, it worked all right.

"I hate to put you to any trouble," said Mama.

"No trouble, Goody Faith," said Taleswapper. "I do little enough to repay your kindness to me."

"Little enough!" The fretfulness was almost gone from Mama's voice now. "Why, my husband says you do the work of two grown men. And when you tell stories to the little ones I get more peace and quiet in this house than I've had since—since *ever*." She turned back to Alvin, but now her anger was more an act than real. "Will you do what Taleswapper tells you, and come to church right quick?"

"Yes, Mama," said Alvin Junior. "Quick as I can."

"All right then. Thank you kindly, Taleswapper. If you can get that boy to obey, that's more than anybody else has managed since he learned to talk."

"He's a real brat," said Mary, from the hallway outside.

"Shut your mouth, Mary," Mama said, "or I'll stuff your lower lip up your nose and tack it there to *keep* it shut."

Alvin sighed in relief. When Mama made impossible threats it meant she wasn't all that angry anymore. Mary put her nose in the air and flounced down the hall, but Alvin didn't even bother with it. He just grinned at Taleswapper, and Taleswapper grinned at him.

"Having trouble getting dressed for church, lad?" asked Taleswapper.

"I'd rather dress myself in lard and walk through a herd of hungry bears," said Alvin Junior.

"More people live through church than survive encounters with bears."

"Not by much, though."

Soon enough he got dressed. But he was able to talk Taleswapper into taking the shortcut, which meant walking through the woods up over the hill behind the house, instead of going around by way of the road. Since it was right cold outside, and hadn't rained in a while, and wasn't about to snow yet, there'd be no mud and Mama'd probably not even guess. And what Mama didn't know wouldn't hurt him.

"I noticed," said Taleswapper as they climbed up the leaf-covered slope, "that your father didn't go with your mother and Cally and the girls."

"He doesn't go to that church," said Alvin. "He says Reverend Thrower is a jackass. Course, he don't say that where Mama can hear."

"I suppose not," said Taleswapper.

They stood at the top of the hill, looking down across

open meadowland toward the church. The church's own hill hid the town of Vigor Church from view. The frost was just beginning to melt off the brown autumn grass, so that the church looked to be the whitest thing in a world of whiteness, and the sun flashed on it like it was another sun. Alvin could see wagons still pulling into place, and horses being tied to the posts on the meadow. If they hurried right now, they'd probably be in their places before Reverend Thrower started up the hymn.

But Taleswapper didn't start down the hill. He just set himself on a stump and started to recite a poem. Alvin listened tight, because Taleswapper's poems often had a real bite to them.

> *"I went to the Garden of Love,*
> *And saw what I never had seen:*
> *A chapel was built in the midst,*
> *Where I used to play on the green.*
>
> *And the gates of this chapel were shut,*
> *And 'Thou shalt not' writ over the door,*
> *So I turned to the Garden of Love,*
> *That so many sweet flowers bore,*
>
> *And I saw it was filled with graves,*
> *And tomb-stones where flowers should be:*
> *And priests in black gowns were walking their rounds,*
> *And binding with briars my joys and desires."*

Oh, Taleswapper had a knack, he did, for as he recited, the very world changed before Alvin's eyes. The meadows and trees looked like the loudest shout of spring, vivid yellow-green with ten thousand blossoms, and the white of the chapel in the midst of it was no longer gleaming, but instead the dusty, chalky white of old bones. "Binding with briars my joys and desires," Alvin repeated. "You ain't got much use for religion."

"I breathe religion with my every breath," said the Taleswapper. "I long for visions, I search for the traces of God's hand. But in this world I see more traces of the other. A trail of glistening slime that burns me when I touch it.

God is a bit standoffish these days, Al Junior, but Satan has no fear of getting down in the muck with mankind."

"Thrower says his church is the house of God."

Taleswapper, he just sat there and said nothing for the longest time.

Finally Alvin asked him right out: "Have you seen devil traces in that church?"

In the days that Taleswapper had been with them, Alvin had come to know that Taleswapper never exactly lied. But when he didn't want to get pinned down with the true answer, he'd say a poem. He said one now.

> *"O Rose, thou art sick.*
> *The invisible worm*
> *That flies in the night*
> *In the howling storm*
>
> *Has found out thy bed*
> *Of crimson joy,*
> *And his dark secret love*
> *Does thy life destroy."*

Alvin was impatient with such twisting answers. "If I want to hear something I don't understand, I can read Isaiah."

"Music to my ears, my lad, to compare me to the greatest of prophets."

"He ain't much of a prophet if nobody can understand a thing he wrote."

"Or perhaps he meant us all to become prophets."

"I don't hold with prophets," said Alvin. "Near as I can tell, they end up just as dead as the next man." It was something he had heard his father say.

"Everybody ends up dead," said Taleswapper. "But some who are dead live on in their words."

"Words never stay straight," said Alvin. "Now, when I *make* a thing, then it's the thing I made. Like when I make a basket. It's a basket. When it gets tore, then it's a tored-up basket. But when I say words, they can get all twisted up. Thrower can take those same very words I said and bend them back and make them mean just contrary to what I said."

"Think of it another way, Alvin. When you make one basket, it can never be more than one basket. But when you say words, they can be repeated over and over, and fill men's hearts a thousand miles from where you first spoke them. Words can magnify, but things are never more than what they are."

Alvin tried to picture that, and with Taleswapper saying it, the picture came easy to his mind. Words as invisible as air, coming out of Taleswapper's mouth and spreading from person to person. Growing larger all the time, but still invisible.

Then, suddenly, the vision changed. He saw the words coming from the preacher's mouth, like a trembling in the air, spreading out, seeping into everything—and suddenly it became his nightmare, the terrible dream that came on him, waking or sleeping, and spiked his heart to his spine till he like to died. The world filling up with an invisible trembling *nothing* that seeped into everything and shook it apart. Alvin could see it, rolling toward him like a huge ball, growing all the time. He knew from all the nightmares before that even if he clenched his fists it would thin itself out and seep between his fingers, and even when he closed his mouth and his eyes it would press on his face and ooze into his nose and ears and—

Taleswapper shook him. Shook him hard. Alvin opened his eyes. The trembling air retreated back to the edges of his sight. That's where Alvin saw it most of the time, waiting just barely out of sight, wary as a weasel, ready to flit away if he turned his head.

"What's wrong with you, lad?" asked Taleswapper. His face looked afraid.

"Nothing," said Alvin.

"Don't tell me nothing," said Taleswapper. "All of a sudden I saw a fear come over you, as if you were seeing a terrible vision."

"It wasn't a vision," said Alvin. "I had a vision once, and I know."

"Oh?" said Taleswapper. "What vision was that?"

"A Shining Man," said Alvin. "I never told nobody about it, and I don't reckon to start now."

Taleswapper didn't press him. "What you saw now, if it wasn't a vision—well, what was it?"

"It was nothing." It was a true answer, but he also knew it was no answer at all. But he didn't *want* to answer. Whenever he told people, they just scoffed at him for being such a baby about nothing.

But Taleswapper wouldn't let him slough off his question. "I've been longing for a true vision all my life, Al Junior, and you saw one, here in broad daylight, with your eyes wide open, you saw something so terrible it made you stop breathing, now tell me what it was."

"I told you! It was nothing!" Then, quieter: "It's *nothing*, but I can see it. Like the air gets wobbly wherever it goes."

"It's nothing, but not invisible?"

"It gets into everything. It gets into all the smallest cracks and shakes everything apart. Just shivers and shivers until there's nothing left but dust, and then it shivers the dust, and I try to keep it out, but it gets bigger and bigger, it rolls over everything, till it like to fills the whole sky and the whole earth." Alvin couldn't help himself. He was shaking with cold, even though he was bundled up thick as a bear.

"How many times have you seen this before?"

"Ever since I can remember. Just now and then it'll come on me. Most times I just think about other things and it stays back."

"Where?"

"Back. Out of sight." Alvin knelt down and then sat down, exhausted. Sat right in the damp grass with his Sunday pants, but he didn't hardly notice. "When you talked about words spreading and spreading, it made me see it again."

"A dream that comes again and again is trying to tell you the truth," said Taleswapper.

The old man was so plainly eager about the whole thing that Alvin wondered if he really understood how frightening it was. "This ain't one of your stories, Tale-swapper."

"It will be," said Taleswapper, "as soon as I understand it."

Taleswapper sat beside him and thought in silence for the longest time. Alvin just sat there, twisting grass in his fingers. After a while he got impatient. "Maybe you can't understand everything," he said. "Maybe it's just a craziness in me. Maybe I get lunatic spells."

"Here," said Taleswapper, taking no notice that Alvin had even spoke. "I've thought of a meaning. Let me say it, and see if we believe it."

Alvin didn't like being ignored. "Or maybe *you* get lunatic spells, you ever think of that, Taleswapper?"

Taleswapper brushed aside Alvin's doubt. "All the universe is just a dream in God's mind, and as long as he's asleep, he believes in it, and things stay real. What you see is God waking up, gradually waking up, and his wakefulness sweeps through the dream, undoes the universe, until finally he sits up, rubs his eyes, and says, 'My, what a dream, I wish I could remember what it was,' and in that moment we'll all be gone." He looked eagerly at Alvin. "How was that?"

"If you believe that, Taleswapper, then you're a blamed fool, just like Armor-of-God says."

"Oh, he says that, does he?" Taleswapper suddenly snaked out his hand and took Alvin by the wrist. Alvin was so surprised he dropped what he was holding. "No! Pick it up! Look what you were doing!"

"I was just fiddling, for pete's sake."

Taleswapper reached down and picked up what Alvin had dropped. It was a tiny basket, not an inch across, made from autumn grasses. "You made this, just now."

"I reckon so," said Alvin.

"Why did you make it?"

"Just made it."

"You weren't even thinking about it?"

"It ain't much of a basket, you know. I used to make them for Cally. He called them bug baskets when he was little. They just fall apart pretty soon."

"You saw a vision of *nothing*, and then you had to make *something*."

Alvin looked at the basket. "Reckon so."

"Do you always do that?"

Alvin thought back to other times he'd seen the shivering air. "I'm always making things," he said. "Don't mean much."

"But you don't feel right again until you've made something. After you see the vision of nothing, you aren't at peace until you put something together."

"Maybe I've just got to work it off."

"Not just *work*, though, is it, lad? Chopping wood doesn't do the job for you. Gathering eggs, toting water, cutting hay, that doesn't ease you."

Now Alvin began to see the pattern Taleswapper had found. It was true, near as he could remember. He'd wake up after such a dream at night, and couldn't stop fidgeting until he'd done some weaving or built a haystack or done up a doll out of corn shucks for one of the nieces. Same thing when the vision came on him in the day—he wasn't no good at whatever chore he was doing, until he built something that hadn't been there before, even if it was nothing more than a pile of rocks or part of a stone wall.

"It's true, isn't it? You do that every time, don't you?"

"Mostly."

"Then let me tell you the name of the nothing. It's the Unmaker."

"Never heard of it," said Alvin.

"Neither did I, till now. That's because it likes to keep itself secret. It's the enemy of everything that exists. All it wants is to break everything into pieces, and break those pieces into pieces, until there's nothing left at all."

"If you break something into pieces, and break the pieces into pieces, you don't get *nothing*," said Alvin. "You just get lots of little pieces."

"Shut up and listen to the story," said Taleswapper.

Alvin was used to him saying that. Taleswapper said it to Alvin Junior more often than to anybody else, even the nephews.

"I'm not talking about good and evil," said

Taleswapper. "Even the devil himself can't afford to break everything down, can he, or he'd cease to be, just like everything else. The most evil creatures don't desire the destruction of everything—they only desire to exploit it for themselves."

Alvin had never heard the word *exploit* before, but it sounded nasty.

"So in the great war between the Unmaker and everything else, God and the devil should be on the same side. But the devil, he doesn't know it, and so he serves the Unmaker as often as not."

"You mean the devil's out to beat himself?"

"My story isn't about the devil," said Taleswapper. He was steady as rain when a story was coming out of him. "In the great war against the Unmaker of your vision, all the men and women of the world should be allies. But the great enemy remains invisible, so that no one guesses that they unwittingly serve him. They don't realize that war is the Unmaker's ally, because it tears down everything it touches. They don't understand that fire, murder, crime, cupidity, and concupiscence break apart the fragile bonds that make human beings into nations, cities, families, friends, and souls."

"You must be a prophet right enough," said Alvin Junior, "cause I can't understand a thing you said."

"A prophet," murmured Taleswapper, "but it was your eyes that saw. Now I know the agony of Aaron: to speak the words of truth, yet never have the vision for himself."

"You're making a big lot out of my nightmares."

Taleswapper was silent, sitting on the ground, his elbows on his knees, his chin propped all dismal on his palms. Alvin tried to figure out what the man was talking about. It was a sure thing that what he saw in his bad dreams wasn't a thing of any kind, so it must be poetical to talk about the Unmaker like a person. Maybe it was true, though, maybe the Unmaker wasn't just something he imagined up in his brain, maybe it was real, and Al Junior was the only person who could see it. Maybe the whole world was in terrible danger, and it was Alvin's job to fight it off, to beat it back, to keep the thing at bay. It was sure enough that when the dream was on him, Alvin couldn't bear it, wanted to drive it away. But he never could figure out how.

"Sposing I believe you," said Alvin. "Sposing there's such a thing as the Unmaker. There ain't a blame thing I can do."

A slow smile crept over Taleswapper's face. He tipped himself to one side, to free up his hand, which slowly reached down to the ground and picked up the little bug basket where it lay in the grass. "Does that look like a blamed thing?"

"That's just a bunch of grass."

"It *was* a bunch of grass," said Taleswapper. "And if you tore it up it'd be a bunch of grass again. But now, right now, it's something more than that."

"A little bug basket is all."

"Something that you made."

"Well, it's a sure thing grass don't grow that way."

"And when you made it, you beat back the Unmaker."

"Not by much," said Alvin.

"No," said Taleswapper. "But by the making of one bug basket. By that much, you beat him back."

It came together in Alvin's mind. The whole story that the Taleswapper was trying to tell. Alvin knew all kinds of opposites in the world: good and evil, light and dark, free and slave, love and hate. But deeper than all those opposites was making and unmaking. So deep that hardly anybody noticed that it was the most important opposite of all. But *he* noticed, and so that made the Unmaker his enemy. That's why the Unmaker came after him in his sleep. After all, Alvin had his knack. His knack for setting things in order, putting things in the shape they ought to be in.

"I think my *real* vision was about the same thing," said Alvin.

"You don't have to tell me about the Shining Man," said Taleswapper. "I never mean to pry."

"You mean you just pry by accident?" said Alvin.

That was the kind of remark that got him a slap across the face at home, but Taleswapper only laughed.

"I did something evil and I didn't even know it," said Alvin. "The Shining Man came and stood by the foot of my bed, and first he showed me a vision of what I done, so I knowed it was bad. I tell you I cried, to know I was so wicked. But then he showed me what my knack was for, and now I see it's the same thing you're talking about. I saw a stone that I pulled out of a mountain, and it was round as a ball, and when I looked close I saw it was the whole world, with forests and animals and oceans and fish and all on it. That's what my knack is for, to try to put things in order."

Taleswapper's eyes were gleaming. "The Shining Man showed you such a vision," he said. "Such a vision as I'd give my life to see."

"Only cause I'd used my knack to cause harm to others, just for my own pleasure," said Alvin. "I made a promise then, my most solemn vow, that I'd never use my knack for my own good. Only for others."

"A good promise," said Taleswapper. "I wish all men and women in the world would take such an oath and keep it."

"Anyway, that's how I know that the—the Unmaker, it isn't a vision. The Shining Man wasn't even a vision. What he *showed* me, *that* was a vision, but him standing there, he was *real*."

"And the Unmaker?"

"Real, too. I don't just see it in my head, it's *there*."

Taleswapper nodded, his eyes never leaving Alvin's face.

"I've got to make things," said Alvin. "Faster than he can tear them down."

"Nobody can make things fast enough for that," said Taleswapper. "If all the men in all the world made all the earth into a million million million million bricks, and built a wall all the days of their lives, the wall would crumble faster than they could build it. Sections of the wall would fall apart even before they built them."

"Now that's silly," said Alvin. "A wall can't fall down

before you build it up."

"If they keep at it long enough, the bricks will crumble into dust when they pick them up, their own hands will rot and slough like slime from their bones, until brick and flesh and bone alike all break down into the same indistinguishable dust. Then the Unmaker will sneeze, and the dust will be infinitely dispersed so that it can never come together again. The universe will be cold, still, silent, dark, and at last the Unmaker will be at rest."

Alvin tried to make sense out of what Taleswapper was saying. It was the same thing he did whenever Thrower talked about religion in school, so Alvin thought of it as kind of a dangerous thing to do. But he couldn't stop himself from doing it, and from asking his questions, even if they made people mad. "If things are breaking down faster than they're getting made, then how come anything's still around? Why hasn't the Unmaker already won? What are we doing here?"

Taleswapper wasn't Reverend Thrower. Alvin's question didn't make him angry. He just knit his brow and shook his head. "I don't know. You're right. We *can't* be here. Our existence is impossible."

"Well we *are* here, in case you didn't notice," said Alvin. "What kind of stupid tale is that, when we just have to look at each other to know it isn't true?"

"It has problems, I admit."

"I thought you only told stories you believe."

"I believed it while I was telling it."

Taleswapper looked so mournful that Alvin reached out and laid his hand on the man's shoulder, though his coat was so thick and Alvin's hand so small that he wasn't altogether sure Taleswapper felt his touch. "I believed it, too. Parts of it. For a while."

"Then there *is* truth in it. Maybe not much, but some." Taleswapper looked relieved.

But Alvin couldn't leave well enough alone. "Just because you believe it doesn't make it so."

Taleswapper's eyes went wide. Now I've done it, thought Alvin. Now I've made him mad, just like I make

Thrower mad. I do it to everbody. So he wasn't surprised when Taleswapper reached out both arms toward him, took Alvin's face between his hands, and spoke with such force as to drive the words deep into Alvin's forehead. "Everything possible to be believed is an image of truth."

And the words *did* pierce him, and he understood them, though he could not have put in words what it was he understood. Everything possible to be believed is an image of truth. If it feels true to me, then there is something true in it, even if it isn't all true. And if I study it out in my mind, then maybe I can find what parts of it are true, and what parts are false, and—

And Alvin realized something else. That all his arguments with Thrower came down to this: that if something just plain didn't make sense to Alvin, he didn't believe it, and no amount of quoting from the Bible would convince him. Now Taleswapper was telling him that he was *right* to refuse to believe things that made no sense. "Taleswapper, does that mean that what I *don't* believe *can't* be true?"

Taleswapper raised his eyebrows and came back with another proverb. "Truth can never be told so as to be understood, and not be believed."

Alvin was fed up with proverbs. "For once would you tell me straight!"

"The proverb *is* the straight truth, lad. I refuse to twist it up to fit a confused mind."

"Well, if my mind's confused, it's all your fault. All your talk about bricks crumbling before the wall is built—"

"Didn't you believe that?"

"Maybe I did. I reckon if I set out to weave all the grass of this meadow into bug baskets, before I got to the far end of the meadow the grass would all have died and rotted to nothing. I reckon if I set out to turn all the trees from here to Noisy River into barns, the trees'd all be dead and fell before I ever got to the last of them. Can't build a house out of rotted logs."

"I was going to say, 'Men cannot build permanent things out of impermanent pieces.' That is the law. But the way you said it was the proverb of the law: 'You can't build a house out of rotted logs.' "

"I said a proverb?"

"And when we get back to the house, I'll write it in my book."

"In the sealed part?" asked Alvin. Then he remembered that he had only seen that book by peeking through a crack in his floor late at night when Taleswapper was writing by candlelight in the room below him.

Taleswapper looked at him sharp. "I hope you never tried to conjure open that seal."

Alvin was offended. He might peek through a crack, but he'd never *sneak*. "Just knowing you don't want me to read that part is better than any old seal, and if you don't know that, you ain't my friend. I don't pry into your secrets."

"My secrets?" Taleswapper laughed. "I seal that back part because that's where my own writings go, and I simply don't want anyone else writing in that part of the book."

"Do other people write in the front part?"

"They do."

"Well, what do they write? Can I write there?"

"They write one sentence about the most important thing they ever did or ever saw with their own eyes. That one sentence is all I need from then on to remind me of their story. So when I visit in another city, in another house, I can open the book, read the sentence, and tell the story."

Alvin thought of a remarkable possibility. Taleswapper had lived with Ben Franklin, hadn't he? "Did Ben Franklin write in your book?"

"He wrote the very first sentence."

"He wrote down the most important thing he ever did?"

"That he did."

"Well, what *was* it?"

Taleswapper stood up. "Come back to the house with me, lad, and I'll show you. And on the way I'll tell you the story to explain what he wrote."

Alvin sprang up spry, and took the old man by his

heavy sleeve, and fairly dragged him toward the path back down to the house. "Come on, then!" Alvin didn't know if Taleswapper had decided not to go on to church, or if he plumb forgot that's where they were supposed to go —whatever the reason, Alvin was happy enough with the result. A Sunday with no church at all was a Sunday worth being alive. Add to that Taleswapper's stories and Maker Ben's own writing in a book, and it was well nigh to being a perfect day.

"There's no hurry, lad. I won't die before noon, nor will you, and stories take some time to tell."

"Was it something he made?" asked Alvin. "The most important thing?"

"As a matter of fact, it was."

"I knew it! The two-glass spectacles? The stove?"

"People used to say to him all the time, Ben, you're a true Maker. But he always denied it. Just like he denied he was a wizard. I've got no knack for hidden powers, he said. I just take pieces of things and put them together in a better way. There were stoves before I made my stove. There were spectacles before I made my spectacles. I never really *made* anything in my life, in the way a true Maker would do it. I give you two-glass spectacles, but a *Maker* would give you new eyes."

"He figured he never made *anything*?"

"I asked him that one day. The very day that I was starting out with my book. I said to him, Ben, what's the most important thing you ever made? And he started in on what I just told you, about how he never really made anything, and I said to him, Ben, you don't believe that, and I don't believe that. And he said, Bill, you found me out. There's one thing I made, and it's the most important thing I ever did, and it's the most important thing I ever saw."

Taleswapper fell silent, just shambling down the slope through leaves that whispered loud underfoot.

"Well, what was it?"

"Don't you want to wait till you get home and read it for yourself?"

Alvin got real mad then, madder than he meant to. "I

hate it when people know something and they won't say!"

"No need to get your dander up, lad. I'll tell you. What he wrote was this: The only thing I ever truly made was Americans."

"That don't make sense. Americans are *born.*"

"Well, now, that's not so, Alvin. *Babies* are born. In England the same as in America. So it isn't being born that makes them American."

Alvin thought about that for a second. "It's being born *in* America."

"Well, that's true enough. But along about fifty years ago, a baby born in Philadelphia was never called an American baby. It was a Pennsylvanian baby. And babies born in New Amsterdam were Knickerbockers, and babies born in Boston were Yankees, and babies born in Charleston were Jacobians or Cavaliers or some such name."

"They still are," Alvin pointed out.

"They are indeed, lad, but they're something else besides. All those names, Old Ben figured, those names divided us up into Virginians and Orangemen and Rhode Islanders, into Whites and Reds and Blacks, into Quakers and Papists and Puritans and Presbyterians, into Dutch, Swedish, French, and English. Old Ben saw how a Virginian could never quite trust a man from Netticut, and how a White man could never quite trust a Red, because they were *different.* And he said to himself, If we've got all these names to hold us apart, why not a name to bind us together? He toyed with a lot of names that already were used. Colonials, for instance. But he didn't like calling us all Colonials because that made us always turn our eyes back to Europe, and besides, the Reds aren't Colonials, are they! Nor are the Blacks, since they came as slaves. Do you see the problem?"

"He wanted a name we could all share the same," said Alvin.

"Just right. There was one thing we all had in common. We all lived on the same continent. North America. So he thought of calling us North Americans. But that was too long. So—"

"Americans."

"That's a name that belongs to a fisherman living on the rugged coast of West Anglia as much as to a baron ruling his slavehold in the southwest part of Dryden. It belongs as much to the Mohawk chief in Irrakwa as to the Knickerbocker shopkeeper in New Amsterdam. Old Ben knew that if people could once start thinking of themselves as Americans, we'd become a nation. Not just a piece of some tired old European country, but a single new nation here in a new land. So he started using that word in everything he wrote. Poor Richard's Almanac was full of talk about Americans this and Americans that. And Old Ben wrote letters to everybody, saying things like, Conflict over land claims is a problem for Americans to solve together. Europeans can't possibly understand what Americans need to survive. Why should Americans die for European wars? Why should Americans be bound by European precedents in our courts of law? Inside of five years, there was hardly a person from New England to Jacobia who didn't think of himself as being, at least partly, an American."

"It was just a name."

"But it is the name by which we call ourselves. And it includes everyone else on this continent who's willing to accept the name. Old Ben worked hard to make sure that name included as many people as possible. Without ever holding any public office except postmaster, he single-handedly turned a name into a nation. With the King ruling over the Cavaliers in the south, and the Lord Protector's men ruling over New England in the north, he saw nothing but chaos and war ahead, with Pennsylvania smack in the middle. He wanted to forestall that war, and he used the name 'American' to fend it off. He made the New Englanders fear to offend Pennsylvania, and made the Cavaliers bend over backward trying to woo Pennsylvanian support. He was the one who agitated for an American Congress to establish trade policies and uniform land law.

"And finally," Taleswapper continued, "just before he invited me over from England, he wrote the American

Compact and got the seven original colonies to sign it. It wasn't easy, you know—even the number of states was the result of a great deal of struggle. The Dutch could see that most of the immigrants to America were English and Irish and Scotch, and they didn't want to be swallowed up—so Old Ben allowed them to divide New Netherland into three colonies so they'd have more votes in the Congress. With Suskwahenny split off from the land claimed by New Sweden and Pennsylvania, another squabble was put to rest."

"That's only six states," said Alvin.

"Old Ben refused to allow anyone to sign the Compact unless the Irrakwa were included as the seventh state, with firm borders, with Reds governing themselves. There were plenty of people who wanted a White man's nation, but Old Ben wouldn't hear of it. The only way to have peace, he said, was for all Americans to join together as equals. That's why his Compact doesn't allow slavery or even bonding. That's why his Compact doesn't allow any religion to have authority over any other. That's why his Compact doesn't let the government close down a press or silence a speech. White, Black, and Red; Papist, Puritan, and Presbyterian; rich man, poor man, beggarman, thief—we all live under the same laws. One nation, created out of a single word."

"American."

"Now do you see why he calls it his greatest deed?"

"How come the Compact itself ain't more important?"

"The Compact was just the words. The name 'American' was the idea that made the words."

"It still doesn't include the Yankees and the Cavaliers, and it didn't stop war, neither, cause the Appalachee folk are still fighting against the King."

"But it *does* include all those people, Alvin. Remember the story of George Washington in Shenandoah? He was Lord Potomac in those days, leading King Robert's largest army against that poor ragtag band that was all Ben Arnold had left. It was plain to see that in the morning, Lord Potomac's Cavaliers would overrun that little fort and seal the doom of Tom Jefferson's free-mountain rebellion. But

Lord Potomac had fought beside those mountain men in the wars against the French. And Tom Jefferson had been his friend in days gone by. In his heart he could not bear to think of the morrow's battle. Who was King Robert, that so much blood should be shed for him? All these rebels wanted was to own their land, and not have the King set barons over them, to tax them dry and turn them into slaves as surely as any Black in the Crown Colonies. He didn't sleep at all that night."

"He was praying," said Alvin.

"That's the way Thrower tells it," Taleswapper said sharply. "But no one knows. And when he spoke to the troops the next morning, he didn't say a word about *prayer*. But he did speak about the word Ben Franklin made. He wrote a letter to the King, resigning from his command and rejecting his lands and titles. He didn't sign it 'Lord Potomac,' he signed it 'George Washington.' Then he rose up in the morning and stood before the blue-coat soldiers of the King and told them what he had done, and told them that they were free to choose, all of them, whether to obey their officers and go into battle, or march instead in defense of Tom Jefferson's great Declaration of Freedom. He said, 'The choice is yours, but as for me—'"

Alvin knew the words, as did every man, woman, and child on the continent. Now the words meant all the more to him, and he shouted them out: "'My American sword will never shed a drop of American blood!'"

"And then, when most of his army had gone and joined the Appalachee rebels, with their guns and their powder, their wagons and their supplies, he ordered the senior officer of the men loyal to the King to arrest him. 'I broke my oath to the King,' he said. 'It was for the sake of a higher good, but still I broke my oath, and I will pay the price for my treason.' He paid, yes sir, paid with a blade through his neck. But how many people outside the court of the King think it was really treason?"

"Not a one," said Alvin.

"And has the King been able to fight a single battle against the Appalachees since that day?"

"Not a one."

"Not a man on that battlefield in Shenandoah was a citizen of the United States. Not a man of them lived under the American Compact. And yet when George Washington spoke of American swords and American blood, they understood the name to mean themselves. Now tell me, Alvin Junior, was old Ben wrong to say that the greatest thing he ever made was a single word?"

Alvin would have answered, but right then they stepped up onto the porch of the house, and before they could get to the door, it swung open, and Ma stood there looking down at him. From the look on her face, Alvin knew that he was in trouble this time, and he knew why.

"I meant to go to church, Ma!"

"Lots of dead people meant to go to heaven," she answered, "and they didn't get there, neither."

"It was my fault, Goody Faith," said Taleswapper.

"It surely was not, Taleswapper," she said.

"We got to talking, Goody Faith, and I'm afraid I distracted the boy."

"The boy was born distracted," said Ma, never taking her eyes from Alvin's face. "He takes after his father. If you don't bridle and saddle him and ride him to church, he never gets there, and if you don't nail his feet to the floor of the church he's out that door in a minute. A ten-year-old boy who hates the Lord is enough to make his mother wish he'd never been born."

The words struck Alvin Junior to the heart.

"That's a terrible thing to wish," said Taleswapper. His voice was real quiet, and Ma finally lifted her gaze to the old man's face.

"I *don't* wish it," she finally said.

"I'm sorry, Mama," said Alvin Junior.

"Come inside," she said. "I left church to come and find you, and now there's not time to get back before the sermon ends."

"We talked about a lot of things, Mama," Alvin said. "About my dreams, and about Ben Franklin, and—"

"The only story I want to hear from you," said Ma, "is

the sound of hymn singing. If you won't go to the church, then you'll sit in the kitchen with me and sing me hymns while I fix the dinner."

So Alvin didn't get to see Old Ben's sentence in Taleswapper's book, not for hours. Ma kept him singing and working till dinnertime, and after dinner Pa and the big boys and Taleswapper sat around planning tomorrow's expedition to bring a millstone down from the granite mountain.

"I'm doing it for you," Pa said to Taleswapper, "so you better come along."

"I never asked you to bring a millstone."

"Not a day since you've been here that you haven't said something about what a shame it is that such a fine mill gets used as nothing but a haybarn, when people hereabouts need good flour."

"I only said it the once, that I remember."

"Well, maybe so," said Pa, "but every time I see you, I think about that millstone."

"That's because you keep wishing the millstone had been there when you threw me."

"He don't wish that!" shouted Cally. "Cause then you'd be dead!"

Taleswapper just grinned, and Papa grinned back. And they went on talking about this and that. Then the wives brought the nephews and nieces over for Sunday supper, and they made Taleswapper sing them the laughing song so many times that Alvin thought he'd scream if he heard another chorus of "Ha, Ha, Hee."

It wasn't till after supper, after the nephews and nieces were all gone, that Taleswapper brought out his book.

"I wondered if you'd ever open that book," Pa said.

"Just waiting for the right time." Then Taleswapper explained about how people wrote down their most important deed.

"I hope you don't expect *me* to write in there," Pa said.

"Oh, I wouldn't let you write in it, not yet. You haven't even told me the story of your most important deed." Taleswapper's voice got even softer. "Maybe you didn't actually *do* your most important deed."

Pa looked just a little angry then, or maybe a little afraid. Whichever it was, he got up and came over. "Show me what's in that book, that other people thought was so all-fired important."

"Oh," said Taleswapper. "Can you read?"

"I'll have you know I got a Yankee education in Massachusetts before I ever got married and set up as a miller in West Hampshire, and *long* before I ever came out here. It may not amount to much compared to a *London* education like you got, Taleswapper, but you don't know how to write a word I can't read, lessen it's Latin."

Taleswapper didn't answer. He just opened the book. Pa read the first sentence. "The only thing I ever truly made was Americans." Pa looked up at Taleswapper. "Who wrote *that*?"

"Old Ben Franklin."

"The way I heard it the only American he ever made was illegitimate."

"Maybe Al Junior will explain it to you later," said Taleswapper.

While they said this, Alvin wormed his way in front of them, to stare at Old Ben's handwriting. It looked no different from other men's writing. Alvin felt a little disappointed, though he couldn't have said what he expected. Should the letters be made of gold? Of course not. There was no reason why a great man's words should look any different on a page than the words of a fool.

Still, he couldn't rid himself of frustration that the words were so plain. He reached out and turned the page, turned many pages, riffling them with his fingers. The words were all the same. Grey ink on yellowing paper.

A flash of light came from the book, blinding him for a moment.

"Don't play with the pages like that," said Papa. "You'll tear one."

Alvin turned around to look at Taleswapper. "What's the page with light on it?" he asked. "What does it say *there*?"

"Light?" asked Taleswapper.

Then Alvin knew that he alone had seen it.

"Find the page yourself," said Taleswapper.

"He'll just tear it," said Papa.

"He'll be careful," said Taleswapper.

But Papa sounded angry. "I said stand away from that book, Alvin Junior."

Alvin started to obey, but felt Taleswapper's hand on his shoulder. Taleswapper's voice was quiet, and Alvin felt the old man's fingers moving in a sign of warding. "The boy saw something in the book," said Taleswapper, "and I want him to find it again for me."

And, to Alvin's surprise, Papa backed down. "If you don't mind getting your book ripped up by that careless lazy boy," he murmured, then fell silent.

Alvin turned to the book and carefully thumbed the pages, one at a time. Finally one fell into place, and from it came a light, which at first dazzled him, but gradually subsided until it came only from a single sentence, whose letters were on fire.

"Do you see them burning?" asked Alvin.

"No," said Taleswapper. "But I smell the smoke of it. Touch the words that burn for you."

Alvin reached out and gingerly touched the beginning of the sentence. The flame, to his surprise, was not hot, though it did warm him. It warmed him through to the bone. He shuddered as the last cold of autumn fled from his body. He smiled, he was so bright inside. But almost as soon as he touched it, the flame collapsed, cooled, was gone.

"What does it say?" asked Mama. She was standing now, across the table from them. She wasn't such a good reader, and the words were upside down to her.

Taleswapper read. "A Maker is born."

"There hasn't been a Maker," said Mama, "since the one who changed the water into wine."

"Maybe not, but that's what she wrote," said Taleswapper.

"Who wrote?" demanded Mama.

"A slip of a girl. About five years ago."

"What was the story that went with her sentence?" asked Alvin Junior.

Taleswapper shook his head.

"You said you never let people write unless you knew their story."

"She wrote it when I wasn't looking," said Taleswapper. "I didn't see it till the next place I stopped."

"Then how did you know it was her?" asked Alvin.

"It was her," he answered. "She was the only one there who could have opened the hex I kept on the book in those days."

"So you don't know what it means? You can't even tell me why I saw those letters burning?"

Taleswapper shook his head. "She was an innkeeper's daughter, if I remember rightly. She spoke very little, and when she did, what she said was always strictly truthful. Never a lie, even to be kind. She was considered to be something of a shrew. But as the proverb says, If you always speak your mind, the evil man will avoid you. Or something like that."

"Her name?" asked Mama. Alvin looked up in surprise. Mama hadn't seen the glowing letters, so why did she look so powerful eager to know about who wrote them?

"Sorry," said Taleswapper. "I don't remember her name right now. And if I remembered her name, I wouldn't tell it, nor will I tell whether I know the place where she lived. I don't want people seeking her out, troubling her for answers that she may not want to give. But I will say this. She was a torch, and saw with true eyes. So if she wrote that a Maker was born, I believe it, and that's why I let her words stay in the book."

"I want to know her story someday," said Alvin. "I want to know why the letters were so bright."

He looked up and saw Mama and Taleswapper looking steadily into each other's eyes.

And then, around the fringes of his own vision, where he could almost but not quite see it, he sensed the Unmaker, trembling, invisible, waiting to shiver the world apart. Without even thinking about it, Alvin pulled the front of his shirt out of his pants and knotted the corners together. The Unmaker wavered, then retreated out of sight.

❖ 11 ❖

Millstone

TALESWAPPER WOKE UP TO SOMEBODY shaking him. Still full dark outside, but it was time to be moving. He sat, flexed himself a little, and took some pleasure in how few knots and pains he had these days, sleeping on a soft bed. I could get used to this, he thought. I could enjoy living here.

The bacon was so fat he could hear it sizzling clear from the kitchen. He was just about to pull his boots on when Mary knocked at the door. "I'm presentable, more or less," he said.

She came in, holding out two pair of long thick stockings. "I knotted them myself," she said.

"I couldn't buy socks this thick in Philadelphia."

"Winter gets right cold here in the Wobbish country, and—" She didn't finish. Got too shy, ducked her head, and scampered out of the room.

Taleswapper pulled on the stockings, and his boots over them, and grinned. He didn't feel bad about accepting a few things like this. He worked as hard as anybody, and he'd done a lot to help ready this farm for winter. He was a good roof man—he liked climbing and didn't get dizzy. So his own hands had made sure the house and barns and coops and sheds all were tight and dry.

And, without anybody ever deciding to do it, he had prepared the millhouse to receive a millstone. He had personally loaded all the hay from the mill floor, five wagons full. The twins, who really hadn't got their two farms going yet, since they married only that summer, did the unloading up in the big barn. It was all done without Miller himself ever touching a pitchfork. Taleswapper saw to that, without making a fuss over it, and Miller never insisted.

Other things, though, weren't going so well. Ta-Kumsaw and his Shaw-Nee Reds were driving off so many folks from down Carthage way that everybody had the jitters. It was fine for the Prophet to have his big town of thousands of Reds across the river, all talking about how they'd never again raise their hands in war for any reason. But there were a lot of Reds who felt the way Ta-Kumsaw did, that the White man ought to be forced to the shores of the Atlantic and floated back to Europe, with or without boats. There was war talk, and word was that Bill Harrison down in Carthage was only too happy to fan that particular flame, not to mention the French in Detroit, always urging the Reds to attack the American settlers in land the French claimed was part of Canada.

Folks in the town of Vigor Church talked about this all the time, but Taleswapper knew that Miller didn't take it all that seriously. He thought of Reds as country clowns that wanted nothing more than to guzzle such whisky as they could find. Taleswapper had seen that attitude before, but only in New England. Yankees never seemed to realize that New England Reds with any gumption had long since moved to the state of Irrakwa. It would surely open Yankee eyes to see that the Irrakwa were working heavily with steam engines brought straight from England, and up in the Finger Lakes country a White named Eli Whitney was helping them make a factory that could turn out guns about twenty times faster than it had ever been done before. Someday those Yankees were going to wake up and find out that the Reds weren't all likker-mad, and some White folks were going to have to scramble fast to catch up.

In the meantime, though, Miller didn't take the war talk very seriously. "Everybody knows there's Reds in the woods. Can't stop them from skulking around, but I haven't missed any chickens so it's no problem yet."

"More bacon?" asked Miller. He shoved the bacon board across the table toward Taleswapper.

"I'm not used to eating so much in the morning," said Taleswapper. "Since I've been here I've had more food at every meal than I used to eat in a whole day."

"Put some meat on your bones," said Faith. She slapped down a couple of hot scones with honey smeared on them.

"I can't eat another bite," protested Taleswapper.

The scones slid right off Taleswapper's plate. "Got em," said Al Junior.

"Don't reach across the table like that," said Miller. "And you can't eat both those scones."

Al Junior proved his father wrong in an alarmingly short time. Then they washed the honey off their hands, put on their gloves, and went out to the wagon. The first light was just showing in the east as David and Calm, who lived townward from the farm, rode up. Al Junior climbed in the back of the wagon, along with all the tools and ropes and tents and supplies—it would be a few days before they came back.

"So—do we wait for the twins and Measure?" asked Taleswapper.

Miller swung up onto the wagon seat. "Measure's on ahead, felling trees for the sledge. And Wastenot and Wantnot are staying back here, riding circuit from house to house." He grinned. "Can't leave the womenfolk unprotected, with all the talk of wild Reds prowling around, can we?"

Taleswapper grinned back. Good to know that Miller wasn't as complacent as he seemed.

It was a good long way up to the quarry. On the road they passed the ruins of a wagon with a split millstone right in the middle of it. "That was our first try," said Miller. "But an axle dried out and jammed up coming down this steep hill, and the whole wagon fell in under the weight of the stone."

They came near a good-sized stream, and Miller told about how they had tried to float two millstones down on a raft, but both times the raft just up and sank. "We've had bad luck," said Miller, but from the set of his face he seemed to take it personally, as if someone had set out to make things fail.

"That's why we're using a sledge and rollers this time," said Al Junior, leaning over the back of the seat. "Nothing can fall off, nothing can break, and even if it does, it's all just logs, and we got no shortage of replacements."

"As long as it don't rain," said Miller. "Nor snow."

"Sky looks clear enough," said Taleswapper.

"Sky's a liar," said Miller. "When it comes to anything I want to do, water always gets in my way."

They got to the quarry when the sun was full up, but still far from noon. Of course, the trip back would be much longer. Measure had already felled six stout young trees and about twenty small ones. David and Calm set right to work, stripping off branches and rounding them smooth as possible. To Taleswapper's surprise, it was Al Junior who picked up the sack of stonecutting tools and headed up into the rocks.

"Where are you going?" asked Taleswapper.

"Oh, I've got to find a good place for cutting," said Al Junior.

"He's got an eye for stone," said Miller. But he wasn't saying all he knew.

"And when you find the stone, what'll you do then?" asked Taleswapper.

"Why, I'll cut it." Alvin sauntered on up the path with all the arrogance of a boy who knows he's about to do a man's job.

"Got a good hand for stone, too," said Miller.

"He's only ten years old," said Taleswapper.

"He cut the first stone when he was six," said Miller.

"Are you saying it's a knack?"

"I ain't saying nothing."

"Will you say this, Al Miller? Tell me if by chance you are a seventh son."

"Why do you ask?"

"It's said, by those who know such things, that a seventh son of a seventh son is born with the knowledge of how things look under the surface. That's why they make such good dowsers."

"Is that what they say?"

Measure walked up, faced his father, put his hands on his hips, and looked plain exasperated. "Pa, what harm is there in telling him? Everybody in the whole country roundabout here knows it."

"Maybe I think Taleswapper here knows more than I want him to know already."

"That's a right ungracious thing to say, Pa, to a man who's proved himself a friend twice over."

"He doesn't have to tell me anything he doesn't want me to know," said Taleswapper.

"Then *I'll* tell you," said Measure. "Pa is a seventh son, all right."

"And so is Al Junior," said Taleswapper. "Am I right? You've never mentioned it, but I'd guess that when a man gives his own name to a son other than his firstborn, it's bound to be his seventh born."

"Our oldest brother Vigor died in the Hatrack River only a few minutes after Al Junior was born," said Measure.

"Hatrack," said Taleswapper.

"Do you know the place?" asked Measure.

"I know *every* place. But for some reason that name makes me think I should have remembered it before now, and I can't think why. Seventh son of a seventh son. Does he conjure the millstone out of the rock?"

"We don't talk about it like that," said Measure.

"He cuts," said Miller. "Just like any stonecutter."

"He's a *big* boy, but he's still just a boy," said Taleswapper.

"Let's just say," said Measure, "that when *he* cuts the stone it's a mite softer than when *I* cut it."

"I'd appreciate it," said Miller, "if you'd stay down here and help with the rounding and notching. We need a nice tight sledge and some smooth true rollers." What he didn't say, but Taleswapper heard just as plain as day, was, Stay down here and don't ask too many questions about Al Junior.

So Taleswapper worked with David and Measure and Calm all morning and well into the afternoon, all the time hearing a steady chinking sound of iron on stone. Alvin Junior's stonecutting set the rhythm for all their work, though no one commented on it.

Taleswapper wasn't the sort of man who could work in silence, though. Since the others weren't too conversational at first, he told stories the whole time. And since they were grown men instead of children, he told stories that weren't all adventure and heroics and tragic death.

Most of the afternoon, in fact, he devoted to the saga of John Adams: How his house was burnt down by a Boston mob after he won the acquittal of ten women accused of witchcraft. How Alex Hamilton invited him to Manhattan Island, where the two of them set up a law practice together. How in ten years they managed to maneuver the Dutch government to allow unlimited immigration of non-Dutch-speaking people, until English, Scotch, Welsh, and Irish were a majority in New Amsterdam and New Orange, and a large minority in New Holland. How they got English declared a second official language in 1780, just in time for the Dutch colonies to become three of the seven original states under the American Compact.

"I'll bet the Dutchmen hated those boys, by the time they were through," said David.

"They were better politicians than *that*," said Taleswapper. "Why, both of them learned to speak Dutch better than most Dutchmen, and had their children grow up speaking Dutch in Dutch schools. They were so dadgum Dutch, boys, that when Alex Hamilton ran for governor of New Amsterdam and John Adams ran for president of the United States, they both did better in the Dutch parts of New Netherland than they did among the Scotch and Irish."

"Reckon if I run for mayor, I could get those Swedes and Dutchmen downriver to vote for me?" said David.

"*I* wouldn't even vote for you," said Calm.

"*I* would," said Measure. "And I hope someday you *do* run for mayor."

"He can't run for mayor," said Calm. "This ain't even a proper town."

"It will be," said Taleswapper. "I've seen it before. Once you get this mill working, it won't be long before three hundred people dwell between your mill and Vigor Church."

"You think so?"

"Right now people come in to Armor's store maybe three or four times a year," said Taleswapper. "But when they can get flour, they'll come in much more often. They'll prefer your mill to any other around here for some time, too, since you've got a smooth road and good bridges."

"If the mill makes money," Measure said, "Pa's sure to send for a Buhr Stone from France. We had one back in West Hampshire, before the flood broke up the mill. And a Buhr Stone means fine white flour."

"And white flour means good business," said David. "We older ones, we remember." He smiled wistfully. "We were almost rich there, once."

"So," said Taleswapper. "With all that traffic here, it won't be just a store and a church and a mill. There's good white clay down on the Wobbish. Some potter's bound to go into business, making redware and stoneware for the whole territory."

"Sure wish they'd hurry with *that*," said Calm. "My wife is sick unto death, she says, of having to serve food on tin plates."

"That's how towns grow," said Taleswapper. "A good store, a church, then a mill, then a pottery. Bricks, too, for that matter. And when there's a town—"

"David can be mayor," said Measure.

"Not me," said David. "All that politics business is too much. It's Armor wants that, not me."

"Armor wants to be king," said Calm.

"That's not kind," said David.

"But it's true," said Calm. "He'd try to be God, if he thought the job was open."

Measure explained to Taleswapper. "Calm and Armor don't get along."

"It ain't much of a husband that calls his wife a witch," said Calm bitterly.

"Why would he call her that?" asked Taleswapper.

"It's sure he doesn't call her that *now*," said Measure. "She promised him to give them up. All her knacks in the kitchen. It's a shame to make a woman run a household with just her own two hands."

"That's enough," David said. Taleswapper caught just a corner of his warning look.

Obviously they didn't trust Taleswapper enough to let him in on the truth. So Taleswapper let them know that the secret was already in his possession. "It seems to me that she uses more than Armor guesses," said Taleswapper. "There's a clever hex out of baskets on the front porch. And she used a calming on him before my eyes, the day I arrived in town."

Work stopped then, for just a moment. Nobody looked at him, but for a second they did nothing. Just took in the fact that Taleswapper knew Eleanor's secret and hadn't told about it to outsiders. Or to Armor-of-God Weaver. Still, it was one thing for him to know, and something else for them to confirm it. So they said nothing, just resumed notching and binding the sledge.

Taleswapper broke the silence by returning to the main topic. "It's just a matter of time before these western lands have enough people in them to call themselves states, and petition to join the American Compact. When that happens, there'll be need for honest men to hold office."

"You won't find no Hamilton or Adams or Jefferson out here in the wild country," said David.

"Maybe not," said Taleswapper. "But if you local boys don't set up your own government, you can bet there'll be plenty of city men willing to do it for you. That's how Aaron Burr got to be governor of Suskwahenny, before Daniel Boone shot him dead in ninety-nine."

"You make it sound like murder," said Measure. "It was a fair duel."

"To my way of thinking," said Taleswapper, "a duel is just two murderers who agree to take turns trying to kill each other."

"Not when one of them is an old country boy in buckskin and the other is a lying cheating city man," said Measure.

"I don't want no Aaron Burr trying to be governor over the Wobbish country," said David. "And that's what kind of man Bill Harrison is, down there in Carthage City. I'd vote for Armor before I'd vote for him."

"And I'd vote for you before I'd vote for Armor," said Taleswapper.

David grunted. He continued weaving rope around the notches of the sledge logs, binding them together. Taleswapper was doing the same thing on the other side. When he got to the knotting place, Taleswapper started to tie the two ends of the rope together.

"Wait on that," said Measure. "I'll go fetch Al Junior." Measure took off at a jog up the slope to the quarry.

Taleswapper dropped the ends of the rope. "Alvin Junior ties the knots? I would have thought grown men like you could tie them tighter."

David grinned. "He's got a knack."

"Don't any of you have knacks?" asked Taleswapper.

"A few."

"David's got a knack with the ladies," said Calm.

"Calm's got dancing feet at a hoedown. Ain't nobody fiddles like him, neither," said David. "It ain't on tune all the time, but he keeps that bow busy."

"Measure's a true shot," said Calm. "He's got an eye for things too far off for most folks to see."

"We got our knacks," said David. "The twins have a way of knowing when trouble's brewing, and getting there just about in time."

"And Pa, he fits things together. We have him do all the wood joints when we're building furniture."

"The womenfolk got women's knacks."

"But," said Calm, "there ain't nobody like Al Junior."

David nodded gravely. "Thing is, Taleswapper, he don't seem to know about it. I mean, he's always kind of surprised when things turn out good. He's right proud when we give him a job to do. I never seen him lord it over nobody because he's got more of a knack than they do."

"He's a good boy," said Calm.

"Kind of clumsy," said David.

"Not *clumsy*," said Calm. "Most times it isn't his *fault*."

"Let's just say that accidents happen more common around him."

"I wouldn't say jinx or nothing," said Calm.

"No, I wouldn't say jinx."

Taleswapper noted that in fact they both had said it. But he didn't comment on their indiscretion. After all, it was the third voice that made bad luck true. His silence was the best cure for their carelessness. And the other two caught on quickly enough. They, too, held their silence.

After a while, Measure came down the hill with Alvin Junior. Taleswapper dared not be the third voice, since he had taken part in the conversation before. And it would be even worse if Alvin himself spoke next, since he was the one who had been linked with a jinx. So Taleswapper kept his eye on Measure, and raised his eyebrows, to show Measure that he was expected to speak.

Measure answered the question that he thought Taleswapper was asking. "Oh, Pa's staying up by the rock. To watch."

Taleswapper could hear David and Calm breathe a sigh of relief. The third voice didn't have jinx in his mind, so Alvin Junior was safe.

Now Taleswapper was free to wonder *why* Miller felt he had to keep watch at the quarry. "What could happen to a rock? I've never heard of Reds stealing rocks."

Measure winked. "Powerful strange things happen sometimes, specially with millstones."

Alvin was joking with David and Calm now, as he tied the knots. He worked hard to get them as tight as he could, but Taleswapper saw that it wasn't in the knot itself that his knack was revealed. As Al Junior pulled the ropes tight, they seemed to twist and bite into the wood in all the notches, drawing the whole sledge tighter together. It was subtle, and if Taleswapper hadn't been watching for it, he wouldn't have seen. But it was real. What Al Junior bound was bound tight.

"That's tight enough to be a raft," said Al Junior, standing back to admire.

"Well, it's floating on solid earth this time," said Measure. "Pa says he won't even piss into water no more."

Since the sun was low in the west, they set to laying the fire. Work had kept them warm today, but tonight they'd need the fire to back off the animals and keep the autumn cold at bay.

Miller didn't come down, even at supper, and when Calm got up to carry food up the hill to his father, Taleswapper offered to come along.

"I don't know," said Calm. "You don't need to."

"I want to."

"Pa—he don't like lots of people gathered at the rock face, time like this." Calm looked a little sheepish. "He's a miller, and it's his stone getting cut there."

"I'm not a lot of people," said Taleswapper. Calm didn't say anything more. Taleswapper followed him up among the rocks.

On the way, they passed the sites of two early stonecuttings. The scraps of cut stone had been used to make a smooth ramp from the cliff face to ground level. The cuts were almost perfectly round. Taleswapper had seen plenty of stone cut before, and he'd never seen one cut this way—perfectly round, right in the cliff. Most times it was a whole slab they cut, then rounded it on the ground. There were several good reasons for doing it that way, but the best of all was that there was no way to cut the back of the stone unless you took a whole slab. Calm didn't slow down for him, so Taleswapper didn't have a chance to look closely, but as near as he could tell there was no possible way that the stonecutter in *this* quarry could have cut the back of the stone.

It looked just the same at the new site, too. Miller was raking chipped rock into a level ramp in front of the millstone. Taleswapper stood back and, in the last specks of daylight, studied the cliff. In a single day, working alone, Al Junior had smoothed the front of the millstone and chipped away the whole circumference. The stone was practically polished, still attached to the cliff face. Not only that, but the center hole had been cut to take the main shaft of the mill machinery. It was fully cut. And there was no way in the world that anybody could get a chisel in position to cut away the back.

"That's some knack the boy has," said Taleswapper.

Miller grunted assent.

"Hear you plan to spend the night up here," said Taleswapper.

"Heard right."

"Mind company?" asked Taleswapper.

Calm rolled his eyes.

But after a little bit, Miller shrugged. "Suit yourself."

Calm looked at Taleswapper with wide eyes and raised eyebrows, as if to say, Miracles never cease.

When Calm had set down Miller's supper, he left. Miller set aside the rake. "You et yet?"

"I'll gather wood for tonight's fire," said Taleswapper. "While there's still light. You eat."

"Watch out for snakes," said Miller. "They're mostly shut in for the winter now, but you never know."

Taleswapper watched out for snakes, but he never saw any. And soon they had a good fire, laid with a heavy log that would burn all night.

They lay there in the firelight, wrapped in their blankets. It occurred to Taleswapper that Miller might have found softer ground a few yards away from the quarry. But apparently it was more important to keep the millstone in plain sight.

Taleswapper began talking. Quietly, but steadily, he talked about how hard it must be for fathers, to watch their sons grow, so full of hope for the boys, but never knowing when death would come and take the child away. It was the right thing to talk about, because soon it was Alvin Miller doing the talking. He told the story of how his oldest boy Vigor died in the Hatrack River, only a few minutes after Alvin Junior was born. And from there, he turned to the dozens of ways that Al Junior had almost died. "Always water," Miller said at the end. "Nobody believes me, but it's so. Always water."

"The question is," said Taleswapper, "is the water evil,

trying to destroy a good boy? Or is it good, trying to destroy an evil power?"

It was a question that might have made some men angry, but Taleswapper had given up trying to guess when Miller's temper would flare. This time it didn't. "I've wondered that myself," said Miller. "I've watched him close, Taleswapper. Of course, he has a knack for making people love him. Even his sisters. He's tormented them unmerciful since he was old enough to spit in their food. Yet there's not a one of them who doesn't find a way to make him something special, and not just at Christmas. They'll sew his socks shut or smear soot on the privy bench or needle up his nightshirt, but they'd also die for him."

"I've found," said Taleswapper, "that some people have a knack for winning love without ever earning it."

"I feared that, too," said Miller. "But the boy doesn't know he has that knack. He doesn't trick people into doing what he wants. He lets me punish him when he does wrong. And he could stop me, if he wanted."

"How?"

"Because he knows that sometimes when I see him, I see my boy Vigor, my firstborn, and then I can't do him any harm, even harm that's for his own good."

Maybe that reason was partly true, Taleswapper thought. But it certainly wasn't the whole truth.

A bit later, after Taleswapper stirred the fire to make sure the log caught well, Miller told the story that Taleswapper had come for.

"I've got a story," he said, "that might belong in your book."

"Give it a try," said Taleswapper.

"Didn't happen to me, though."

"Has to be something you saw yourself," said Taleswapper. "I hear the craziest stories that somebody heard happened to a friend of a friend."

"Oh, I saw this happen. It's been going on for years now, and I've had some discussions with the fellow. It's one of the Swedes downriver, speaks English good as I do. We helped him put up his cabin and his barn when he first come here, the year after us. And I watched him a little bit even then. See, he has a boy, a blond Swede boy, you know how they get."

"Hair almost white?"

"Like frost in the first morning sun, white like that, and shiny. A beautiful boy."

"I can see him in my mind," said Taleswapper.

"And that boy, his papa loved him. Better than his life. You know that Bible story, about that papa who gave his boy a coat of many colors?"

"I've heard tell of it."

"He loved his boy like that. But I saw them two walking alongside the river, and the father all of a sudden lurched kind of, just bumped his boy, and sent the lad tumbling down into the Wobbish. Now, it happened that the boy caught onto a log and his father and I helped pull him in, but it was a scary thing to see that the father might have killed his own best-loved child. It wouldn't've been a-purpose, mind you, but that wouldn't make the boy any less dead, or the father any less blameful."

"I can see the father might never get over such a thing."

"Well, of course *not*. Yet not long after that, I seen him a few more times. Chopping wood, and he swung that axe wild, and if the boy hadn't slipped and fell right at that very second, that axe would've bit into the boy's head, and I never seen nobody live after something like that."

"Nor I."

"And I tried to imagine what must be happening. What that father must be thinking. So I went to him one day, and I said, 'Nels, you ought to be more careful round that boy. You're likely to take that boy's head off someday, if you keep swinging that axe so free.'

"And Nels, he says to me, 'Mr. Miller, that wasn't no accident.' Well, you could've blowed me down with a baby's burp. What does he mean, no accident? And he says to me, 'You don't know how bad it is. I think maybe a witch cursed me, or the devil takes me, but I'm just working there, thinking how much I love the boy, and suddenly I have this wish to kill him. It came on me first when he was just a baby, and I stood at the top of the stairs, holding him, and it was like a voice inside my head, it said, "Throw him down," and I wanted to do it, even though I also knew it would be the most terrible thing in the world. I was hungry to throw him off, like a boy gets when he wants to smash a bug with a stone. I *wanted* to see his head break open on the floor.

"'Well, I just fought off that feeling, just swallowed it back and held that boy so tight I like to smothered him. Finally when I got him back into his cradle, I knew that from then on I wasn't going to carry him up those stairs no more.

"'But I couldn't just leave him alone, could I? He was my boy, and he grew up so bright and good and beautiful that I had to love him. If I stayed away, he cried cause his papa didn't play with him. But if I stayed with him, then those feelings came back, again and again. Not every day, but many a day, sometimes so fast that I did it afore I even knew what I was doing. Like the day I bumped him into the river, I just took a wrong step and tripped, but I knew even as I took that step that it was a wrong step, and that I'd trip, and that I'd bump him, I *knew* it, but I didn't have time to stop myself. And someday I know that I won't be able to stop myself, I won't mean to do it, but someday when that boy is under my hand, I'll kill him.'"

Taleswapper could see Miller's arm move, as if to wipe tears away from his cheek.

"Ain't that the strangest thing?" Miller asked. "A man having that kind of feeling for his own son."

"Does that fellow have any other sons?"

"A few. Why?"

"I just wondered if he ever felt a desire to kill them."

"Never, not a speck. I asked him that, matter of fact. I asked him, and he said not a speck."

"Well, Mr. Miller, what did you tell him?"

Miller breathed in and out a few times. "I didn't know what to tell him. Some things are just too big for a man like me to understand. I mean, the way that water is out to kill my boy Alvin. And then this Swede fellow with his son. Maybe there's some children that wasn't meant to grow up. Do you think so, Taleswapper?"

"I think there are some children that are so important, that someone—some force in the world—may want them dead. But there are always other forces, maybe stronger forces, that want them alive."

"Then why don't those forces show theirselves, Taleswapper? Why don't some power from heaven come and say—come to that poor Swedish man and say, 'Don't you fear no more, your boy is safe, even from you!'"

"Maybe those forces don't speak out loud in words. Maybe those forces just show you what they're doing."

"The only force that shows itself in this world is the one that kills."

"I don't know about that Swedish boy," said Taleswapper, "but I'd guess that there's a powerful protection on *your* son. From what you said, it's a miracle he isn't dead ten times over."

"That's the truth."

"I think he's being watched over."

"Not well enough."

"The water never got him, did it?"

"It came so close, Taleswapper."

"And as for that Swedish boy, I *know* he's got somebody watching over him."

"Who?" asked Miller.

"Why, his own father."

"His father is the enemy," said Miller.

"I don't think so," said Taleswapper. "Do you know how many fathers kill their sons by accident? They're out hunting, and a shot goes wrong. Or a wagon crushes the boy, or he takes a fall. Happens all the time. Maybe those fathers just didn't *see* what was happening. But this Swedish man is sharp, he sees what's happening, and he watches himself, catches himself in time."

Miller sounded a little more hopeful. "You make it sound like maybe the father ain't all bad."

"If he were all bad, Mr. Miller, that boy would be dead and buried long ago."

"Maybe. Maybe."

Miller thought for a while more. So long, in fact, that

Taleswapper dozed a little. He snapped awake with Miller already talking.

"—and it's just getting worse, not better. Harder to fight off those feelings. Not all that long ago, he was standing up in a loft in the—in his barn—and he was pitching down hay. And there below him was his boy, and all it would take is to let fly with the pitchfork, easiest thing in the world, he could say the pitchfork slipped and no one would ever know. Just let it fly, and stick that boy right through. And he was going to do it. Do you understand me? It was so hard to fight off those feelings, harder than ever before, and he just *gave up*. Just decided to have it done with, to give in. And in that very moment, why, a stranger appeared in the doorway, and shouted, 'No,' and I set down the pitchfork—that's what he said, 'I set down the pitchfork, but I was shaking so bad I could hardly walk, knowing that the stranger saw me with murder in my heart, he must think I'm the most terrible man in the world to think of killing my own boy, he can't even guess how hard I've struggled all those years before—' "

"Maybe that stranger knew something about the powers that can work inside a man's heart," said Taleswapper.

"Do you think so?"

"Oh, I can't be sure, but maybe that stranger also saw how much that father loved the boy. Maybe the stranger was confused for a long time, but finally began to realize that the child was extraordinary, with powerful enemies. And then maybe he came to understand that no matter how many enemies the boy had, his father wasn't one of them. Wasn't an enemy. And he wanted to say something to that father."

"What did he want to say?" Miller brushed his eyes with his sleeve again. "What do you think that stranger might want to say?"

"Maybe he wanted to say, 'You've done all you can do, and now it's too strong for you. Now you ought to send that boy away. To relatives back east, maybe, or as a prentice in some town.' That might be a hard thing for the father to do, since he loves the boy so much, but he'll do it because he knows that real love is to take the boy out of danger."

"Yes," said Miller.

"For that matter," said Taleswapper, "maybe you ought to do something like that with your own boy, Alvin."

"Maybe," said Miller.

"He's in some danger from the water around here, wouldn't you say? Somebody's protecting him, or some-*thing*. But maybe if Alvin weren't living here—"

"Then some of the dangers would go away," said Miller.

"Think about it," said Taleswapper.

"It's a terrible thing," said Miller, "to send your boy away to live with strangers."

"It's a worse thing, though, to put him in the ground."

"Yes," said Miller. "That's the worst thing in the world. To put your child in the ground."

They didn't talk any more, and after a while they both slept.

The morning was cold, with a heavy frost, but Miller wouldn't even let Al Junior come up to the rock until the sun burned it away. Instead they all spent the morning preparing the ground from the cliff face to the sledge, so they could roll the stone down the mountain.

By now, Taleswapper was sure that Al Junior used a hidden power to get the millstone away from the cliff face, even if he didn't realize it himself. Taleswapper was curious. He wanted to see just how powerful this power was, so he could understand more about its nature. And since Al Junior didn't realize what he was doing, Taleswapper's experiment had to be subtle, too. "How do you dress your stone?" asked Taleswapper.

Miller shrugged. "Buhr Stone is what I used before. They all come with sickle dress."

"Can you show me?" asked Taleswapper.

Using a corner of the rake, Miller drew a circle in the frost. Then he drew a series of arcs, radiating from the center of the circle out to the edges. Between each pair of arcs he drew a shorter arc, which began at the edge but never came closer than two-thirds of the way toward the center. "Like that," said Miller.

"Most millstones in Pennsylvania and Suskwahenny are quarter dress," said Taleswapper. "You know that cut?"

"Show me."

So Taleswapper drew another circle. It didn't show up as well, since the frost was burning off now, but it was good enough. He drew straight lines instead of curved ones from the center to the edge, and the shorter lines branched directly from the long ones and ran straight to the edge. "Some millers like this better, because you can keep it sharp longer. Since all the lines are straight, you get a nice even draw when you're tooling the stone."

"I can see that," said Miller. "I don't know, though. I'm used to those curvy lines."

"Well, suit yourself," said Taleswapper. "I've never been a miller, so I don't know. I just tell stories about what I've seen."

"Oh, I don't mind you showing me," said Miller. "Don't mind a bit."

Al Junior stood there, studying both circles.

"I think if we once get this stone home," said Miller, "I'll try that quarter dress on it. Looks to me like it might be easier to keep up a clean grind."

Finally the ground was dry, and Al Junior walked to the cliff face. The other boys were all down below, breaking camp or bringing the horses up to the quarry. Only Miller and Taleswapper watched as Al Junior finally carried his hammer to the cliff face. He had a little more cutting to do, to get the circle to its full depth all around.

To Taleswapper's surprise, when Al Junior set the chisel in place and gave a whang with the hammer, a whole section of stone, some six inches long, split away from the cliff face and crumbled to the ground.

"Why, that stone's as soft as coal," said Taleswapper. "What kind of millstone can it make, if it's as weak as that?"

Miller grinned and shook his head.

Al Junior stepped away from the stone. "Oh, Taleswapper, it's *hard* stone, unless you know just the right place to crack it. Give it a try, you'll see."

He held out the chisel and hammer. Taleswapper took

them and approached the rock. Carefully he laid the chisel onto the stone, a slight angle away from perpendicular. Then, after a few trial taps, he laid on a blow with the hammer.

The chisel practically jumped out of his left hand, and the shock of impact was so great that he dropped the hammer. "Sorry," he said, "I've done this before, but I must have lost the skill—"

"Oh, it's just the stone," said Al Junior. "It's kind of temperamental. It only likes to give in certain directions."

Taleswapper inspected the place where he had tried to cut. He couldn't find the spot. His mighty blow had left no mark at all.

Al Junior picked up the tools and laid the chisel against the stone. It looked to Taleswapper as though he put it in exactly the same place. But Al acted as though he had placed it quite differently. "See, it's getting just the angle on it. Like this."

He whanged with the hammer, the iron rang out, there was a cracking of stone, and once again crumbled stone pattered on the ground.

"I can see why you have him do all the cutting," Taleswapper said.

"Seems like the best way," said Miller.

In only a few minutes, the stone was fully rounded. Taleswapper said nothing, just watched to see what Al would do.

He set down his tools, walked to the millstone, and embraced it. His right hand curled around the lip of it. His left hand probed back into the cut on the other side. Alvin's cheek pressed against the stone. His eyes were closed. It looked for all the world as though he were listening to the rock.

He began to hum softly. A mindless little tune. He moved his hands. Shifted his position. Listened with the other ear.

"Well," Alvin said, "I can't hardly believe it."

"Believe what?" asked his father.

"Those last few cuts must have set up a real shiver in the rock. The back is already split right off."

"You mean that millstone is standing free?" asked Taleswapper.

"I think we can rock it forward now," said Alvin. "It takes a little rope work, but we'll get it out of there without too much trouble."

The brothers arrived with the ropes and horses. Alvin passed a rope back behind the stone. Even though not a single cut had been made against the back, the rope dropped easily into place. Then another rope, and another, and soon they were all tugging, first left, then right, as they slowly walked the heavy stone out of its bed in the cliff face.

"If I hadn't seen it," murmured Taleswapper.

"But you did," said Miller.

It was only a few inches clear when they changed the ropes, passing four lines through the center hole and hitching them to a team of horses uphill of the stone. "It'll roll on downhill just fine," Miller explained to Taleswapper. "The horses are there as a drag, pulling against it."

"It looks heavy."

"Just don't lie down in front of it," said Miller.

They started it rolling, very gently. Miller took hold of Alvin's shoulder and kept the boy well back from the stone—and uphill of it, too. Taleswapper helped with the horses, so he didn't get a good look at the back surface of the stone until it was down on level ground by the sledge.

It was smooth as a baby's backside. Flat as ice in a basin. Except that it was scored in a quarter dress pattern, straight lines radiating from the lip of the center hole to the edge of the stone.

Alvin came up to stand beside him. "Did I do it right?" he asked.

"Yes," said Taleswapper.

"It was the luckiest thing," said the boy. "I could just feel that stone ready to split right along those lines. It just wanted to split, easy as you please."

Taleswapper reached out and drew his finger gently along the edge of a dress cut. It stung. He brought his finger to his mouth, sucked, and tasted blood.

"Stone holds a nice sharp edge, don't it?" said Measure. He sounded as if this sort of thing happened every day. But Taleswapper could see the awe in his eyes.

"Good cut," said Calm.

"Best one yet," said David.

Then, with horses bracing against a rapid fall, they gently tipped it to lie on the sledge, dress side up.

"Will you do me a favor, Taleswapper?" asked Miller.

"If I can."

"Take Alvin back home with you now. His work's done."

"No, Papa!" Alvin shouted. He ran over to his father. "You can't make me go home *now*."

"Don't need no ten-year-old boys underfoot while we're manhandling a stone that size," said his father.

"But I've got to watch the stone, to make sure it don't split or chip, Pa!"

The older sons looked at their father, waiting. Taleswapper wondered what they hoped for. They were too old now, surely, to resent their father's particular love for his seventh son. They also must hope to keep the boy safe from harm. Yet it meant much to all of them that the stone arrive safely, unbroken, to begin its service in the mill. There could be no doubt that young Alvin had the power to keep it whole.

"You can ride with us till sundown," Miller finally said. "By then we'll be close enough to home that you and Taleswapper can head back and spend the night in beds."

"Fine with me," said Taleswapper.

Alvin Junior plainly wasn't satisfied, but he didn't answer back.

They got the sledge under way before noon. Two horses in front and two behind, for stopping, were hitched to the stone itself. The stone rested on the wooden raft of the sledge, and the sledge rode atop seven or eight of the small rollers at a time. The sledge moved forward, passing over new rollers waiting in front. As the rollers emerged from the back, one of the boys immediately yanked the roller out from under the ropes hitched to the trailing team, raced to the front, and laid it in place directly behind the lead team.

It meant that each man ran about five miles for every mile the stone traveled.

Taleswapper tried to take his turn, but David, Calm, and Measure wouldn't hear of it. He ended up tending the trailing team, with Alvin perched atop one of the horses. Miller drove the leading team, walking backward half the time to make sure he wasn't going too fast for the boys to keep up.

Hour after hour they went on. Miller offered to let them stop and rest, but they seemed not to tire, and Taleswapper was amazed to see how the rollers held up. Not a one split on a rock or from the sheer weight of the stone. They got scuffed and dented, but that was about all.

And as the sun sank to about two fingers above the horizon, awash in the ruddy clouds of the western sky, Taleswapper recognized the meadow opening up before them. They had made the whole journey in a single afternoon.

"I think I got the strongest brothers in the whole world," Alvin murmured.

I have no doubt of it, Taleswapper said silently. You who can cut a stone from the mountain without hands, because you "find" the right fractures in the rock, it's no surprise that your brothers find in themselves exactly as much strength as you believe they have. Taleswapper tried again, as he had tried so many times before, to puzzle out the nature of the hidden powers. Surely there was some natural law that governed their use—Old Ben had always said so. And yet here was this boy who, by mere belief and desire, could cut stone like butter and give strength to his brothers. There was a theory that the hidden power came from friendship with a particular element, but which was it that could do all that Alvin did? Earth? Air? Fire? Certainly not water, for Taleswapper knew that Miller's stories were all true. Why was it that Alvin Junior could wish for something, and the earth itself would bend to his will, while others could long for things and never cause so much as a breeze to blow?

They needed lanterns inside the millhouse by the time

they rolled the stone through the doors. "Might as well lay it in place tonight," said Miller. Taleswapper imagined the fears that ran through Miller's mind. If he left the stone upright, it would surely roll in the morning and crush a particular child as he innocently carried water up to the house. Since the stone had miraculously come down from the mountain in a single day, it would be foolish to leave it anywhere but in its proper place, on the foundation of rammed earth and stone in the millhouse.

They brought a team inside and hitched it to the stone, as they had when they lowered it on the sledge back by the quarry. The team would pull against the weight of the stone as they levered it downward onto the foundation.

At the moment, though, the stone was resting on built-up earth just outside the circle of foundation stones. Measure and Calm were working their lever poles under the outside edge of the stone, ready to pry it up and make it fall into place. The stone rocked a little as they worked. David was holding the horses, since it would be a disaster if they pulled too soon and rocked the stone over the wrong way, to lie on its dress face in the plain dirt.

Taleswapper stood aside, watching as Miller directed his sons with useless calls of "Careful there" and "Steady now." Alvin had been beside him ever since they brought the millstone inside. One of the horses got jumpy. Miller reacted at once. "Calm, go help your brother with the horses!" Miller also took a step that way.

At that moment, Taleswapper realized that Alvin was *not* beside him, after all. He was carrying a broom, walking briskly toward the millstone. Perhaps he had seen some loose stones lying on the foundation; he had to sweep them away, didn't he? The horses backed up; the lines went slack. Taleswapper realized, just as Alvin got behind the stone, that with ropes so slack there'd be nothing to keep the stone from falling all the way over, if it should fall at just this moment.

Surely it would not fall, in a reasonable world. But Taleswapper knew by now that it was *not* a reasonable world at all. Alvin Junior had a powerful, invisible enemy, and it would not miss such a chance as this.

Taleswapper bounded forward. Just as he came level with the stone, he felt a lurching in the earth under his feet, a collapse of the firm dirt. Not much, just a few inches, but it was enough to let the inside lip of the millstone fall that much, which rocked the top of the great wheel more than two feet, and so quickly that the momentum could not be stopped. The millstone would fall all the way down, right into its proper place on the foundation, with Alvin Junior underneath, ground like grain under the stone.

With a shout, Taleswapper caught hold of Alvin's arm and yanked him back, away from the stone. Only then did Alvin see the great stone falling upon him. Taleswapper had enough force in his movement to carry the boy several feet back, but it was not quite enough. The boy's legs still lay in the stone's shadow. It was falling fast now, too fast for Taleswapper to respond, to do anything but watch it crush Alvin's legs. He knew that such an injury was the same as death, except that it would take longer. He had failed.

In that moment, though, as he watched the stone in its murderous fall, he saw a crack appear in the stone and, in less than an instant, it became a clean split right through the stone. The two halves leapt apart from each other, each with such a movement that it would fall beside Alvin's leg, not touching him.

No sooner had Taleswapper seen lantern light through the middle of the stone than Alvin himself cried, "No!"

To anyone else, it would seem the boy was shouting at the fall of the stone, at his impending death. But to Taleswapper, lying on the ground beside the boy, with the light of the lantern dazzling through the split in the millstone, the cry meant something else altogether. Heedless of his own danger, as children usually are, Alvin was crying out against the breaking of the millstone. After all his work, and the labors in bringing the stone home, he could not bear to see it breaking.

And because he could not bear it, it did not happen. The halves of the stone jumped back together like a needle jumping at a magnet, and the stone fell in one piece.

The shadow of the stone had exaggerated its footprint on the ground. It did not crush both Alvin's legs. His left leg, in fact, was completely clear of the stone, tucked up under him as it was. The right leg, however, lay so that the rim of the stone overlapped his shin by two inches at the widest point. Since Alvin was still pulling his legs away, the blow from the stone pushed it further in the direction it was already going. It peeled off all the skin and muscle, right down to the bone, but it did not catch the leg directly when it came to rest. The leg might not even have broken, had the broom not been lying crosswise under it. The stone drove Alvin's leg downward against the broom handle, just hard enough to snap both bones of the lower leg clean in half. The sharp edges of the bone broke the skin and came to rest like two sides of a vise, gripping the broom handle. But the leg was not under the millstone, and the bones were broken cleanly, not ground to dust under the rock.

The air was filled with the crash of stone on stone, the great-throated shouts of men surprised by grief, and above all the piercing cry of agony from one boy who was never so young and frail as now.

By the time anyone else could get there, Taleswapper had seen that both Alvin's legs were free of the stone. Alvin tried to sit up and look at his injury. Either the sight or the pain of it was too much for him, and he fainted. Alvin's father reached him then; he had not been nearest, but he had moved faster than Alvin's brothers. Taleswapper tried to reassure him, for with the bones gripping the broom handle, the leg did not look broken. Miller lifted his son, but the leg would not come, and even unconscious the pain wrung a cruel moan from the boy. It was Measure who steeled himself to pull on the leg and free it from the broom handle.

David already held a lantern, and as Miller carried the boy, David ran alongside, lighting the way. Measure and Calm would have followed, but Taleswapper called to them. "The womenfolk are there, and David, and your father," he said. "Someone needs to see to all this."

"You're right," said Calm. "Father won't be eager to come down here soon."

The young men used levers to raise the stone enough that Taleswapper could pull out the broom handle and the ropes that were still tied to the horses. The three of them cleared all the equipment out of the millhouse, then stabled the horses and put away the tools and supplies. Only then did Taleswapper return to the house to find that Alvin Junior was sleeping in Taleswapper's bed.

"I hope you don't mind," said Anne anxiously.

"Of course not," said Taleswapper.

The other girls and Cally were clearing away the supper dishes. In the room that had been Taleswapper's, Faith and Miller, both ashen and tight-lipped, sat beside the bed, where Alvin lay with his leg splinted and bandaged.

David stood near the door. "It was a clean break," he whispered to Taleswapper. "But the cuts in the skin—we fear infection. He lost all the skin off the front of his shin. I don't know if bare bone like that can ever heal."

"Did you put the skin back?" asked Taleswapper.

"Such as was left, we pressed into place, and Mother sewed it there."

"That was well done," said Taleswapper.

Faith lifted her head. "Do you know aught of physicking, then, Taleswapper?"

"Such as a man learns after years trying to do what he can among those who know as little as he."

"How could this happen?" Miller said. "Why now, after so many other times that did him no injury?" He looked up at Taleswapper. "I had come to think the boy had a protector."

"He has."

"Then the protector failed him."

"It did not fail," said Taleswapper. "For a moment, as the stone fell, I saw it split, wide enough that it wouldn't have touched him."

"Like the ridgebeam," whispered Faith.

"I thought I saw it too, Father," said David. "But when it came down whole, I decided I must have seen what I wished for, and not what was."

"There's no split in it now," said Miller.

"No," said Taleswapper. "Because Alvin Junior refused to let it split."

"Are you saying he knit it back together? So it would

strike him and wreck his leg?"

"I'm saying he had no thought of his leg," said Taleswapper. "Only of the stone."

"Oh, my boy, my good boy," murmured his mother, gently caressing the arm that extended thoughtlessly toward her. As she moved his fingers, they limply bent as she pushed them, then sprang back.

"Is it possible?" asked David. "That the stone split and was made whole again, as quickly as that?"

"It must be," said Taleswapper, "because it happened."

Faith moved her son's fingers again, but this time they did not spring back. They extended even further, then flexed into a fist, then extended flat again.

"He's awake," said his father.

"I'll fetch some rum for the boy," said David. "To slack the pain. Armor'll have some in his store."

"No," murmured Alvin.

"The boy says no," said Taleswapper.

"What does he know, in pain as he is?"

"He has to keep his wits about him, if he can," said Taleswapper. He knelt by the bed, just to the right of Faith, so he was even nearer to the boy's face. "Alvin, do you hear me?"

Alvin groaned. It must have meant yes.

"Then listen to me. Your leg is very badly hurt. The bones are broken, but they've been set in place—they'll heal well enough. But the skin was torn away, and even though your mother has sewn it back in place, there's a good chance the skin will die and take gangrene, and kill you. Most surgeons would cut off your leg to save your life."

Alvin tossed his head back and forth, trying to shout. It came out as a moan: "No, no, no."

"You're making things worse!" Faith said angrily.

Taleswapper looked at the father for permission to go on.

"Don't torment the boy," said Miller.

"There's a proverb," said Taleswapper. "The apple tree never asks the beech how he shall grow, nor the lion the horse, how he shall take his prey."

"What does that mean?" asked Faith.

"It means that I have no business trying to teach *him* how to use powers that I can't begin to understand. But since he doesn't know how to do it himself, I'll have to try, won't I?"

Miller pondered a moment. "Go ahead, Taleswapper. Better for him to know how bad it is, whether he can heal himself or not."

Taleswapper held the boy's hand gently between his own. "Alvin, you want to keep your leg, don't you? Then you have to think of it the way you thought of the stone. You have to think of the skin of your leg, growing back, attaching to the bone as it should. You have to study it out. You'll have plenty of time for it, lying here. Don't think about the pain, think about the leg as it should be, whole and strong again."

Alvin lay there, squinting his eyes closed against the pain.

"Are you doing that, Alvin? Can you try?"

"No," said Alvin.

"You have to fight against the pain, so you can use your own knack to make things right."

"I never will," said Alvin.

"Why not!" cried Faith.

"The Shining Man," said Alvin. "I promised him."

Taleswapper remembered Alvin's oath to the Shining Man, and his heart sank.

"What's the Shining Man?" asked Miller.

"A—visitation he had, when he was little," said Taleswapper.

"How come we never heard of this afore now?" Miller asked.

"It was the night the ridgebeam split," said Taleswapper. "Alvin promised the Shining Man that he'd never use his power for his own benefit."

"But Alvin," said Faith. "This isn't to make you rich or nothing, this is to save your *life*."

The boy only winced against the pain and shook his head.

"Will you leave me with him?" said Taleswapper. "Just

for a few minutes, so I can talk to him?"

Miller was rushing Faith out the door of the room before Taleswapper even finished his sentence.

"Alvin," said Taleswapper. "You must listen to me, listen carefully. You know I won't lie to you. An oath is a terrible thing, and I'd never counsel a man to break his word, even to save his own life. So I won't tell you to use your power for your own good. Do you hear me?"

Alvin nodded.

"Just think, though. Think of the Unmaker going through the world. Nobody sees him as he does his work, as he tears down and destroys things. Nobody but one solitary boy. Who is that boy, Alvin?"

Alvin's lips formed the word, though no sound came out. Me.

"And that boy has been given a power that he can't even begin to understand. The power to build against the enemy's unbuilding. And more than that, Alvin, the *desire* to build as well. A boy who answers every glimpse of the Unmaker with a bit of making. Now, tell me, Alvin, those who help the Unmaker, are they the friend or the enemy of mankind?"

Enemy, said Alvin's lips.

"So if you help the Unmaker destroy his most dangerous foe, you're an enemy of mankind, aren't you?"

Anguish wrung sound from the boy. "You're twisting it," he said.

"I'm straightening it," said Taleswapper. "Your oath was never to use your power for your own benefit. But if you die, only the Unmaker benefits, and if you live, if that leg is healed, then that's for the good of all mankind. No, Alvin, it's for the good of the world and all that's in it."

Alvin whimpered, more against the pain in his mind than the pain in his body.

"But your oath was clear, wasn't it? Never to your own benefit. So why not satisfy one oath with another, Alvin? Take an oath now, that you will devote your whole *life* to building up against the Unmaker. If you keep *that* oath —and you will, Alvin, you're a boy who keeps his word—if you keep that oath, then saving your own life is truly for the benefit of others, and not for your private good at all."

Taleswapper waited, waited, until at last Alvin nodded slightly.

"Do you take an oath, Alvin Junior, that you will live your life to defeat the Unmaker, to make things whole and good and right?"

"Yes," whispered the boy.

"Then I tell you, by the terms of your own promise, you must heal yourself."

Alvin gripped Taleswapper's arm. "How," he whispered.

"That I don't know, boy," said Taleswapper. "How to use your power, you have to find that out inside yourself. I can only tell you that you must try, or the enemy has his victory, and I'll have to end your tale with your body being lowered into a grave."

To Taleswapper's surprise, Alvin smiled. Then Taleswapper understood the joke. His tale would end with the grave no matter what he did today. "Right enough, boy," said Taleswapper. "But I'd rather have a few more pages about you before I put finis to the Book of Alvin."

"I'll try," whispered Alvin.

If he tried, then surely he would succeed. Alvin's protector had not brought him this far only to let him die. Taleswapper had no doubt that Alvin had the power to heal himself, if he could only figure out the way. His own body was far more complicated than the stone. But if he was to live, he had to learn the pathways of his own flesh, bind the fissures in the bones.

They made a bed for Taleswapper out in the great room. He offered to sleep on the floor beside Alvin's bed, but Miller shook his head and answered, "That's my place."

Taleswapper found it hard to sleep, though. It was the middle of the night when he finally gave up, lit a lantern with a match from the fire, bundled on his coat, and went outside.

The wind was brisk. There was a storm coming, and from the smell in the air, it would be snow. The animals were restless in the big barn. It occurred to Taleswapper that he might not be alone outside tonight. There might be Reds in the shadows, or even wandering among the buildings of the farm, watching him. He shuddered once, then shrugged off the fear. It was too cold a night. Even the most bloodthirsty, White-hating Choc-Taws or Cree-Eks spying from the south were too smart to be outside with such a storm coming.

Soon the snow would fall, the first of the season, but it would be no slight trace. It would snow all day tomorrow, Taleswapper could feel it, for the air behind the storm would be even colder than this, cold enough for the snow to be fluffy and dry, the kind of snow that piled deeper and deeper, hour after hour. If Alvin had not hurried them home with the millstone in a single day, they would have been trying to sledge the stone home in the midst of the snowfall. It would have become slippery. Something even worse might have happened.

Taleswapper found himself in the millhouse, looking at the stone. It was so solid-looking, it was hard to imagine anyone ever moving it. He touched the face of it again, being careful not to cut himself. His fingers brushed over the shallow dress cuts, where flour would collect when the great water wheel turned the shaft and made the grindstone roll around and around atop the millstone, as steadily as the Earth rolled around and around the sun, year after year, turning time into dust as surely as the mill turned grain into flour.

He glanced down, to the place where the earth had given way slightly under the millstone, tipping it and nearly killing the boy. The bottom of the depression glistened in the lantern light. Taleswapper knelt and dipped his finger into a half-inch of water. It must have collected there, weakening the ground, carrying away the soil. Not so that it would ever be visibly moist. Just enough that when great weight was placed on it, it would give way.

Ah, Unmaker, thought Taleswapper, show yourself to me, and I'll build such a building that you'll be trussed up and held captive forever. But try as he might, he could not make his eyes see the trembling air that had shown itself to Alvin Miller's seventh son. Finally Taleswapper took up the lantern and left the millhouse. The first flakes were falling. The wind had almost died. The snow came faster and faster, dancing in the light of his lantern. By the time he reached the house, the ground was grey with snow, the forest invisible in the distance. He went inside the house, lay down on the floor without removing even his boots, and fell asleep.

✳ 12 ✳

Book

THEY KEPT A THREE-LOG FIRE, night and day, so the stones of the wall seemed to glow with heat, and the air in his room was dry. Alvin lay unmoving on his bed, his right leg heavy with splints and bandages, pressing into the bed like an anchor, the rest of his body afloat, adrift, pitching and rolling and yawing. He was dizzy, and a little sick.

But he hardly noticed the weight of his leg, or the dizziness. The pain was his enemy, throbs and stabs of it taking his mind away from the task that Taleswapper had set him: to heal himself.

Yet the pain was his friend, too. It built a wall around him so he scarce knew he was in a house, in a room, on a bed. The outside world could burn up and turn to ash and he'd never notice it. It was the world inside that he was exploring now.

Taleswapper didn't know half what he was talking about. It wasn't a matter of making pictures in his mind. His leg wouldn't get better from just pretending it was all healed up. But Taleswapper still had the right idea. If Alvin could feel his way through the rock, could find the weak and strong places and teach them where to break and where to hold firm, why couldn't he do it with skin and bone?

Trouble was, skin and bone was all mixed up. The rock was pretty much the same thing through and through, but the skin changed with every layer, and it wasn't no easy trick figuring where everything went. He lay there with his eyes closed, looking into his own flesh for the first time. At first he tried following the pain, but that didn't get nowhere, just led him to where everything was mashed and cut and messed up so he couldn't tell up from down. After a long while he tried a different tack. He listened to his heart beating. At first the pain kept tearing him away, but after a while he closed in on that sound. If there was noise in the world outside he didn't know about it, because the pain shut all that out. And the rhythm of the heartbeat, that shut out the pain, or mostly, anyway.

He followed the tracks of his blood, the big strong stream, the little streams. Sometimes he got lost. Sometimes a stab from his leg just broke in and demanded to be heard. But by and by he found his way to healthy skin and bone in the other leg. The blood wasn't half so strong there, but it led him where he wanted to go. He found all the layers, like the skin of an onion. He learned their order, saw how the muscle was tied together, how the tiny veins linked up, how the skin stretched taut and bonded tight.

Only then did he find his way to the bad leg. The patch of skin Mama sewed on was pretty much dead, just turning to rot. Alvin Junior knew what it needed, though, if any part of it was to live. He found the mashed-off ends of the arteries around the wound, and began to urge them to grow, just the way he made cracks travel through stone. The stone was easy, compared to this—to make a crack, it just had to let go, that's all. The living flesh was slower to do what he wanted, and pretty soon he gave up on all but the strongest artery.

He began to see how it was using bits and pieces of this and that to build with. A lot was happening that was far too small and fast and complicated for Alvin to get hold of with his mind. But he could get his body to free up what the artery needed in order to grow. He could send it where it was needed, and after a while the artery linked up with the rotted tissue. It took some doing, but he finally found the end of a shriveled artery and linked them up, and sent the blood flowing into the sewn-on patch.

Too soon, too fast. He felt the heat on his leg from

blood pouring out of the dead flesh at a dozen points; it couldn't hold in all the blood he sent. Slow, slow, slow. He followed the blood, now seeping instead of pumping, and again linked up blood vessels, arteries to veins, trying to match it, as best he could, to the other leg.

Finally it was done, or well enough. The normal flow of blood could be contained. Many parts of the patch of skin came back to life as the blood returned. Other parts stayed dead. Alvin kept going around and around with the blood, stripping away the dead parts, breaking them up into bits and pieces too small for him to recognize. But the living parts recognized them well enough, took them up, put them to work. Wherever Alvin explored, he made the flesh grow.

Until he was so weary in his mind from thinking so small and working so hard that he fell asleep in spite of himself.

"I don't want to wake him."

"No way to change the bandage without touching it, Faith."

"All right, then—oh, be careful, Alvin! No, let me!"

"I've done this before—"

"On cows, Alvin, not on little boys!"

Alvin Junior felt pressure on his leg. Something pulling at the skin there. The pain wasn't as bad as yesterday. But he was still too tired even to open his eyes. Even to make a sound to let them know he was awake, he could hear them.

"Good laws, Faith, he must have bled something awful in the night."

"Mama, Mary says I have to—"

"Hush up and get on out of here, Cally! Can't you see your ma's worried about—"

"No need to yell at the boy, Alvin. He's only seven."

"Seven's old enough to keep his mouth shut and leave grown-ups alone when we've got things to—look at that."

"I can hardly believe it."

"I thought to see pus coming out like cream from a cow's tit."

"Clean as can be."

"And skin growing back, will you look at that? Your sewing must've took."

"I hardly dared to hope that skin would live."

"Can't even see no bone under there."

"The Lord is blessing us. I prayed all night, Alvin, and look what God has done."

"Well, you should've prayed harder, then, and got it healed up tight. I need this boy for chores."

"Don't you get blasfemious with me, Alvin Miller."

"It just gripes me hollow, the way God always sneaks in to take the credit. Maybe Alvin's just a good healer, you ever think of that?"

"Look, your nastiness is waking the boy."

"See if he wants a drink of water."

"He's getting one whether he wants it or not."

Alvin wanted it badly. His body was dry, not just his mouth; it needed to make back what it lost in blood. So he swallowed as much as he could, from a tin cup held to his mouth. A lot of it spilled around his face and neck but he didn't hardly notice that. It was the water that trickled into his belly that mattered. He lay back and tried to find out from the inside how his wound was doing. But it was too hard to get back there, too hard to concentrate. He dropped off before he was halfway there.

He woke again, and thought it must be night again, or maybe the curtains were drawn. He couldn't find out cause it was too hard to open his eyes, and the pain was back, fierce again, and something maybe even worse: the wound was a-tickling till he could hardly keep himself from reaching down to scratch. After a while, though, he was able to find the wound and once again help the layers to grow. By the time he slept, there was a thin, complete layer of skin over the whole wound. Underneath, the body was still working to renew the ravaged muscles and knit the broken bones. But there'd be no more loss of blood, no more open wound to get infected.

"Look at this, Taleswapper. You ever seen the like of this?"

"Skin like a newborn baby."

"Maybe I'm crazy, but except for the splint I can't see no reason to leave this leg bound up no more."

"Not a sign of a wound. No, you're right, there's no

need for a bandage now."

"Maybe my wife is right, Taleswapper. Maybe God just rared back and passed a miracle on my boy."

"Can't prove anything. When the boy wakes up, maybe he'll know something about it."

"Not a chance of that. He hasn't even opened his eyes this whole time."

"One thing's certain, Mr. Miller. The boy isn't about to die. That's more than I could have guessed yesterday."

"I was set to build him a box to hold him underground, that I was. I didn't see no chance him living. Will you look at how healthy he is? I want to know what's protecting him, or who."

"Whatever is protecting him, Mr. Miller, the boy is stronger. That's something to think about. His protector split that stone, but Al Junior put it back together and not a thing his protector could do about it."

"Reckon he even knew what he was doing?"

"He must have some notion of his powers. He knew what he could do with the stone."

"I never heard of a knack like this, to tell you straight. I told Faith what he did with that stone, dressing it on the backside without ever laying on a tool, and she starts reading from the Book of Daniel and crying about fulfillment of the prophecy. Wanted to rush in here and warn the boy about clay feet. Don't that beat all? Religion makes them crazy. Not a woman I ever met wasn't crazy with religion."

The door opened.

"Get out of here! Are you so dumb I have to tell you twenty times, Cally? Where's his mother, can't she keep one seven-year-old boy away from—"

"Be easy on the lad, Miller. He's gone now, anyway."

"I don't know what's wrong with him. As soon as Al Junior is down, I see Cally's face wherever I look. Like an undertaker hoping for a fee."

"Maybe it's strange to him. To have Alvin hurt."

"As many times as Alvin's been an inch from death—"

"But never injured."

A long silence.

"Taleswapper."

"Yes, Mr. Miller?"

"You've been a good friend to us here, sometimes in spite of ourselfs. But I reckon you're still a walking man."

"That I am, Mr. Miller."

"What I'm saying is, not to rush you off, but if you go anytime soon, and you happen to be heading generally eastward, do you think you could carry a letter for me?"

"I'd be glad to. And no fee, to sender or receiver."

"That's right kind of you. I been thinking on what you said. About a boy needing to be sent far off from certain dangers. And I thought, in all the world where's there some folks I can trust to look after the boy? We got no kin worth speaking of back in New England—I don't want the boy raised Puritan on the brink of hell anyway."

"I'm relieved to hear that, Mr. Miller, because I have no great longing to see New England again myself."

"If you just follow back on the road we made coming west, sooner or later you come along to a place on the Hatrack River, some thirty miles north of the Hio, not all that far downriver from Fort Dekane. There's a road house there, or leastwise there was, with a graveyard out back where a stone says 'Vigor he died to save his kin.'"

"You want me to take the boy?"

"No, no, I'll not send him now that the snow's come. Water—"

"I understand."

"There's a blacksmith there, and I thought he might want a prentice. Alvin's young, but he's big for his age, and I reckon he'll be a bargain for the smith."

"Prentice?"

"Well, I sure won't make him a bond slave, now, will I? And I got no money to send him off to school."

"I'll take the letter. But I hope I can stay till the boy is awake, so I can say good-bye."

"I wasn't going to send you out tonight, was I? Nor tomorrow, with new snow deep enough to smother bunnies."

"I didn't know if you had noticed the weather."

"I always notice when there's water underfoot." He laughed wryly, and they left the room.

Alvin Junior lay there, trying to figure why Pa wanted to send him away. Hadn't he done right all his life, as best he could? Hadn't he tried to help all he knew how? Didn't he go to Reverend Thrower's school, even though the preacher was out to make him mad or stupid? Most of all, didn't he finally get a perfect stone down from the mountain, holding it together all the time, teaching it the way to go, and at the very end risking his leg just so the stone wouldn't split? And now they were going to send him away.

Prentice! To a blacksmith! In his whole life he never even saw a blacksmith up to now. They had to ride three days to the nearest smithy, and Pa never let him go along. In his whole life he never even been ten mile from home one way or any other.

In fact, the more he thought about it the madder he got. Hadn't he been begging Mama and Papa just to let him go out walking in the woods alone, and they wouldn't let him. Had to have somebody with him all the time, like he was a captive or a slave about to run off. If he was five minutes late getting somewhere, they came to look for him. He never got to go on long trips—the longest one ever was to the quarry a few times. And now, after they kept him penned up like a Christmas goose all his life, they were set to send him off to the end of the whole earth.

It was so blame unfair that tears come to his eyes and squeezed out and tickled down his cheeks right into his ears, which felt so silly it made him laugh.

"What you laughing at?" asked Cally.

Alvin hadn't heard him come in.

"Are you all better now? It ain't bleeding nowhere, Al."

Cally touched his cheek.

"You crying cause it hurts so bad?"

Alvin probably could have spoke to him, but it seemed like too much work to open up his mouth and push words out, so he kind of shook his head, slow and gentle.

"You going to die, Alvin?" asked Cally.

He shook his head again.

"Oh," said Cally.

He sounded so disappointed that it made Alvin a little mad. Mad enough to get his mouth working after all. "Sorry," he croaked.

"Well it ain't fair, anyhow," said Cally. "I didn't want you dead, but they all said you was going to die. And I got to thinking what it'd be like if *I* was the one they all took care of. All the time, everybody watching out for you, and when I say one little thing they just say, Get out of here, Cally, Just shut up, Cally. Nobody asked you, Cally, Ain't you spose to be in bed, Cally? They don't care what I do. Except when I start hitting *you*, then they all say, Don't get in fights, Cally."

"You wrestle real good for a field mouse." At least that was what Alvin meant to say, but he didn't know for sure if his lips even moved.

"You know what I did one time when I was six? I went out and got myself lost in the woods. I just walked and walked. Sometimes I closed my eyes and spun around a few times so I'd sure not know where I was. I must have been lost half the day. Did one soul come looking for me? I finally had to turn around and find my own way home. Nobody said, Where you been all day, Cally? Mama just said, Your hands are dirty as the back end of a sick horse, go wash yourself."

Alvin laughed again, near silently, his chest heaving.

"It's funny for *you*. Everybody looks after *you*."

Alvin worked hard to make a sound this time. "You want me gone?"

Cally waited a long time to answer. "No. Who'd play with me then? Just the dumb old cousins. There ain't a good wrassler in the bunch of them."

"I'm going," whispered Alvin.

"No you ain't. You're the seventh son and they'll never let you go."

"Going."

"Course the way I count up it's *me* that's number seven. David, Calm, Measure, Wastenot, Wantnot, Alvin Junior that's you, and then me, that's seven."

"Vigor."

"He's dead. He's been dead a long time. Somebody ought to tell that to Ma and Pa."

Alvin lay there, near wore out from the few things he said. Cally didn't say anything much after that. Just sat there, still as could be. Holding Alvin's hand real tight. Pretty soon Alvin started drifting, so he wasn't sure altogether whether Cally really spoke or it was in a dream. But he heard Cally say, "I don't never wish you dead, Alvin." And then he might have said, "I wish I was you." But anyway Alvin drifted off to sleep, and when he woke up again there was nobody with him and the house was still except for nightsounds, the wind rattling the shutters, the timbers popping as they shrunk from the cold, the log snapping in the hearth.

One more time Alvin went inside himself and worked his way down to the wound. Only this time he didn't have much to do with the skin and muscle. It was the bones he worked on now. It surprised him how lacy it was, pocked with little hollows all over, not solid straight through like the millstone was. But he learned the way of it soon enough, and it was easy after a while to knit the bones up tight.

Still, there was something wrong with that bone. Something in his bad leg just wouldn't get exactly like the good leg. But it was so small he couldn't see it clear. Just knew that whatever it was, it made the bone sick inside, just a little patch of sickness, but he couldn't figure how to make it better. Like trying to pick up snowflakes off the ground, whenever he thought he had ahold of something, it turned out to be nothing, or maybe just too small to see.

Maybe, though, it would just go away. Maybe if everything else got better, that sick place on his bone would get better by itself.

Eleanor was late getting back from her mother's house. Armor believed that a wife should have strong ties with her family, but coming home at dusk was too dangerous.

"There's talk of wild Reds up from the south," said Armor-of-God. "And you traipsing about after dark."

"I hurried home," she said. "I know the way in the dark."

"It's not a question of knowing the way," he said sternly. "The French are giving guns as bounty on White scalps now. It won't tempt the Prophet's people, but there's many a Choc-Taw who'd be glad to come up to Fort Detroit, gathering scalps along the way."

"Alvin isn't going to die," said Eleanor.

Armor hated it when she turned the subject like that. But it was such news that he couldn't very well not ask after it. "They decide to take off the leg, then?"

"I saw the leg. It's getting better. And Alvin Junior was awake late this afternoon. I talked to him awhile."

"I'm glad he was awake, Elly, I truly am, but I hope you don't expect the leg to get better. A big wound like that may look to be healing for a while, but the rot'll set in pretty soon."

"I don't think so this time," she said. "You want supper?"

"I must have gnawed down two loaves just pacing back and forth wondering whether you were even coming home."

"It isn't good for a man to get a belly."

"Well, I got one, and it calls out for food just like any other man's."

"Mama gave me a cheese to bring home." She set it out on the table.

Armor had his doubts. He figured half the reason Faith Miller's cheeses turned out so good was because she *did* things to the milk. At the same time, there wasn't no better cheese on the banks of the Wobbish, nor up Tippy-Canoe Creek neither.

It put him out of sorts when he caught himself compromising with witchery. And being out of sorts, he wasn't about to let anything lie, even though he knew Elly plain didn't want to talk about it. "Why don't you think the leg will rot?"

"It's just getting better so fast," she said.

"How much better?"

"Oh, pert near fixed."

"How near?"

She turned around, rolled her eyes, and turned back

away from him. She started cutting up an apple to eat with the cheese.

"I said *how* near, Elly? How near fixed?"

"Fixed."

"Two days after a millstone rips off the front half of his leg, and it's fixed?"

"Only two days?" she said. "Seems like a week to me."

"Calendar says it's two days," said Armor. "Which means there's been witchery up there."

"As I read the gospels, the one that healed people wasn't no witch."

"Who did it? Don't tell me your pa or ma suddenly figured out something as strong as that. Did they conjure up a devil?"

She turned around, the knife in her hands still poised for cutting. There was a flash in her eyes. "Pa may be no kind of church man, but the devil never set foot in our house."

That wasn't what Reverend Thrower said, but Armor knew better than to bring *him* into the conversation. "It's that beggar, then."

"He works for his room and board. Hard as anyone."

"They say he knew that old wizard Ben Franklin. And that atheist from Appalachee, Tom Jefferson."

"He tells good stories. And he didn't heal the boy neither."

"Well, *somebody* did."

"Maybe he just healed up himself. Anyway, the leg's still *broke*. So it ain't a miracle or nothing. He's just a fast healer."

"Well maybe he's a fast healer cause the devil takes care of his own."

From the look in her eye when she turned around, Armor kind of wished he hadn't said it. But dad-gum it, Reverend Thrower as much as said the boy was as bad as the Beast of the Apocalypse.

But beast or boy, he was Elly's brother, and whereas she might be as quiet as you please most of the time, when she got her dander up she could be a terror.

"Take that back," she said.

"Now, that's about as silly a thing as I ever heard. How can I take back what I said?"

"By saying you know it ain't so."

"I don't know it is and I don't know it ain't. I said maybe, and if a man can't say his maybes to his wife then he might as well be dead."

"I reckon that's about true," she said. "And if you don't take that back you'll wish you was dead!" And she started coming after him with two chunks of apple, one in each hand.

Now, most times she came for him like that, even if she was really mad, if he let her chase him around the house awhile she usually ended up laughing. But not this time. She mushed one apple in his hair and threw the other one at him, and then just sat down in the upstairs bedroom, crying her eyes out.

She wasn't one to cry, so Armor figured this had got right out of hand.

"I take it back, Elly," he said. "He's a good boy, I know that."

"Oh, I don't care what you think," she said. "You don't know a thing about it anyway."

There weren't many husbands who'd let their wife say such a thing without slapping her upside the head. Armor wished sometimes that Elly'd appreciate how him being a Christian worked to her advantage.

"I know a thing or two," he said.

"They're going to send him off," she said. "Once spring comes, they're going to prentice him out. He's none too happy about it, I can tell, but he don't argue none, he just lies there in his bed, talking real quiet, but looking at me and everybody else like he was saying good-bye all the time."

"What are they wanting to send him off for?"

"I told you, to prentice him."

"The way they baby that boy, I can't hardly believe they'd let him out of their sight."

"They ain't talking about nothing close by, neither. Clear back at the east end of Hio Territory, near Fort Dekane. Why, that's halfway to the ocean."

"You know, it just makes sense, when you think about it."

"It does?"

"With Red trouble starting up, they want him plumb gone. The others can all stick around to get an arrow in their face, but not Alvin Junior."

She looked at him with withering contempt. "Sometimes you're so suspicious you make me want to puke, Armor-of-God."

"It ain't suspicion to say what's really happening."

"You can't tell real from a rutabaga."

"You going to wash this apple out of my hair, or do I have to make you lick it out?"

"I expect I'll have to do something, or you'll rub it all over the bed linen."

Taleswapper felt almost like a thief, to take so much with him as he left. Two pair of thick stockings. A new blanket. An elkhide cloak. Jerky and cheese. A good whetstone.

And things they couldn't even know they gave him. A rested body, free of aches and bruises. A jaunty step. Kind faces fresh in his mind. And stories. Stories jotted in the sealed-up part of the book, the ones he wrote down himself. And true stories painfully inscribed by their own hands.

Still, he gave them fair return, or tried to. Roofs patched for winter, other jobs here and there. More important, they'd seen a book with Ben Franklin's own handwriting in it, with sentences from Tom Jefferson, Ben Arnold, Pat Henry, John Adams, Alex Hamilton—even Aaron Burr, from before the duel, and Daniel Boone, from after. Before Taleswapper came they were part of their family, and part of the Wobbish country, and that's all. Now they belonged to much larger stories. The War of Appalachee Independence. The American Compact. They saw their own trek through the wilderness as one thread among many, and felt the strength of the whole tapestry woven from those threads. Not a tapestry, really. A rug. A good, thick, solid rug that generations of Americans after them could tread on. There was a poem in that; he'd work that into a poem sometime.

He left them a few other things, too. A beloved son he pulled from under a falling millstone. A father who now had the strength to send away his son before he killed him. A name for a young man's nightmare, so he could understand that his enemy was real. A whispered encouragement for a broken child to heal himself.

And a single drawing, burnt into a fine slab of oakwood with the tip of a hot knife. He'd rather have worked with wax and acid on metal, but there was neither to be had in this place. So he burnt lines into the wood, making of it what he could. A picture of a young man caught in a strong river, bound up in the roots of a floating tree, gasping for breath, his eyes facing death fearlessly. It would have earned nothing but scorn at the Lord Protector's Academy of Art, being so plain. But Goody Faith cried out when she saw it, and hugged it to her, dropping her tears over it like the last drips from the eaves after a rainstorm. And Father Alvin, when he saw it, nodded and said, "That's your vision, Taleswapper. You got his face perfect, and you never even saw him. That's Vigor. That's my boy." Then he cried, too.

They set it right up on the mantel. It might not be great art, thought Taleswapper, but it was true, and it meant more to these folks than any portrait could mean to some fat old lord or parliamentarian in London or Camelot or Paris or Vienna.

"It's fair morning now," said Goody Faith. "You've got long to go before dark."

"You can't blame me for being reluctant to leave. Though I'm glad you trusted me with this errand, and I won't fail you." He patted his pocket, wherein lay the letter to the blacksmith of Hatrack River.

"You can't go without you say good-bye to the boy," said Miller.

He'd put it off as long as it could be delayed. He nodded once, then eased himself from the comfortable chair by the fire and went on into the room where he'd slept the best nights of his life. It was good to see Alvin Junior's eyes wide open, his face lively, no longer slack the way it was for a while, or winced up with pain. But the pain was still there, Taleswapper knew.

"You going?" asked the boy.

"I'm gone, except for saying good-bye to you."

Alvin looked a little angry. "So you ain't even going to let me write in your book?"

"Not everybody does, you know."

"Pa did. And Mama."

"And Cally, too."

"I bet that looks good," said Alvin. "He writes like a, like a—"

"Like a seven-year-old." It was a rebuke, but Alvin had no intention of squirming.

"Why not me, then? Why Cally and not me?"

"Because I only let people write the most important thing they ever did or ever saw with their own eyes. What would *you* write?"

"I don't know. Maybe about the millstone."

Taleswapper made a face.

"Then maybe my vision. That's important, you said so yourself."

"And that got written up somewhere else, Alvin."

"I want to write in the book," he said. "I want my sentence in there along with Maker Ben's."

"Not yet," said Taleswapper.

"When!"

"When you've whipped that old Unmaker, lad. That's when I'll let you write in this book."

"What if I don't ever whip him?"

"Then this book won't amount to much, anyway."

Tears sprang to Alvin's eyes. "What if I die?"

Taleswapper felt a thrill of fear. "How's the leg?"

The boy shrugged. He blinked back the tears. They were gone.

"That's no answer, lad."

"It won't stop hurting."

"It'll be that way till the bone knits."

Alvin Junior smiled wanly. "Bone's all knit."

"Then why don't you walk?"

"It pains me, Taleswapper. It never goes away. It's got a bad place on the bone, and I ain't figured out yet how to make it right."

"You'll find a way."

"I ain't found it yet."

"An old trapper once said to me, 'It don't matter if you start at the bung or the breastbone, any old way you get the skin off a panther is a good way.'"

"Is that a proverb?"

"It's close. You'll find a way, even if it isn't what you expect."

"Nothing's what I expect," said Alvin. "Nothing turns out like anything I figured."

"You're ten years old, lad. Weary of the world already?"

Alvin kept rubbing folds of the blanket between his thumb and fingers. "Taleswapper, I'm dying."

Taleswapper studied his face, trying to see death there. It wasn't. "I don't think so."

"The bad place on my leg. It's growing. Slow, maybe, but it's growing. It's invisible, and it's eating away at the hard places of the bone, and after a while it'll go faster and faster and—"

"And Unmake you."

Alvin started to cry for real this time, and his hands were shaking. "I'm scared to die, Taleswapper, but it got inside me and I can't get it out."

Taleswapper laid a hand on his, to still the trembling. "You'll find a way. You've got too much work to do in this world, to die now."

Alvin rolled his eyes. "That's about as dumb a thing as I've heard this year. Just because somebody's got things to do don't mean he won't die."

"But it does mean he won't die *willingly*."

"I ain't willing."

"That's why you'll find a way to live."

Alvin was silent for a few seconds. "I've been thinking. About if I do live, what I'll do. Like what I done to make my leg get mostly better. I can do that for other folks, I bet. I can lay hands on them and feel the way it is inside, and fix it up. Wouldn't that be good?"

"They'd love you for it, all the folks you healed."

"I reckon the first time was the hardest, and I wasn't partickler strong when I done it. I bet I can do it faster on other people."

"Maybe so. But even if you heal a hundred sick people every day, and move on to the next place and heal a hundred more, there'll be ten thousand people die behind you, and ten thousand more ahead of you, and by the time you die, even the ones you healed will almost all be dead."

Alvin turned his face away. "If I know how to fix them, then I got to fix them, Taleswapper."

"Those you can, you must," said Taleswapper. "But not as your life's work. Bricks in the wall, Alvin, that's all they'll ever be. You can never catch up by repairing the crumbling bricks. Heal those who chance to fall under your hand, but your life's work is deeper than that."

"I know how to heal people. But I don't know how to beat down the Un—the Unmaker. I don't even know what it is."

"As long as you're the only one that can see him, though, you're also the only one who has a hope of beating him."

"Maybe."

Another long silence. Taleswapper knew it was time to go.

"Wait."

"I've got to leave now."

Alvin caught at his sleeve. "Not yet."

"Pretty soon."

"At least—at least let me read what the others wrote."

Taleswapper reached into his bag and pulled out the book pouch. "I can't promise I'll explain what they mean," he said, sliding the book out of its waterproof cover.

Alvin quickly found the last, newest writings.

In his mother's hand: "Vigor he push a log and he don die til the boy is bornd."

In David's hand: "A mil ston splits in two then it suks bak not a crak."

In Cally's hand: "A sevent sunn."

Alvin looked up. "He ain't talking about me, you know."

"I know," said Taleswapper.

Alvin looked back at the book. In his father's hand: "He dont kil a boy cus a stranjer com in time."

"What's Pa talking about?" asked Alvin.

Taleswapper took the book from his hands and closed it. "Find a way to heal your leg," he said. "There's a lot more souls than you who need it to be strong. It's not for yourself, remember?"

He bent over and kissed the boy on the forehead. Alvin reached up and held him with both arms, hanging on him so that he couldn't stand up without lifting the boy clear out of bed. After a while, Taleswapper had to reach up and pull the boy's arms away. His cheek was wet with Alvin's tears. He didn't wipe them away. He let the breeze dry them as he trudged along the cold dry path, with fields of half-melted snow stretching left and right.

He paused a moment on the second covered bridge. Just long enough to wonder if he'd ever come back here, or see them again. Or get Alvin Junior's sentence for his book. If he were a prophet, he'd know. But he hadn't the faintest idea.

He walked on, setting his feet toward morning.

✳ 13 ✳

Surgery

THE VISITOR SAT COMFORTABLY upon the altar, leaning casually on his left arm, so that his body had a jaunty tilt. Reverend Thrower had seen just such an informal pose taken by a dandy from Camelot, a rakehell who clearly despised everything that the Puritan churches of England and Scotland stood for. It made Thrower more than a little uncomfortable to see the Visitor in such an irreverent pose.

"Why?" asked the Visitor. "Just because the only way you can maintain control over your bodily passions is to sit straight in your chair, knees together, hands delicately arranged in your lap, fingers tightly intertwined, does not mean that I am required to do the same."

Thrower was embarrassed. "It isn't fair to chastise me for my thoughts."

"It is, when your thoughts chastise me for my actions. Beware of hubris, my friend. Do not fancy yourself so righteous that *you* can judge the acts of angels."

It was the first time the Visitor had ever called himself an angel.

"I did not call myself *anything*," said the Visitor. "You must learn to control your thoughts, Thrower. You leap to conclusions far too easily."

"Why have you come to me?"

"It's a matter of the maker of this altar," said the

Visitor. He patted one of the crosses Alvin Junior had burnt into the wood.

"I've done my best, but the boy is unteachable. He doubts everything, and contests each point of theology as if it were required to meet the same tests of logic and consistency that prevail in the world of science."

"In other words, he expects your doctrines to make sense."

"He is unwilling to accept the idea that some things remain mysteries, comprehensible only to the mind of God. Ambiguity makes him saucy, and paradox causes open rebellion."

"An obnoxious child."

"The worst I have ever seen," said Thrower.

The Visitor's eyes flashed. Thrower felt a stab in his heart.

"I've tried," said Thrower. "I've tried to turn him to serve the Lord. But the influence of his father—"

"It is a weak man who blames his failures on the strength of others," said the Visitor.

"I haven't failed yet!" said Thrower. "You told me I had until the boy was fourteen—"

"No. I told you *I* had until the boy was fourteen. *You* only have him as long as he lives here."

"I've heard nothing about the Millers moving. They just got their millstone in place, they're going to start grinding in the spring, they wouldn't leave without—"

The Visitor stood up from the altar. "Let me put a case to you, Reverend Thrower. Purely hypothetical. Let us suppose you were in the same room with the worst enemy of all that I stand for. Let us suppose that he were ill, and lay helpless in his bed. If he recovered, he would be removed from your reach, and would thus go on to destroy all that you and I love in this world. But if he died, our great cause would be safe. Now suppose that someone put a knife into your hand, and begged you to perform a delicate surgery upon the boy. And suppose that if you were to slip, just the tiniest bit, your knife could cut a great artery. And suppose that if you simply delayed, his lifeblood would flow out so quickly that in moments he would die. In that case,

Reverend Thrower, what would be your duty?"

Thrower was aghast. All his life he had prepared to teach, persuade, exhort, expound. Never to perform a bloody-handed act like the one the Visitor suggested. "I'm not suited for such things," he said.

"Are you suited for the kingdom of God?" asked the Visitor.

"But the Lord said Thou shalt not kill."

"Oh? Is that what he said to Joshua, when he sent him into the promised land? Is that what he said to Saul, when he sent him against the Amalekites?"

Thrower thought of those dark passages in the Old Testament, and trembled with fear at the thought of taking part in such things himself.

But the Visitor did not relent. "The high priest Samuel commanded King Saul to kill all the Amalekites, every man and woman, every *child*. But Saul hadn't the stomach for it. He saved the king of the Amalekites and brought him back alive. For that crime of disobedience, what did the Lord do?"

"Chose David to be king in his place," murmured Thrower.

The Visitor stood close to Thrower, his eyes wounding him with their fire. "And then Samuel, the high priest, the *gentle* servant of God, what did he do?"

"He called for Agag the king of the Amalekites to be brought before him."

The Visitor would not relent. "And what did Samuel *do*?"

"Killed him," whispered Thrower.

"What does the scripture say that he did!" roared the Visitor. The walls of the meetinghouse shook, the glass of the windows rattled.

Thrower wept in fear, but he spoke the words that the Visitor demanded: "Samuel hacked Agag in pieces—in the presence of the Lord."

Now the only sound in the church was Thrower's own ragged breath as he tried to control his hysterical weeping. The Visitor smiled at him, his eyes filled with love and forgiveness. Then he was gone.

Thrower sank to his knees before the altar and prayed. O Father, I would die for Thee, but do not ask me to kill. Take away this cup from my lips, I am too weak, I am unworthy, do not lay this burden upon my shoulders.

His tears fell on the altar. He heard a sizzling sound and jumped back from the altar, startled. His tears skittered along the surface of the altar like water on a hot skillet, until finally they were consumed.

The Lord has rejected me, he thought. I pledged to serve Him however He required, and now, when He asks something difficult, when He commands me to be as strong as the great prophets of old, I discover myself to be a broken vessel in the hands of the Lord. I cannot contain the destiny He wanted to pour into me.

The door of the church opened, letting in a wave of freezing air that rushed along the floor and sent a chill through the minister's flesh. He looked up, fearing that it was an angel sent to punish him.

It was no angel, though. Merely Armor-of-God Weaver.

"I didn't mean to interrupt you in prayer," said Armor.

"Come in," said Thrower. "Close the door. What can I do for you?"

"Not for me," said Armor.

"Come here. Sit down. Tell me."

Thrower hoped that perhaps it was a sign from God that Armor had come just now. A member of the congregation, coming to him for help, right after he prayed—surely the Lord was letting him know that he was accepted after all.

"It's my wife's brother," said Armor. "The boy, Alvin Junior."

Thrower felt a thrill of dread run through him, freezing him to the bone. "I know him. What about him?"

"You know he got his leg mashed."

"I heard of it."

"You didn't happen to go visit and see him afore it healed up?"

"I've been given to believe that I'm not welcome in that house."

"Well, let me tell you, it was bad. A whole patch of skin tore off. Bones broke. But two days later, it was healed right up. Couldn't even see no scar. Three days later he was *walking*."

"It must not have been as bad as you thought."

"I'm telling you, that leg was *broke* and the wound was *bad*. The whole family figured the boy was bound to die. They asked me about buying nails for a coffin. And they looked so bad from grieving that I wasn't sure but what we'd bury the boy's ma and pa, too."

"Then it can't be as fully healed as you say."

"Well, it ain't *fully* healed, and that's why I come to you. I know you don't believe in such things, but I tell you they witched the boy's leg to heal somehow. Elly says the boy did the witching himself. He was even walking on the leg for a few days, no splint even. But the pain never let up, and now he says there's a sick place on his bone. He's got a fever, too."

"There's a perfectly natural explanation for everything," said Thrower.

"Well, be that as you like, the way I see it the boy invited the devil with his witchery, and now the devil's eating him alive inside. And seeing how you're an ordained minister of God, I thought maybe you could cast out that devil in the name of the Lord Jesus."

Superstitions and sorceries were nonsense, of course, but when Armor brought up the possibility of a devil being in the boy, it made sense, it fit with what he knew from the Visitor. Maybe the Lord wanted him to exorcise the child, to purge the evil from him, not to kill the boy at all. It was a chance for him to redeem himself from his failure of will a few minutes before.

"I'll go," he said. He reached for his heavy cloak and whipped it around his shoulders.

"I better warn you, nobody up at their house asked me to bring you."

"I'm prepared to deal with the anger of the unfaithful,"

said Thrower. "It's the victim of deviltry that concerns me, not his foolish and superstitious family."

Alvin lay on his bed, burning with the heat of his fever. Now, in the daylight, they kept his shutters closed, so the light wouldn't hurt his eyes. At night, though, he made them open things up, let some of the cold air in. He would breathe it in relief. During the few days when he could walk, he had seen the snow covering the meadow. Now he tried to imagine himself lying under that blanket of snow. Relief from the fire burning through his body.

He just couldn't see small enough inside himself. What he did with the bone, with the strands of muscle and layers of skin, it was harder than ever it was to find the cracks in the quarry stone. But he could feel his way through the labyrinth of his body, find the large wounds, help them to close. Most of what went on, though, was too small and fast for him to comprehend. He could see the result, but he couldn't see the pieces, couldn't make out how it happened.

That's how it was with the bad place in his bone. Just a patch of it that was weakening, rotting away. He could feel the difference between the bad place and the good healthy bone, he could find the borders of the sickness. But he couldn't actually see what was happening. He couldn't undo it. He was going to die.

He wasn't alone in the room, he knew. Someone always sat at his bedside. He would open his eyes and see Mama, or Papa, or one of the girls. Sometimes even one of the brothers, even though it meant he had left his wife and his chores. It was a comfort to Alvin, but it was also a burden. He kept thinking he ought to hurry up and die so they could all get back to their regular lives.

This afternoon it was Measure sitting there. Alvin said howdy to him when he first came, but there wasn't much to talk about. Howdy do? I'm dying, thanks, and you? Kind of hard to keep chatting. Measure talked about how he and the twins had tried to cut a grindstone. They chose a softer stone than what Alvin worked with, and still they had a devil of a time cutting. "We finally gave right up," said Measure. "It's just going to have to wait till you can go up the mountain and get us a stone yourself."

Alvin didn't answer that, and they neither one said a word since then. Alvin just lay there, sweating, feeling the rot in his bone as it slowly, steadily grew. Measure sat there, lightly holding his hand.

Measure started to whistle.

The sound of it startled Alvin. He'd been so caught up inside himself that the music seemed to come from a great distance, and he had to travel some distance to discover where it was coming from.

"Measure," he cried; but the sound of his voice was a whisper.

The whistling stopped. "Sorry," said Measure. "Does it bother you?"

"No," said Alvin.

Measure started in whistling again. It was a strange tune, one that Alvin didn't recollect he ever heard before. In fact it didn't sound like any kind of tune at all. It never did repeat itself, just went on with new patterns all the time, like as if Measure was making it up on the way. As Alvin lay there and listened, the melody seemed like it was a map, winding through a wilderness, and he started to follow it. Not that he *saw* anything, the way he would following a real map. It just seemed always to show him the center of things, and everything he thought about, he thought about as if he was standing in that place. Almost like he could see all the thinking he had done before, trying to figure out a way to fix the bad place on his bone, only now he was looking from a ways off, maybe higher up a mountain or in a clearing, somewhere that he could see *more.*

Now he thought of something he never thought of before. When his leg was first broke, with the skin all tore up, everybody could see how bad off he was, but nobody could help him, only himself. He had to fix it all from inside. Now, though, nobody else could see the wound that was killing him. And even though *he* could see it, he couldn't do a blame thing to make it better.

So maybe this time, somebody else could fix him up. Not using any kind of hidden power at all. Just plain old bloody-handed surgery.

"Measure," he whispered.

"I'm here," said Measure.

"I know a way to fix my leg," he said.

Measure leaned in close. Alvin didn't open his eyes, but he could feel his brother's breath on his cheek.

"The bad place on my bone, it's growing, but it ain't spread all over yet," Alvin said. "I can't make it better, but I reckon if somebody cut off that part of my bone and took it right out of my leg, I could heal it up the rest of the way."

"Cut it out?"

"Pa's bone saw that he uses when he's cutting up meat, that'd do the trick I think."

"But there ain't a surgeon in three hundred mile."

"Then I reckon somebody better learn how real quick, or I'm dead."

Measure was breathing quicker now. "You think cutting your bone would save your life?"

"It's the best I can think of."

"It might mess up your leg real bad," said Measure.

"If I'm dead, I won't care. And if I live, it'll be worth a messed-up leg."

"I'm going to fetch Pa." Measure scuffed back his chair and thumped out of the room.

Thrower let Armor lead the way onto the Millers' porch. They couldn't very well turn away their daughter's husband. His concern was unfounded, however. It was Goody Faith who opened the door, not her pagan husband.

"Why, Reverend Thrower, if you ain't being too kind to us, stopping up here," she said. The cheerfulness of her voice was a lie, though, if her haggard face was telling the truth. There hadn't been much good sleep in this house lately.

"I brought him along, Mother Faith," said Armor. "He come only cause I asked him."

"The pastor of our church is welcome in my home whenever it pleases him to come by," said Faith.

She ushered them into the great room. A group of girls making quilt squares looked up at him from their chairs near the hearth. The little boy, Cally, was doing his letters on a board, writing with charcoal from the fire.

"I'm glad to see you doing your letters," said Thrower.

Cally just looked at him. There was a hint of hostility in his eyes. Apparently the boy resented having his teacher look at his work here at home, which he had supposed was a sanctuary.

"You're doing them well," said Thrower, trying to put the boy at ease. Cally said nothing, just looked down again at his makeshift slate and kept on scrawling out words.

Armor brought up their business right away. "Mother Faith, we come cause of Alvin. You know how I feel about witchery, but I never before said a word against what you folks do in your house. I always reckoned that was your business and none of mine. But that boy is paying the price for the evil ways that you've let go on here. He witched his leg, and now there's a devil in him, killing him off, and I brought Reverend Thrower here to wring that devil on out of him."

Goody Faith looked puzzled. "There ain't no devil in this house."

Ah, poor woman, said Thrower silently. If you only knew how long a devil has dwelt here. "It is possible to become so accustomed to the presence of a devil as not to recognize that it is present."

A door by the stairs opened up, and Mr. Miller stepped backward through the doorway. "Not me," he said, talking to whoever was in that room. "I'll not lay a knife to the boy."

Cally jumped up at the sound of his father's voice and ran to him. "Armor brung old Thrower here, Papa, to kill the devil."

Mr. Miller turned around, his face twisted with un-identified emotion, and looked at the visitors as if he hardly recognized them.

"I've got good strong hexes on this house," said Goody Faith.

"Those hexes are a summons for the devil," said Armor. "You think they protect your house, but they drive away the Lord."

"No devil ever came in here," she insisted.

"Not by itself," said Armor. "You called it in with all your conjuring. You forced the Holy Spirit to leave your house by your witchery and idolatry, and having swept goodness from your home, the devils naturally come right in. They always come in, where they see a fair chance to do mischief."

Thrower became a little concerned that Armor was saying too much about things he didn't really understand. It would have been better had he simply asked if Thrower could pray for the boy at Alvin's bedside. Now Armor was drawing battle lines that should never have been drawn.

And whatever was going on in Mr. Miller's head right now, it was plain to see that this wasn't the best of times to provoke the man. He slowly walked toward Armor. "You telling me that what comes into a man's house to do mischief is the devil?"

"I bear you my witness as one who loves the Lord Jesus," Armor began, but before he could get any further into his testimony, Miller had him by the shoulder of his coat and the waist of his pants, and he turned him right toward the door.

"Somebody better open this door!" roared Miller. "Or there's going to be a powerful big hole right in the middle of it!"

"What do you think you're doing, Alvin Miller!" shouted his wife.

"Casting out devils!" cried Miller. Cally had swung the door open by then, and Miller walked his son-in-law to the edge of the porch and sent him flying. Armor's cry of outrage ended up muffled by the snow on the ground, and there wasn't much chance to hear his yelling after that because Miller closed and barred the door.

"Ain't you a big man," said Goody Faith, "throwing out your own daughter's husband."

"I didn't do but what he said the Lord wanted done," said Miller. Then he turned his gaze upon the pastor.

"Armor didn't speak for me," said Thrower mildly.

"If you lay a hand on a man of the cloth," said Goody Faith, "you'll sleep in a cold bed for the rest of your life."

"Wouldn't think of touching the man," said Miller.

"But the way I figure it, I stay out of his place, and he ought to stay out of mine."

"You may not believe in the power of prayer," said Thrower.

"I reckon it depends on who's doing the praying, and who's doing the listening," said Miller.

"Even so," said Thrower, "your wife believes in the religion of Jesus Christ, in the which I have been called and ordained a minister. It is her belief, and my belief, that for me to pray at the boy's bedside might be efficacious in his cure."

"If you use words like that in your praying," said Miller, "it's a wonder the Lord even knows what you're talking about."

"Though you don't believe such prayer will help," Thrower went on, "it certainly can't hurt, can it?"

Miller looked from Thrower to his wife and back again. Thrower had no doubt that if Faith had not been there, he would have been eating snow alongside Armor-of-God. But Faith *was* there and had already uttered the threat of Lysistrata. A man does not have fourteen children if his wife's bed holds no attraction to him. Miller gave in. "Go on in," he said. "But don't pester the boy too long."

Thrower nodded graciously. "No more than a few hours," he said.

"Minutes!" Miller insisted. But Thrower was already headed for the door by the stairs, and Miller made no move to stop him. He could have hours with the boy, if he wanted to. He closed the door behind him. No sense in letting any of the pagans interfere with this.

"Alvin," he said.

The boy was stretched out under a blanket, his forehead beaded with sweat. His eyes were closed. After a while, though, he opened his mouth a little. "Reverend Thrower," he whispered.

"The very same," said Thrower. "Alvin, I've come to pray for you, so the Lord will free your body of the devil that is making you sick."

Again a pause, as if it took a while for Thrower's words to reach Alvin and just as long again for his answer to return. "Ain't no devil," he said.

"One can hardly expect a child to be well-versed in matters of religion," said Thrower. "But I must tell you that healing comes only to those who have the faith to be healed." He then devoted several minutes to recounting the story of the centurion's daughter and the tale of the woman who had an issue of blood and merely touched the Savior's robe. "You recall what he said to her. Thy faith hath made thee whole, he said. So it is, Alvin Miller, that your faith must be strong before the Lord can make you whole."

The boy didn't answer. Since Thrower had used his considerable eloquence in the telling of both stories, it offended him a bit that the boy might have fallen asleep. He reached out a long finger and poked Alvin's shoulder.

Alvin flinched away. "I heard you," he muttered.

It wasn't good that the boy could still be sullen, after hearing the light-giving word of the Lord. "Well?" asked Thrower. "Do you believe?"

"In what," murmured the boy.

"In the gospel! In the God who would heal you, if you only soften your heart!"

"Believe," he whispered. "In God."

That should have been enough. But Thrower knew too much of the history of religion not to press for more detail. It was not enough to confess faith in a deity. There were so many deities, and all but one was false. "*Which* God do you believe in, Al Junior?"

"God," said the boy.

"Even the heathen Moor prays toward the black stone of Mecca and calls it God! Do you believe in the true God, and do you believe in Him correctly? No, I understand, you're too weak and fevered to explain your faith. I will help you, young Alvin. I'll ask you questions, and you tell me, yes or no, whether you believe."

Alvin lay still, waiting.

"Alvin Miller, do you believe in a God without body, parts, or passions? The great Uncreated Creator, Whose center is everywhere, yet Whose circumference can never be found?"

The boy seemed to ponder this for a while before he spoke. "That don't make a bit of sense to me," he said.

"He isn't supposed to make sense to the carnal mind," Thrower said. "I merely ask if you *believe* in the One who sits atop the Topless Throne; the self-existing Being who is so large He fills the universe, yet so penetrating that He lives in your heart."

"How can he sit on the top of something that ain't got no top?" the boy asked. "How can something that big fit inside my heart?"

The boy was obviously too uneducated and simple-minded to grasp sophisticated theological paradox. Still, it was more than a life or even a soul at stake here—it was all the souls that the Visitor had said this boy would ruin if he could not be converted to the true faith. "That's the beauty of it," said Thrower, letting emotion fill his voice. "God is beyond our comprehension; yet in His infinite love He condescends to save us, despite our ignorance and foolishness."

"Ain't love a passion?" asked the boy.

"If you have trouble with the idea of God," said Thrower, "then let me pose another question, which may be more to the point. Do you believe in the bottomless pit of hell, where the wicked writhe in flames, yet are never burned up? Do you believe in Satan, the enemy of God, who wishes to steal your soul and take you captive into his kingdom, to torment you through all eternity?"

The boy seemed to perk up a little, turning his head toward Thrower, though he still didn't open his eyes. "I might believe in something like that," he said.

Ah, yes, thought Thrower. The boy *has* had some experience with the devil. "Have you seen him, child?"

"What's *your* devil look like?" whispered the boy.

"He is not *my* devil," said Thrower. "And if you had listened in services, you would have known, for I have described him many times. Where a man has hair on his head, the devil has the horns of a bull. Where a man has hands, the devil has the claws of a bear. He has the hooves of a goat, and his voice is the roar of a ravening lion."

To Thrower's amazement, the boy smiled, and his chest bounced silently with laughter. "And you call *us* superstitious," he said.

Thrower would never have believed how firm a grip the devil could have on a child's soul, had he not seen the boy laugh with pleasure at the description of the monster Lucifer. That laughter must be stopped! It was an offense against God!

Thrower slapped his Bible down on the boy's chest, causing Alvin to wheeze out his breath. Then, with his hand pressing on the book, Thrower felt himself fill up with inspired words, and he cried out with more passion than he had ever felt before in his life: "Satan, in the name of the Lord I rebuke you! I command you to depart from this boy, from this room, from this house forever! Never again seek to possess a soul in this place, or the power of God will wreak destruction unto the uttermost bounds of hell!"

Then silence. Except for the boy's breathing, which seemed labored. There was such peace in the room, such exhausted righteousness in Thrower's own heart, that he felt convinced the devil had heeded his peroration and retreated forthwith.

"Reverend Thrower," said the boy.

"Yes, my son?"

"Can you take that Bible off my chest now? I reckon if there was any devils here, they're all gone now."

Then the boy began to laugh again, causing the Bible to jump up and down under Thrower's hand.

In that moment Thrower's exultation turned to bitter disappointment. Indeed, the fact that the boy could laugh so devilishly with the Bible itself resting on his body was proof that no power could purge him of evil. The Visitor had been right. Thrower should never have refused the mighty work that the Visitor had called him to do. It had been in his power to be the slayer of the Beast of the Apocalypse, and he had been too weak, too sentimental to accept the divine calling. I could have been a Samuel, hewing to death the enemy of God. Instead I am a Saul, a weakling, who cannot kill what the Lord commands must die. Now I will see this boy rise up with the power of Satan in him, and I will know that he thrives only because I was weak.

Now the room was stifling hot, choking him. He had not realized until now how his clothing sogged with sweat. It was hard to breathe. But what should he expect? The hot breath of hell was in this room. Gasping, he took the Bible, held it out between him and the satanic child who lay giggling feverishly under the blanket, and fled.

In the great room he stopped, breathing heavily. He had interrupted a conversation, but he scarcely took notice of it. What did the conversations of these benighted people amount to, compared to what he had just experienced? I have stood in the presence of Satan's minion, masquing it as a young boy; but his mockery revealed him to me. I should have known what the boy was years ago, when I felt his head and found it to be so perfectly balanced. Only a counterfeit would be so perfect. The child was never *real*. Ah, that I had the strength of the great prophets of old, so I could confound the enemy and bear the trophy back to my Lord!

Someone was tugging at his sleeve. "Are you well, Reverend?" It was Goody Faith, but Reverend Thrower did not think to answer her. Her tugging pulled him around, though, so he faced the fireplace. There on the mantel he saw a carven image, and in his distracted state he could not at once determine what it was. It seemed to be the face of a soul in torment, surrounded by writhing tendrils. Flames, that's what they are, he thought, and that is a soul drowning in brimstone, burning in hellfire. The image was a torment to him, and yet it was also satisfying, for its presence in this house signified how closely bound this family was to hell. He stood in the midst of his enemies. A phrase from the Psalmist came to his mind: Bulls of Bashan stare upon me, and I can tell all my bones. My God, my God, why hast Thou forsaken me?

"Here," said Goody Faith. "Sit down."

"Is the boy all right?" demanded Miller.

"The boy?" asked Thrower. Words could hardly come to his mouth. The boy is a fiend from Sheol, and you ask how he is? "As well as can be expected," said Thrower.

They turned away from him then, back to their conversation. Gradually he came to understand what they were discussing. It seemed that Alvin wanted someone to cut away the diseased portion of his bone. Measure had even brought a fine-toothed bone saw from the butchery shed. The argument was between Faith and Measure, because Faith didn't want anyone cutting her son, and between Miller and the other two, because Miller refused to do it, and Faith would only consent if Alvin's father did the cutting.

"If you think it ought to be done," said Faith, "then I don't see how you'd be willing to have anyone but yourself cut into him."

"Not me," said Miller.

It struck Thrower that the man was afraid. Afraid to lay the knife against his own son's flesh.

"He asked for you, Pa. He said he'd draw the marks for cutting, right on his own leg. You just cut a flap of skin and peel it back, and right under it there's the bone, and you just cut a wedge in the bone that takes out the whole bad place."

"I'm not the fainting kind," said Faith, "but my head is getting light."

"If Al Junior says it's got to be done, then do it!" said Miller. "But not me!"

Then, like a rush of light into a dark room, Reverend Thrower saw his redemption. The Lord was clearly offering him exactly the opportunity that the Visitor had prophesied. A chance to hold a knife in his hand, to cut into the boy's leg, and *accidently* sever the artery and spill the blood until the life was gone. What he had shrunk to do in the church, thinking of Alvin as a mere boy, he would do gladly, now that he had seen the evil that disguised itself in child-shape.

"I'm here," he said.

They looked at him.

"I'm no surgeon," he said, "but I have some knowledge of anatomy. I *am* a scientist."

"Head bumps," said Miller.

"You ever butchered cattle or pigs?" asked Measure.

"Measure!" said his mother, horrified. "Your brother is not a beast."

"I just wanted to know if he was going to throw up when he saw blood."

"I've seen blood," said Thrower. "And I have no fear, when the cutting is for salvation."

"Oh, Reverend Thrower, it's too much to ask of you," said Goody Faith.

"Now I see that perhaps it *was* inspiration that brought me up here today, after so long being away from this house."

"It was my pebble-headed son-in-law brought you here," said Miller.

"Well," said Thrower, "it was just a thought. I can see that you don't want me to do it, and I can't say that I blame you. Even if it means saving your son's life, it's still a dangerous thing to let a stranger cut into your own child's body."

"You're no stranger," insisted Faith.

"What if something went wrong? I might slip. His previous injury might have changed the path of certain blood vessels. I might cut an artery, and he could bleed to death in moments. Then I'd have the blood of your child on my hands."

"Reverend Thrower," said Faith, "we can't blame you for chance. All we can do is try."

"It's sure that if we don't do something he'll die," said Measure. "He says we got to cut right away, before the bad place spreads too far."

"Perhaps one of your older sons," said Thrower.

"We got no time to fetch them!" cried Faith. "Oh, Alvin, he's the boy you chose to have your name. Are you set to let him die, just cause you can't abide the preacher here?"

Miller shook his head miserably. "Do it, then."

"He'd rather *you* did, Pa," said Measure.

"No!" said Miller vehemently. "Better anyone than me. Better even him than me."

Thrower saw disappointment, even contempt, on Measure's face. He stood and walked to where Measure sat, holding a knife and the bone saw in his hands. "Young man," he said, "do not ajudge any man to be a coward. You cannot guess what reasons he hides in his heart."

Thrower turned to Miller and saw a look of surprise and gratitude on the man's face. "Give him them cutting tools," Miller said.

Measure held out the knife and the bone saw. Thrower pulled out a handkerchief, and had Measure lay the implements carefully within it.

It had been so easy to do. In just a few moments he had them all asking him to take the knife, absolving him in advance of any accident that might happen. He had even won the first scrap of friendship from Alvin Miller. Ah, I have deceived you all, he thought triumphantly. I am a match for your master the devil. I have deceived the great deceiver, and will send his corrupt progeny back to hell within the hour.

"Who will hold the boy?" asked Thrower. "Even with wine in him, the pain will make him jump if he isn't held down."

"I'll hold him," said Measure.

"He won't take no wine," said Faith. "He says he has to have his head clear."

"He's a ten-year-old boy," said Thrower. "If you insist that he drink it, he's bound to obey you."

Faith shook her head. "He knows what's best. He bears up right smart under pain. You never seen the like."

I imagine not, said Thrower silently. The devil within the boy no doubt revels in the pain, and doesn't want the wine to dim the ecstasy. "Very well, then," he said. "There's no reason to delay further." He led the way into the bedroom and boldly pulled the blanket off Alvin's body. The boy immediately began trembling in the sudden cold, though he continued sweating from the fever. "You say that he has marked the place to cut?"

"Al," said Measure. "Reverend Thrower here is going to do the cutting."

"Papa," said Alvin.

"It's no use asking him," said Measure. "He just plain won't."

"Are you sure you won't have some wine?" asked Faith.

Alvin started to cry. "No," he said. "I'll be all right if Pa holds me."

"That does it," said Faith. "He may not do the cutting, but he'll be here with the boy or he'll be stuffed up the chimney, one or the other." She stormed out of the room.

"You said the boy would mark the place," Thrower said.

"Here, Al, let me set you up here. I got some charcoal, and you mark right on your leg here just exactly where you want that flap of skin took up."

Alvin moaned as Measure lifted him to a sitting position, but his hand was steady as he marked a large rectangle on his shin. "Cut it from the bottom, and leave the top attached," he said. His voice was thick and slow, each word an effort. "Measure, you hold that flap back out of the way while he cuts."

"Ma'll have to do that," said Measure. "I got to hold you down so you don't jump."

"I won't jump," said Alvin. "If Pa's holding me."

Miller came slowly into the room, his wife right behind. "I'll be holding you," he said. He took Measure's place, sitting behind the boy with his arms wrapped clear around him. "I'm holding you," he said again.

"Very well, then," said Thrower. He stood there, waiting for the next step.

He waited for a good little while.

"Ain't you forgetting something, Reverend?" asked Measure.

"What?" asked Thrower.

"The knife and the saw," he said.

Thrower looked at his handkerchief, wadded in his left hand. Empty. "Why, they were right here."

"You set them down on the table on the way in," said Measure.

"I'll fetch them," said Goody Faith. She hurried out of the room.

They waited and waited and waited. Finally Measure got up. "I can't guess what's keeping her."

Thrower followed him out of the room. They found Goody Faith in the great room, piecing together quilt squares with the girls.

"Ma," said Measure. "What about the saw and the knife?"

"Good laws," said Faith, "I can't imagine what's got into me. I clean forgot why I come out here." She picked up the knife and saw and marched back to the room. Measure shrugged at Thrower and followed her. Now, thought Thrower. Now I'll do all that the Lord ever expected of me. The Visitor will see that I am a true friend to my Savior, and my place in heaven will be assured. Not like this poor, miserable sinner caught up in the flames of hell.

"Reverend," said Measure. "What are you doing?"

"This drawing," said Thrower.

"What about it?"

Thrower looked closely at the drawing over the hearth. It wasn't a soul in hell at all. It was a depiction of the family's oldest boy, Vigor, drowning. He had heard the story at least a dozen times. But why was he standing here looking at it, when he had a great and terrible mission to perform in the other room?

"Are you all right?"

"Perfectly all right," said Thrower. "I just needed a moment of silent prayer and meditation before I undertook this task."

He strode boldly into the room and sat down on the chair beside the bed where Satan's child lay trembling, waiting for the knife. Thrower looked around for his tools of holy murder. They were nowhere in sight. "Where is the knife?" he asked.

Faith looked at Measure. "Didn't you bring them back in with you?" she asked.

"You're the one brought them in here," said Measure.

"But when you went back out to get the preacher, you took them," she said.

"Did I?" Measure looked confused. "I must have set them down out there." He got up and left the room.

Thrower began to realize that something strange was going on here, though he couldn't quite put his finger on it.

He walked to the door and waited for Measure to return.

Cally was standing there, holding his slate, looking up at the minister. "You going to kill my brother?" he asked.

"Don't even think of such a thing," Thrower answered.

Measure looked sheepish as he handed the implements to Thrower. "I can't believe I just set them on the mantel like that." Then the young man pushed past Thrower into the room.

A moment later, Thrower followed him into Alvin's room and took his place beside the exposed leg, with the box drawn in black.

"Well where'd you put them?" asked Faith.

Thrower realized that he didn't have the knife or the saw. He was completely confused. Measure handed them to him just outside the door. How could he have lost them?

Cally stood in the doorway. "Why'd you give me these?" he asked. He was, in fact, holding both blades.

"That's a good question," said Measure, eyeing the pastor with a frown. "Why'd you give them to Cally?"

"I didn't," said Thrower. "*You* must have given them to him."

"I put them right in your hands," said Measure.

"The preacher give them to me," said Cally.

"Well, bring them here," said his mother.

Cally obediently started into the room, brandishing the blades like trophies of war. Like the attack of a great army. Ah, yes, a great army, like the army of the Israelites that Joshua led into the promised land. This is how they held their weapons, high above their heads, as they marched around and around the city of Jericho. Marched and marched. Marched and marched. And on the seventh day they stopped and blew their trumpets and gave a great shout, and *down* came the walls, and they held their swords and knives high over their heads and charged into the city, hacking men, women, and children, all the enemies of God, so the promised land would be purged of their filthiness and be ready to receive the people of the Lord. They were spattered in blood by the end of the day, and Joshua stood in their midst, the great prophet of God, holding a bloody sword above his head, and he shouted. What did he shout?

I can't remember what he shouted. If I could only remember what he shouted, I'd understand why I'm standing here on the road, surrounded by snow-covered trees.

Reverend Thrower looked at his hands, and looked at the trees. He had somehow walked half a mile away from the Millers' house. He wasn't even wearing his heavy cloak.

Then the truth came clear. He hadn't fooled the devil at all. Satan had transported him here, in the twinkling of an eye, rather than let him kill the Beast. Thrower had failed in his one opportunity for greatness. He leaned against a cold black trunk and cried bitterly.

Cally walked into the room, holding the blades above his head. Measure was all set to get a grip on the leg, when all of a sudden old Thrower stood right up and walked out of the room just as quick as if he was trotting to the privy.

"Reverend Thrower," cried Ma. "Where are you going?"

But Measure understood now. "Let him go, Ma," he said.

They heard the front door of the house open, and the minister's heavy steps on the porch.

"Go shut the front door, Cally," said Measure.

For once Cally obeyed without a speck of backsass. Ma looked at Measure, then at Pa, then at Measure again. "I don't understand why he left like that," she said.

Measure gave her a little half-smile and looked at Pa. "*You* know, don't you, Pa?"

"Maybe," he said.

Measure explained to his mother. "Them knives and that preacher, they can't be in this room with Al Junior at the same time."

"But why not!" she said. "He was going to do the surgery!"

"Well, he sure ain't going to do it now," said Measure.

The knife and the bone saw lay on the blanket.

"Pa," said Measure.

"Not me," said Pa.

"Ma," said Measure.

"I can't," Faith said.

"Well then," said Measure, "I reckon I just turned surgeon." He looked at Alvin.

The boy's face had a deathly pallor to it that was even worse than the ruddiness of the fever. But he managed a sort of smile, and whispered, "Reckon so."

"Ma, you're going to have to hold back that flap of skin."

She nodded.

Measure picked up the knife and brought the blade to rest against the bottom line.

"Measure," Al Junior whispered.

"Yes, Alvin?" Measure asked.

"I can stand the pain and hold right still, iffen you whistle."

"I can't keep no tune, if I'm trying to cut straight at the same time," said Measure.

"Don't want no tune," said Alvin.

Measure looked into the boy's eyes and had no choice but to do as he asked. It was Al's leg, after all, and if he wanted a whistling surgeon, he'd get one. Measure took a deep breath and started in whistling, no kind of tune at all, just notes. He put the knife on the black line again and began to cut. Shallow at first, cause he heard Al take a gasp of air.

"Keep whistling," Alvin whispered. "Right to the bone."

Measure whistled again, and this time he cut fast and deep. Right to the bone in the middle of the line. A deep slit up both sides. Then he worked the knife under the two corners and peeled the skin and muscle right back. At first it bled more than a little bit, but almost right away the bleeding stopped. Measure figured it must be something Alvin did inside himself, to stop the bleeding like that.

"Faith," said Pa.

Ma reached over and laid her hand on the bloody flap of skin. Al reached out a trembling hand and traced a wedge on the red-streaked bone of his own leg. Measure laid down the knife and picked up the saw. It made an awful, squeaky sound as he cut. But Measure just whistled and sawed,

sawed and whistled. And pretty soon he had a wedge of bone in his hand. It didn't look no different from the rest of the bone.

"You sure that was the right place?" he asked.

Al nodded slowly.

"Did I get it all?" Measure asked.

Al sat for a few moments, then nodded again.

"You want Ma to sew this back up?" Measure asked.

Al didn't say a thing.

"He fainted," said Pa.

The blood started to flow again, just a little, seeping into the wound. Ma had a needle and thread on the pincushion she wore around her neck. In no time she had that flap of skin right back down, and she was stitching away at it, making a fine tight seam.

"You just keep on whistling, Measure," she said.

So he kept right on whistling and she kept right on sewing, till they had the wound all bandaged up and Alvin was laying back sleeping like a baby. They all three stood up to go. Pa laid a hand on the boy's forehead, as gentle as you please.

"I think his fever's gone," he said.

Measure's tune got downright jaunty as they slipped on out the door.

❧ 14 ❧

Chastisement

As soon as Elly saw him, she was sweet as could be, brushing snow off him, helping with his cloak, and never so much as whispering a question of how it happened.

Didn't make no difference how kindly she might be. He was shamed afore his own wife, cause sooner or later she'd hear the tale from one of those children. Soon enough the tale would be all up and down the Wobbish. How Armor-of-God Weaver, storekeeper for the western country, future governor, got throwed right off a porch into the snow by his old father-in-law. They'd be laughing behind their hands, all right. They'd laugh him up and down. Never to his face, of course, cause there was hardly a soul between Lake Canada and the Noisy River who didn't owe him money or need his maps to prove their claims. Come the time when the Wobbish country was made a state, they'd tell that story at every polling place. They might like a man they laughed at, but they wouldn't respect him, and they wouldn't vote for him.

It was the death of his plans he was facing, and his wife just had too much of that Miller family look about her. She was pretty enough, for a frontier woman, but he didn't care about pretty right now. He didn't care about sweet nights and gentle mornings. He didn't care about her working alongside him in the store. All he cared about was shame and rage.

"Don't do that."

"You got to get that wet shirt off. How'd you get snow clear down your shirt?"

"I said get your hands off me!"

She stepped back, surprised. "I was just—"

"I know what you 'was just.' Poor little Armor, you just pat him like a little boy and he'll feel better."

"You could catch your death—"

"Tell that to your pa! If I cough my guts out, you tell him what it means to throw a man in the snow!"

"Oh no!" she cried. "I can't believe Papa would—"

"See? You don't even believe your own husband."

"I *do* believe you, it just ain't like Pa—"

"No ma'am, it's like the devil himself, that's what it's like! That's what fills that house of yours up there! The spirit of evil! And when a body tries to speak the words of God in that house, they throw him right out in the snow!"

"What were you doing up at the house?"

"Trying to save your brother's life. He's no doubt dead by now."

"How could *you* save him?"

Maybe she didn't mean to sound so contemptuous. It didn't matter. He knew what she meant. That him having no hidden power, there wasn't a thing he could do to help anybody. After years of being married, she still put her faith in witchery, just like her kin. He hadn't changed her a bit. "You're just the same," he said. "Evil's in you so deep that I can't *pray* it out of you, and I can't *preach* it out of you, and I can't *love* it out of you, and I can't *yell* it out of you!" When he said "pray," he shoved her a little, just to make his point. When he said "preach," he shoved her harder, and she stumbled back. When he said "love," he took her by the shoulders and gave her such a shake her hair broke right out of the bun she'd made of it, and fluttered around her head. When he said "yell," he knocked her back so far she stumbled down on the floor.

Seeing her falling, even before she hit the floor, he felt such a shame go through him, even worse than when her father threw him in the snow. A strong man makes me feel weak, so I go home and shove around my wife, what a big man that makes me. Here I been a Christian who never hit or hurt a man or woman, and I knock my own wife, flesh of my flesh, right down on the floor.

That was his thinking, and he was about to throw himself on his knees and bawl like a baby and beg forgiveness. He would've done it, too, except that when she saw the look on his face, all twisted up with shame and rage, she didn't know that he was angry at himself, she just knew that he was hurting her, and so she did what come natural to a woman who grew up like she did. She moved her fingers to make a fending, and whispered a word to hold him back.

He couldn't fall on his knees before her. He couldn't take one step toward her. He couldn't even *think* of taking a step toward her. Her fending was so strong he staggered back, he headed for the door, he opened it and ran outside in just his shirt. Everything he'd been afraid of came true today. He probably lost his future in politics, but that was nothing compared to this: his own wife did witchery in his own home, and she did it against *him,* and he had no defense against it. She was a witch. She was a witch. And his house was unclean.

It was cold. He had no coat, not even his waistcoat. His shirt was already wet, and now it clung to him and froze him to the bone. He had to get indoors, but he couldn't bear to knock on anybody's door. There was only one place he could go. Up the hill to the church. Thrower had firewood there, so he'd be warm. And in the church he could pray and try to understand why the Lord didn't help him. Haven't I served you, Lord?

Reverend Thrower opened the door of the church and walked slowly, fearfully inside. He could not bear to face the Visitor, knowing how he had failed. For it had been his own failure, he knew that now. Satan should have had no power over him, to drive him from the house that way. An ordained minister, acting as the emissary of the Lord, following instructions given to him by an angel—Satan should not have been able to thrust him out of the house like that, before he even knew what was happening.

He stripped off his cloak, and his topcoat as well. The church was hot. The fire in the stove must have burned longer than he expected. Or maybe he felt the heat of shame.

It could not be that Satan was stronger than the Lord. The only possible explanation was that Thrower himself was too weak. It was his own faith that faltered.

Thrower knelt at the altar and cried out the name of the Lord. "Forgive thou my unbelief!" he cried. "I held the knife, but Satan stood against me, and I had no strength!" He recited a litany of self-excoriation, he rehearsed all his failures of the day, until at last he was exhausted.

Only then, with his eyes sore from crying, his voice feeble and hoarse, did he realize the moment when his faith was undermined. It was when he stood in Alvin's room, asking the boy to confess his faith, and the boy scoffed at the mysteries of God. "How can he be on top of something that ain't got no top?" Even though Thrower had rejected the question as the result of ignorance and evil, the question had nevertheless pierced his heart and penetrated to the core of his belief. Certainties that had sustained him most of his life were suddenly split through by the questions of an ignorant boy. "He stole my faith," said Thrower. "I went into his room a man of God, and came out as a doubter."

"Indeed," said a voice behind him. A voice he knew.

A voice that now, in his moment of failure, he both feared and longed for. Oh, forgive me, comfort me, my Visitor, my friend! Yet do not fail also to chastise me with the terrible wrath of a jealous God.

"Chastise you?" asked the Visitor. "How could I chastise you, such a glorious specimen of humanity?"

"I am not glorious," said Thrower miserably.

"You're barely human, for that matter," said the Visitor. "In whose image were *you* made? I sent you to bring my word into that house, and instead they have nearly converted *you*. What do I call you now? A heretic? Or merely a skeptic?"

"A Christian!" cried Thrower. "Forgive me and call me once again a Christian."

"You had the knife in your hand, but you set it down."

"I didn't mean to!"

"Weak, weak, weak, weak, weak . . ." Each time the Visitor repeated the word, he stretched it longer and longer, until each repetition became a song in itself. As he sang, he began to walk around the church. He did not run, but he walked quickly, far faster than any man could walk. "Weak, weak . . ." He was moving so fast that Thrower had to turn constantly just to keep him in sight. The Visitor was no longer walking on the floor. He was skittering along the walls, as smooth and fast in his motion as a cockroach, then even faster, until he became a blur, and Thrower could not keep up with him by turning. Thrower leaned on the altar, facing the empty pews, watching the Visitor race by again and again and again.

Gradually Thrower realized that the Visitor had changed shape, that he had stretched himself, like a long slender beast, a lizard, an alligator, bright-scaled and shining, longer and longer, until finally the Visitor's body was so long that it circled the room, a vast worm that gripped its own tail between its teeth.

And in his mind Thrower realized how very small and worthless he was, compared to this glorious being that sparkled with a thousand different colors, that glowed with inner fire, that breathed in darkness and exhaled light. I worship thee! he shouted inside himself. Thou art all that I desire! Kiss me with your love, so I may taste your glory!

Suddenly the Visitor stopped, and the great jaws came toward him. Not to devour, for Thrower knew he was unworthy even to be consumed. He saw now the terrible predicament of man: he saw that he dangled over the pit of hell like a spider on a slender thread, and the only reason God did not let him fall was because he was not even worthy of destruction. God did not hate him. He was so vile that God disdained him.

Thrower looked into the Visitor's eyes and despaired. For there was neither love, nor forgiveness, nor anger, nor contempt. The eyes were utterly empty. The scales dazzled, scattering the light of an inner fire. But that fire did not shine through the eyes. They were not even black. They simply were not there at all, a terrible emptiness that trembled, that would not hold still, and Thrower knew that this was his own reflection, that he was nothing, that for him to continue to exist was a cruel waste of precious space, that the only choice left to him was to be annihilated, uncreated, to restore the world to the greater glory it would have had if Philadelphia Thrower had never been born.

It was Thrower's praying that woke Armor up. He was curled up by the Franklin stove. Maybe he stoked that stove a mite too hot, but that's what it took to beat back the cold. Why, by the time he got to the church his shirt was solid ice. He'd get more charcoal to pay back the parson.

Armor meant to speak right up and let Thrower know he was there, but when he heard the words that Thrower was praying, he couldn't find no words to say. Thrower was talking about knives and arteries, and how he should've cut up the enemies of God. After a minute it came clear: Thrower hadn't gone up there to save that boy, he'd gone up to kill him! What's wrong around here, thought Armor, when a Christian man beats his wife, and a Christian wife witches her husband, and a Christian minister plots murder and prays for forgiveness cause he failed to commit the crime!

All of a sudden, though, Thrower stopped praying. He was so hoarse and his face so red that Armor thought he might have had the apoplexy. But no. Thrower lifted his head like he was listening to somebody. Armor listened, too, and he could hear something, like people talking in a windstorm, so you couldn't never hear what they were saying.

I know what this is, thought Armor. Reverend Thrower's having himself a vision.

Sure enough, Thrower talked, and the faint voice answered, and pretty soon Thrower started turning around and around, faster and faster, like he was watching something on the walls. Armor tried to see what it was he was watching, but he couldn't never make it out. It was like a shadow passing across the sun—you couldn't see it coming and you couldn't see it go, but for a second it was darker and colder. That's what Armor saw.

Then it stopped. Armor saw a shimmering in the air, a
dazzle here and there like when a pane of glass catches the
sunlight. Was Thrower seeing the glory of God, like Moses
saw? Not likely, looking at the parson's face. Armor never
did see such a face as that before. Like a man's face might
look if he had to watch his own baby being killed.

The shimmering and dazzle went away. The church
was quiet. Armor wanted to run to Thrower and ask him,
What did you see! What was your vision! Was it a prophecy?

But Thrower didn't look much like he wanted to
answer questions. That look of wishing to die was still on
his face. The preacher walked real slow away from the altar.
He wandered around among the pews, bumping into them
sometimes, not watching or caring where his body went.
Finally he ended up by the window, facing the glass, but
Armor knew he didn't see nothing, he was just standing
there, his eyes wide open, looking like death.

Reverend Thrower lifted up his right hand, the fingers
spread, and he laid his palm on a pane of glass. He pressed.
He pressed and pushed so hard that Armor could see the
glass bowing outward. "Stop it!" shouted Armor. "You'll
cut yourself!"

Thrower didn't even make a sign that he heard. Just
kept pressing. Armor started walking toward him. Got to
make that man stop before he breaks the glass and cuts up
his arm.

With a crash the glass shattered. Thrower's arm went
right through, up to the shoulder. The preacher smiled. He
pulled his arm partway back into the church. Then he
began to slide his arm around the frame, jamming it right
into the shards of glass that hung there in the putty.

Armor tried to pull Thrower away from the window,
but the man had a strength on him like Armor never seen
before. Finally Armor had to take a run at him and knock
him right down to the floor. Blood was spattered everywhere. Armor grabbed at Thrower's arm, which was drip-
ping all over with blood. Thrower tried to roll away from
him. Armor didn't have no choice. For the first time since

he became a Christian man he made his hand into a fist and popped Thrower right on the chin. It slammed the preacher's head back into the floor and knocked him silly.

Got to stop the bleeding, Armor thought. But first he had to get the glass out. Some of the big pieces were only stuck in a little way, and he could brush them right off. But other pieces, some of the little pieces, were in deep, only a bit of their top showing, and that was slimy with blood so he couldn't get much of a grip on it. Finally, though, he got all the glass he could find. Lucky enough there wasn't a single cut a-pumping blood, which told Armor that the big veins hadn't been cut. He stripped off his shirt, which left him naked to the waist with that cold draft coming in from the broken window, but he didn't hardly notice. He just ripped up the shirt and made bandages. He bound up the wounds and stopped the bleeding. Then he sat there and waited for Thrower to wake up.

Thrower was surprised to find he wasn't dead. He was lying on his back on a hard floor, covered up with heavy cloth. His head hurt. His arm hurt worse. He remembered trying to cut up that arm, and he knew he ought to try again, but he just couldn't work up the same wish for death that he had felt before. Even remembering the Visitor in the form of a great lizard, even remembering those empty eyes, Thrower just couldn't remember how it felt. He only knew that it was the worst feeling in the world.

His arm was bandaged tight. Who had bandaged him?

He heard the sloshing of water. Then the flopping sound of wet rags slapping against wood. In the winter twilight coming through the window, he could make out somebody washing the wall. One of the window panes was covered over with a piece of wood.

"Who is it?" asked Thrower. "Who are you?"

"Just me."

"Armor-of-God."

"Washing down the walls. This is a church, not a butcher shed."

Of course there'd be blood all over. "Sorry," said Thrower.

"I don't mind cleaning up," said Armor. "I think I got all the glass out of your arm."

"You're naked," said Thrower.

"Your arm is wearing my shirt."

"You must be cold."

"Maybe I was, but I got the window covered and the stove het up. You're the one with a face so white you look like you been dead a week."

Thrower tried to sit up, but he couldn't. He was too weak; his arm hurt too bad.

Armor pushed him back down. "Now, you just lay back, Reverend Thrower. You just lay back. You been through a lot."

"Yes."

"I hope you don't mind, but I was here in the church when you come in. I was asleep by the stove—my wife threw me out of the house. I been thrown out twice today." He laughed, but there was no mirth in it. "So I saw you."

"Saw?"

"You were having a vision, weren't you?"

"Did you see him?"

"I didn't see much. I mostly saw *you,* but there was a few glimpses, if you know what I mean. Running around the walls."

"You saw," said Thrower. "Oh, Armor, it was terrible, it was beautiful."

"Did you see God?"

"See *God*? God has no body to be seen, Armor. No, I saw an angel, an angel of chastisement. Surely this was what Pharaoh saw, the angel of death that came through the cities of Egypt and took the firstborn."

"Oh," said Armor, sounding puzzled. "Was I spose to let you die, then?"

"If I were supposed to die, you could not have saved me," said Thrower. "Because you saved me, because you were here at the moment of my despair, it is a sure sign that I am meant to live. I was chastised, but not destroyed.

Armor-of-God, I have another chance."

Armor nodded, but Thrower could see that he was worried about something. "What is it?" Thrower asked. "What is it that you want to ask me?"

Armor's eyes widened. "Can you hear what I'm thinking?"

"If I could, I wouldn't have to ask you."

Armor smiled. "Reckon not."

"I'll tell you what you want to know, if I can."

"I heard you praying," said Armor. He waited, as if that were the question.

Since Thrower didn't know what the question was, he wasn't sure what to answer. "I was in despair, because I failed the Lord. I was given a mission to perform, but at the crucial moment my heart was filled with doubt." With his good hand he reached out and clutched at Armor. All he could touch was the cloth of Armor's trousers, where he knelt beside him. "Armor-of-God," he said, "never let doubt enter your heart. Never question what you know is true. It's the doorway to let Satan have power over you."

But that wasn't the answer to Armor's question.

"Ask me what you want to ask me," said Thrower. "I'll tell you the truth, if I can."

"You prayed about killing," said Armor.

Thrower had not thought to tell anyone about the burden the Lord had placed upon him. Yet if the Lord had wanted the secret kept from Armor, He would not have allowed the man to be there in the church to overhear. "I believe," said Thrower, "that it was the Lord God that brought you to me. I am weak, Armor, and I failed at what the Lord required. But now I see that you, a man of faith, have been given to me as a friend and helper."

"What did the Lord require?" asked Armor.

"Not murder, my brother. The Lord never asked me to kill a man. It was a devil I was sent to kill. A devil in man-shape. Living in that house."

Armor pursed his lips, deep in thought. "The boy ain't just possessed, is that what you're saying? It ain't something you can cast right out?"

"I tried, but he laughed at the Holy Book and mocked

my words of exorcism. He is not possessed, Armor-of-God. He is the devil's own kin."

Armor shook his head. "My wife ain't a devil, and she's his own sister."

"She has given up witchcraft, and so she has been made pure," said Thrower.

Armor gave one bitter laugh. "I thought so."

Thrower understood, now, why Armor had taken refuge in the church, in the house of God: His own house had been polluted.

"Armor-of-God, will you help me purge this country, this town, that house, that *family,* of the evil influence that has corrupted them?"

"Will it save my wife?" asked Armor. "Will it end her love of witchery?"

"It may," said Thrower. "Perhaps the Lord has brought us together so we can purify both our houses."

"Whatever it takes," said Armor. "I'm with you against the devil."

❖ 15 ❖

Promises

THE BLACKSMITH LISTENED as Taleswapper read the letter from beginning to end.

"Do you remember the family?" asked Taleswapper.

"I do," said Makepeace Smith. "The graveyard almost began with their oldest boy. I pulled his body from the river with my own hands."

"Well then, will you take him as your prentice?"

A youth, perhaps sixteen years old, walked into the forge carrying a bucket of snow. He glanced at the visitor, ducked his head, and walked to the cooling barrel that stood near the hearth.

"You see I have a prentice," said the smith.

"He looks like a big one," said Taleswapper.

"Getting on," the smith agreed. "Ain't that right, Bosey? You ready to go on your own?"

Bosey smiled a bit, stifled it, nodded. "Yes, sir," he said.

"I'm not an easy master," said the smith.

"Alvin's a good-hearted boy. He'll work hard for you."

"But will he obey me? I like to be obeyed."

Taleswapper looked again at Bosey. He was busy scooping snow into the barrel.

"I said he's a good-hearted boy," said Taleswapper. "He'll obey you if you're fair with him."

The smith met his gaze. "I give honest measure. I don't

233

beat the boys I take on. Have I ever laid hand on you, Bosey?"

"Never, sir."

"You see, Taleswapper, a prentice can obey out of fear, and he can obey out of greed. But if I'm a good master, he'll obey me cause he knows that's how he'll learn."

Taleswapper grinned at the smith. "There's no fee," said Taleswapper. "The boy will earn it out. And he gets his schooling."

"No need for a smith to have letters, as I should know."

"Won't be long before Hio's part of the United States," said Taleswapper. "The boy's got to vote, I think, and read the newspapers. A man who can't read only knows what other folks tell him."

Makepeace Smith looked at Taleswapper with a grin half-hid on his face. "That so? And ain't it you telling me? So don't I only know this cause other folks, namely you, is telling me so?"

Taleswapper laughed and nodded. The smith had shot the head clean off the turkey with that one. "I make my way in the world telling tales," said Taleswapper, "so I know you can get much with just the sound of a man's voice. He already reads above his years, so it won't do him harm to miss a bit of school. But his ma is set on him having letters and ciphering like a scholar. So just promise me you won't stand between him and schooling, if he wants it, and we'll leave it at that."

"Got my word on that," said Makepeace Smith. "And you don't have to write it down. A man who keeps his word doesn't have to read and write. But a man who has to write down his promises, you got to watch him all morning. I know that for a fact. We got lawyers in Hatrack these days."

"The curse of civilized man," said Taleswapper. "When a man can't get folks to believe his lies anymore, then he hires him a professional to lie in his place."

They laughed together over that one, setting there on two stout stumps just inside the door of the forge, the fire smoldering in its brick chimney place behind them, the sun shining on half-melted snow outside. A redbird flew across the grassy, trampled, dunged-up ground in front of the forge. It dazzled Taleswapper's eyes for a moment, it was such a startlement against the whites and greys and browns of late winter.

In that moment of amazement at the redbird's flight, Taleswapper knew for certain, though he couldn't say why, that it would be a while yet before the Unmaker let young Alvin come to this place. And when he came he'd be like a redbird out of season, to dazzle folks all hereabouts, them thinking he was just as natural as a bird flying, not knowing what a miracle it was every minute that the bird stayed in the air.

Taleswapper shook himself, and the moment's clear vision passed. "Then it's done, and I'll write to them to send the boy."

"I'll look for him the first of April. No later!"

"Unless you expect the boy to control the weather, you'd best be flexible about the date."

The smith grumbled and waved him away. All in all, a successful meeting. Taleswapper left feeling good—he had discharged his duty. It'd be easy to send a letter with a westbound wagon—several groups passed through the town of Hatrack every week.

Though it had been a long time since he passed through this place, he still knew the way from the forge to the inn. It was a well-traveled road, and not a long one. The inn was much larger now than it had been, and there were several shops a bit farther up the road. An outfitter, a saddler, a cobbler. The kind of service traveling folk could use.

He hardly set foot on the porch when the door opened and Old Peg Guester came out, her arms spread wide to embrace him. "Ah, Taleswapper, you've been away too long, come in, come in!"

"It's good to see you again, Peg," he said.

Horace Guester growled at him from behind the bar in the common room, where he was serving several thirsty visitors. "What I don't need here is another teetotaling man!"

"Good news, then, Horace," Taleswapper answered

cheerfully. "I gave up tea as well."

"What do you drink, *water*?"

"Water and the blood of greasy old men," said Taleswapper.

Horace gestured to his wife. "You keep that man away from me, Old Peg, you hear?"

Old Peg helped him strip off a few layers of clothing. "Look at you," said Old Peg, sizing him up. "There ain't enough meat on you to make a stew."

"The bears and panthers pass me by in the night, looking for richer fare," said Taleswapper.

"Come in and tell me stories while I fix up a mess of supper for the company."

There was talk and chatter, especially once Oldpappy came in to help. He was getting feeble now, but he still had a hand in the kitchen, which was all to the benefit of those who ate here; Old Peg meant well and worked hard, but some folks had the knack and some folks didn't. But it wasn't food that Taleswapper came for, nor conversation either, and after a while he realized he'd have to bring it up himself. "Where's your daughter?"

To his surprise, Old Peg stiffened, and her voice went cold and hard. "She ain't so little no more. She's got a mind of her own, she's the first to tell you."

And you don't much like it, thought Taleswapper. But his business with the daughter was more important than any family squabbles. "Is she still a—"

"A torch? Oh, yes, she does her duty, but it's no pleasure for folks to come for her. Snippy and cold, that's what she is. It's got her a name for being sharp-tongued." For a moment Old Peg's face softened. "She used to be such a soft-hearted child."

"I've never seen a soft heart turn hard," said Taleswapper. "At least not without good reason."

"Well, whatever her reason, she's one whose heart has crusted up like a waterbucket on a winter's night."

Taleswapper held his tongue and didn't sermonize, didn't talk about how if you chip the ice it'll freeze up again right away, but if you take it inside, it'll warm up fresh as you please. No use stepping in the middle of a family squabble. Taleswapper knew enough of the way people lived that he took this particular quarrel as a natural event, like cold winds and short days in autumn, like thunder after lightning. Most parents didn't have much use for a half-grown child.

"I have a matter to discuss with her," said Taleswapper. "I'll take the risk of having my head bitten off."

He found her in Dr. Whitley Physicker's office, working on his accounts. "I didn't know you were a bookkeeper," he said.

"I didn't know you held much with physicking," she answered. "Or did you just come to see the miracle of a girl who does sums and ciphers?"

Oh, yes, she was as sharp as could be. Taleswapper could see how a wit like that might discommode a few folks who expected a young woman to cast down her eyes and speak softly, glancing upward only now and then under heavy-lidded eyes. There was none of that young ladyness about Peggy. She looked Taleswapper in the face, plain as could be.

"I didn't come to be healed," said Taleswapper. "Or to have my future told. Or even to have my accounts added up."

And there it was. The moment a man answered her right back instead of getting his dander up, why, she flashed a smile fit to charm the warts off a toad. "I don't recollect you having much to add or subtract anyhow," she said. "Naught plus naught is naught, I think."

"You've got it wrong, Peggy," said Taleswapper. "I own this whole world, and folks haven't been keeping up too well on the payments."

She smiled again, and set aside the doctor's account book. "I keep his records for him, once a month, and he brings me things to read from Dekane." She talked about the things she read, and Taleswapper began to see that her heart yearned for places far beyond Hatrack River. He also saw other things—that she, being a torch, knew the folks around here too well, and thought that in faraway places she'd find people with jewel-like souls that would never disappoint a girl who could see clean into their heart.

She's young, that's all. Give her time, and she'll learn to love such goodness as she finds, and forgive the rest.

After a while the doctor came in, and they chatted a bit, and it was well into the afternoon by the time Taleswapper was alone with Peggy again and could ask her what he came to ask.

"How far off can you see, Peggy?"

He could almost see wariness fall across her face like a thick velvet curtain. "I don't reckon you're asking me whether I need spectacles," she said.

"I just wonder about a girl who once wrote in my book, A Maker is born. I wonder if she still keeps an eye on that Maker, now and then, so she can see how he fares."

She looked away from him, gazing at the high window above where the curtain gave privacy. The sun was low and the sky outside was grey, but her face was full of light, Taleswapper saw that right enough. Sometimes you didn't have to be a torch to know full well what was in a person's heart.

"I wonder if that torch saw a ridgebeam falling on him one time," said Taleswapper.

"I wonder," she said.

"Or a millstone."

"Could be."

"And I wonder if somehow she didn't have some way to split that ridgebeam clean in twain, and crack that millstone so a certain old taleswapper could see lantern light right through the middle of that stone."

Tears glistened in her eyes, not like she was about to cry, but like she was looking into the sun straight on, and it made her water up: "A scrap of his birth caul, rubbed into dust, and a body can use the boy's own power to work a few clumsy makings," she said softly.

"But now he knows something of his own knack, and he undid what you did for him."

She nodded.

"Must be lonely, watching out for him from so far

away," said Taleswapper.

She shook her head. "Not to me. I got folks all around me, all the time." She looked at Taleswapper and smiled wanly. "It's almost a relief to spend time with that one boy who doesn't want a thing from me, because he doesn't even know that I exist."

"I know, though," said Taleswapper. "And I don't want a thing from you, either."

She smiled. "You old fraud," she said.

"All right, I *do* want something from you, but not something for myself. I've met that boy, and even if I can't see into his heart the way you can, I think I know him. I think I know what he might be, what he might do, and I want you to know that if you ever need my help for anything, just send me word, just tell me what to do, and if it's in my power I'll do it."

She didn't answer, nor did she look at him.

"So far you didn't need help," said Taleswapper, "but now he has a mind of his own, and you can't always do for him the things he'll need. The dangers won't come just from things that fall on him or hurt him in the flesh. He's in as much danger from what he decides to do himself. I'm just telling you that if you see such danger and you need me to help, I'll come no matter what."

"That's a comfort," she said. That was honest enough, Taleswapper knew; but she was feeling more than she said, he knew that too.

"And I wanted to tell you he was coming here, first of April, to prentice with the smith."

"I know he's coming," she said, "but it won't be the first of April."

"Oh?"

"Or even this year at all."

Fear for the boy stabbed at Taleswapper's heart. "I guess I did come to hear the future after all. What's in store for him? What's to come?"

"All kinds of things might happen," she said, "and I'd be a fool to guess which one. I see it open like a thousand roads before him, all the time. But there's precious few of those roads that bring him here by April, and a whole lot more that leave him dead with a Red man's hatchet in his head."

Taleswapper leaned across the doctor's writing table and rested his hand on hers. "Will he live?"

"As long as I have breath in my body," she said.

"Or I in mine," he answered.

They sat in silence for a moment, hand on hand, eye to eye, until she burst into laughter and looked away.

"Usually when folks laugh I get the joke," said Taleswapper.

"I was just thinking we're a poor excuse for a conspiracy, the two of us, against the enemies that boy will face."

"True," said Taleswapper, "but then, our cause is good, and so all nature will conspire with us, don't you think?"

"And God, too," she added firmly.

"I can't say about that," said Taleswapper. "The preachers and priests seem to have him so fenced up with doctrine that the poor old Father hardly has room to act anymore. Now that they've got the Bible safely interpreted, the last thing they ever want is for him to speak another word, or show his hand of power in this world."

"I saw his hand of power in the birth of a seventh son of a seventh son, some years back," she said. "Call it nature if you want to, since you've got all kinds of learning from philosophers and wizards. I just know that he's tied as tight to my life as if we was born from the same womb."

Taleswapper didn't plan his next question, it just came unthought-of from his lips. "Are you glad of it?"

She looked at him with terrible sadness in her eyes. "Not often," she said. She looked so weary then that Taleswapper couldn't help himself, he walked around the table and stood beside her chair and held her tight like a father holds his daughter, held her for a good long while. If she was crying or just holding on, he couldn't say. They spoke not a word. Finally she let go of him and turned back to the account book. He left without breaking the silence.

Taleswapper wandered on over to the inn to take his supper. There were tales to tell and chores to do in order to earn his keep. Yet all the stories seemed to pale beside the one story that he could *not* tell, the one story whose end he didn't know.

On the meadow around the millhouse were a half dozen farm wagons, watched over by farmers who had come a good long way to get high-quality flour. No more would their wives sweat over a mortar and pestle to make coarse meal for hard and lumpy bread. The mill was in business, and everyone for miles around would bring their grain to the town of Vigor Church.

The water poured through the millrace, and the great wheel turned. Inside the millhouse, the force of the wheel was carried by interlocking gears, to make the grindstone roll around and around, riding on the face of a quarter dress millstone.

The miller poured out the wheat upon the stone. The grindstone passed over it, crushing it to flour. The miller swept it smooth for a second pass, then brushed it off into a basket held by his son, a ten-year-old boy. His son poured the flour into a sieve, and shook the good flour into a cloth sack. He emptied what stayed in the sieve into a silage barrel. Then he returned to his father's side for the next basket of wheat.

Their thoughts were remarkably alike, as they worked silently together. This is what I want to do forever, each one thought. Rise in the morning, come to the mill, and work all day with him beside me. Never mind that the wish was impossible. Never mind that they might never see each other again, once the boy left for his apprenticeship back in the place of his birth. That only added to the sweetness of the moment, which would soon become a memory, would soon become a dream.

4/05